The Review

Annette Mori

The Review

Annette Mori

2016

The Review

Affinity E-Book Press NZ LTD
Canterbury, New Zealand

1st Edition

ISBN: 978-0-908351-95-4

Editor: JoSelle Vanderhooft
Proof Editor: Alexis Smith
Cover Design: Irish Dragon Designs

Acknowledgments

A huge thank you to all of my beta readers, Gail Dodge, Cathie Williamson, Ameliah Faith, Carrie Camp, Ali Spooner, and my sister, who made great suggestions to improve the initial draft. Of course, once again I have to acknowledge Erin O'Reilly, who is a constant support and encouragement to me. She continues to mentor me so that I improve as a writer, giving her time freely, without the expectation of anything in return. I am honored to call her a friend and have her support me in my journey.

I would also like to express my gratitude to Affinity Press and the wonderful trio (JM Dragon, Erin O'Reilly and Nancy Kaufman) who continue to provide feedback to tighten up manuscripts that need assistance and publish my sometimes unconventional work. I am eternally grateful for the opportunities they give me to let my stories see the light of day.

My other family members who are also very supportive include my nephew Aaron, his wife Chelsea, and my little sister Kim. I always enjoy working with the beta editor Kay who helped to improve my story. Thanks to JoSelle Vanderhooft for her thorough editing to tighten the story even further. Inevitably, there are those pesky final errors that slip through, and I am thankful the final proof editor, Alexis Smith, caught those before the book went to print.

Nancy Kaufman is a rock star with her covers and a promoter extraordinaire. Over the past year, fellow authors Lynn Lawler, Dawn Carter, Melissa Grace, Suzie Carr, Darla Baker, Linda North, Fran Heckrotte, Alicia Joseph, Holly Anne Weaver, Ali Spooner, Jen Silver, Lacey Schmidt, Renee Mackenzie, K'Anne Meinel, and Charlene Neil have been particularly supportive.

A huge thanks to all the other readers and fellow writers who have sent personal emails, written reviews, and posted nice things on Facebook (you know who you are). A few of those particularly supportive readers include Sue Collins, Amelia Faith, AE Cavalieri, Gail Dodge, Carrie Camp, Cathie Williamson, Charlotte Demescko, Robin Hicks, Marian Dries, Sue Rossman, Karen Cobb, Susan Barnes, Elaine Mattern, Fran Alsbrook, Ethel Barker, Susan Hall, Toni Lambert, and so many more (the list continues to grow) I am forgetting due to old age! The Affinity authors are an especially supportive group and often share posts or send words of encouragement.

Finally, my wife, Jody, continues her support even when it interferes with our weekend time.

Dedication

To all the readers, who continue to support my books. To my wife, who I love dearly for her patience and her ability to take care of me when I fail to do that myself.

Table of Contents

Also by Annette Mori

The Ultimate Betrayal

Locked Inside

Out of This World

Asset Management

The Incredibly True Adventure of Two Elves in Love
(Affinity 2014 Christmas Collection)

Love Forever, Live Forever

The True Story of Valentine's Day

Vampire Pussy…Cat
Nicky's Christmas Miracle X3
(*It's in Her Kiss*, Affinity's Charity Anthology)

Chapter One

Silver Lining stared at her property through the dirty sliding glass door. Her wife would have hated how much grime she'd allowed to accumulate on every glass surface. The sun was shining, and the picture-perfect view of the mountains was probably a sight that would lift most people's spirits, but not hers.

Silver Lining wasn't her real name, and it didn't particularly suit her anymore. It did at one time because she used to be the kind of person who recognized the good in everyone and everything—a glass-half-full type. Ten years ago her wife, Naomi, had picked that pen name for her, and she'd laughed and said, why not? Naomi had tactfully argued that Helen Carson was an ordinary name, but Silver Lining would stand out.

Naomi had always been brutally honest with Silver. Of all the things she missed, Naomi's honesty was in the top five. They'd been together so long—just shy of twenty-two years, and they'd evolved to the point of finishing each other's thoughts—that was another thing she missed about her wife.

Damn the infection that took the love of her life from her. Having to watch Naomi's organs shut down as she withered away before Silver's eyes was the worst thing that could ever have happened to Silver. Unless they'd been through it, no one could relate to how painful it had been to watch her wife die and not be able to do a damn thing about it.

Silver was lonely, angry, and petrified—in no particular order.

In a moment of insanity, she'd thought up that ridiculous contest, and now she had to follow through on her commitment. Blasted integrity. Why hadn't she dumped that along with her positive outlook on life? But she couldn't put the genie back in the bottle now because she'd already made the arrangements. She was due to pick Jasmine up at the airport in exactly three and a half hours.

As a mildly successful lesbian romance author, she'd offered a home-cooked dinner at her house to the first fan who posted a review for her latest novel, *Resurrection*. She knew before putting the contest on her Facebook page that Jasmine would be the first to respond, and at the time, this was the outcome she believed she wanted, but now that the reality of the situation had smacked her in the face, she was terrified.

Jasmine was her most loyal fan, but not in that crazy Kathy Bates sort of way. Silver shuddered as she thought of the movie *Misery*, where Kathy Bates did an Oscar-worthy performance as a nutcase who kidnaps an author so he'll write another story in her favorite series. Jasmine was sweet and supportive and had been a fan from the very beginning, long before Silver's life went to shit. Jasmine never stepped over the line, because she knew how much Silver loved her wife.

Silver never thought about Jasmine in any other way than a loyal reader, and after a while as a friend—until recently. Lately the tone of their private messages had subtly changed. That was the root of this current evil—that and the bottle of wine she'd consumed right before posting the contest message on Facebook. She hadn't been able to pull it back before Jasmine took the bait.

The review had been so insightful that Silver had memorized nearly every word. She pulled the crumpled piece of paper from her pocket. She'd printed it out after reading what Jasmine had written because they were beautiful words and she needed to read them again and again.

Silver Lining's latest book, Resurrection, has a depth of emotion that brings the reader to tears. When a book can do that for me, the author has reached the pinnacle of greatness. This isn't Silver's normal storyline, nor is it typical for this genre, but it is by far her best work and something no reader who enjoys Silver's books should miss. I felt the anguish and despair of Angela, the main character, as Silver brilliantly brought the reader into her world. Although this was a world of pain, grief, and at times despondency, Silver left me with the feeling that in the end Angela was finally on a path of rebirth. A rebirth into a world where love could be just around the corner. This is a story that needed to be told, and that is evident in her words.

Silver glanced at her watch again and noted that in exactly three hours and twenty minutes, she would be picking up Jasmine from the airport. She'd insisted on personally meeting her there and had offered her the guest bedroom for the long weekend. Demonic possession—that had to be the only logical reason for her rash behavior.

Silver turned back to her great room, looked up at the ceiling, and, upon spying the old water stain, smiled as she remembered how it got there and why she never wanted to have a painter fix it. Silver had started to run a bath and then completely forgot about it when Naomi distracted her. It started with an innocent kiss to the back of her neck, and before Silver knew it, they were rolling around in the bed, arms and legs tangled together, panting, and screaming each other's names. By the time they realized the water was overflowing in their Jacuzzi tub, it was too late.

"God, Naomi, I miss you. Why did you have to leave me all alone to fend for myself? You know I need a keeper. I don't want to move on. Can you ever forgive me for what I've just done? Stupid social media," Silver grumbled.

Socrates, her gray kitten jumped on the island in the kitchen and pulled Silver from her reverie. He pranced around as if he owned the place.

"Socrates, get down. You know Mommy doesn't like it when you get on the counters."

Artemis, her other kitten and sister to Socrates jumped up and joined him. Silver thought they were far too brazen for their own good, but then she was a terrible disciplinarian and somehow they knew that.

"Oh for crying out loud, get down," Silver chastised.

She lifted both kittens from the island and tossed them on the floor. Stereo meows reminded her she hadn't given them their treat yet. For such little things, they sure could bellow loudly, which brought the other three cats waddling into the kitchen.

Silver knew she shouldn't feed them so much, because Sinbad, Plato, and Freud were not fluffy, they were obese. With their bellies practically dragging on the ground, she was amazed they could jump on the counters as easily as the kittens.

Sinbad wove his furry body between her legs and bellowed as loud as the youngsters. Plato and Freud waited patiently sitting a few feet away. Silver imagined this was only because they knew the chorus of meows would spur their minion into action.

"Okay, okay, I'm getting right to it," Silver placated. She chuckled as she thought of the joke about dogs versus cats that Naomi had told her six months before her death. They were relaxing in front of the fire, Silver working on her book, when Naomi started laughing.

"What's so funny?" Silver asked.

"I was thinking about the joke my nephew told me today."

"I could use a good laugh. Tell me," Silver encouraged.

"Oh, I'll probably screw it up, but here goes. So… the dog is patiently waiting for its owner to feed it when it thinks, '*She feeds me, she takes care of me, she pets my head, she loves me. She must be God.* The cat is also waiting, and it thinks, '*she feeds me, she takes care of me, she pets my head, she loves me. I must be God.*'" Naomi burst out laughing.

"You know, that is so true. Remind me why we have cats and not dogs."

Silver pulled the raw food from the refrigerator and distributed it evenly on five plates. After the kittens and cats had gobbled up the treats, she returned to the sliding glass doors and looked out again at the vast property.

The house and the grounds were too much for her to handle on her own and some of the landscaping beds were beyond overgrown, but Silver couldn't part with Naomi's pride and joy. She'd kept the large house on five acres and suffered the dirty looks from her distant neighbors. At first, they'd been sympathetic, but recently they'd started leaving cards with the names of yard management companies. Silver tossed them into the wooden bowl on the kitchen counter and promptly forgot about them. She'd get around to taking care of it once she got a handle on her emotions, but, after three years, letting the yard go had become a habit. A lot of things had become routine, and her perpetual melancholy mood became another bad pattern.

A few days ago, she'd laughed for what felt like the first time in three years after reading one of Jasmine's posts. It was a start.

†

Jasmine peered out the tiny airplane window and gasped as she took in Mt. Rainier in all its glory. The sight, however, did nothing to settle her nerves. *What the hell was I thinking?*

Jasmine had jumped on the challenge the minute Silver had put it on Facebook. She'd never admit it to anyone, but she'd fallen in love, lust, or something else she couldn't quite name with Silver the first time she'd laid eyes on her at the Lesbian Literary Society conference. Silver's first book was good, but since then she'd only gotten better, and now she was a well-known author with her own loyal fan base.

Silver tended to weave her words and characters in a way that sucked a reader in and took them for a wild ride all the way to the inevitable happy conclusion. No book was the same, and the emotions Jasmine felt each time she absorbed Silver's words were nothing short of a miracle. No other author had touched Jasmine as Silver had. If a book could make love to you, Silver's books would and did.

When Jasmine had asked her for her autograph, Silver looked surprised and overwhelmed. She'd blushed, chuckled, and bent her head to scribble her name and a personal message in the book. Her beautiful wife had smiled down at her and said, "See, honey? You're a hit."

Jasmine had been the very first person to ask for Silver's autograph. She'd remained a loyal fan ever since. Since that initial meeting five years ago, a lot had happened. Four years ago, Silver had won her first literary award. Six months later, *The Ellen DeGeneres Show* featured her as an up-and-coming star. Silver had the right combination of good looks, humor, positive messages, humility, and ability to connect with her readers that put her on a trajectory to success.

Jasmine had already developed a solid Facebook friendship with Silver and had a front-row seat to the tragedy that occurred six months after her appearance on *Ellen*. Nothing had been the same since.

Silver was polite when responding to the well-wishes from her readers, but her playful banter had stopped and she hadn't written a single word until six months ago. But Jasmine wouldn't let Silver stop communicating with her and checked in on a weekly basis. She'd gently prodded Silver to start writing again, and finally, Silver had published her most recent book. It was dark, depressing, and devoid of Silver's unique brand of humor. This book was not a lighthearted romance with a happy ending. Instead, she'd written about devastating loss. She captured the emotions so completely the reader fell right into the hole along with the narrator. It was probably her best novel, but that didn't mean it would sell well.

Jasmine knew it wasn't fair, but she'd managed to reveal very little of her own life in their five-year friendship. Silver knew Jasmine had an on-again, off-again relationship with her supervisor, but that was nearly all she'd learned about Jasmine. The only other personal tidbit Silver had asked about and Jasmine had shared, was the broad strokes of what she did for a living.

Jasmine considered all of this as she moved closer to her destination. With each mile the plane traveled through the clouds, her anxiety grew, until the passenger next to her interrupted her panic attack.

The young man had ignored her for the entire flight, choosing to bob his head to the music in his ears while scrolling through his phone. She wasn't sure why he'd suddenly turned his head in her direction and yanked out his earphones, because she was perfectly content with him ignoring her. It clearly wasn't her lucky day.

"Darling, are you all right?" he asked.

Jasmine shook her head and focused on her breathing.

"You know, flying is one of the safest ways to travel. No need to be nervous, but if you're gonna hurl, um, there's a barf bag in the pocket," he offered.

"I'm not afraid of flying. Just stick your earphones back in your ears and ignore me," Jasmine responded.

He shrugged, replaced his earbuds, and turned his attention back to his phone.

Jasmine glanced at her watch and noted the time. In thirty minutes, she would be face-to-face with the object of her desire. She'd probably say something stupid and the rest of the day would be awkward.

Jasmine racked her brain to come up with a clever greeting. She glanced over at her neighbor, and her gaydar pinged loudly. She could tell someone had neatly pressed his shirt and styled his hair perfectly in that messy, but controlled way many gay men always insisted on achieving. He also had those precise mannerisms that screamed persnickety. Since no one else was around to give her solid advice, she tapped him on the shoulder. She didn't know why she'd want his opinion, but she was desperate.

He smiled at her and pulled out his earbuds. "You still look scared. Do you need a distraction or something?"

"Can I ask you a question?"

"Only if we learn each other's names first, because I don't talk to just anybody on an airplane. Preston, at your service." Preston held out his hand, and she tentatively shook it.

"Jasmine," she replied.

"Okay, shoot, since it appears as though our conversation has distracted you from your panic attack." Preston grinned.

"What would you say to a woman you're about to spend the weekend with, that you're secretly in love or lust with, but she doesn't really think about you in the same way and you were only invited because you won a contest? I need a good line or something. She's a writer, so words matter, you know," she blurted out.

"Oh, girlfriend, take a breath." Preston narrowed his eyes. "You're serious," he declared. Jasmine nodded.

"Wow, is she famous or something?" he asked.

"Um…yeah, kinda, I guess, but in a limited, subculture kind of way. You know, lesbians might know her, but you wouldn't. Her name is Silver Lining," Jasmine clarified.

"Nice name. I suppose it's a pen name. Anyway, I guess that makes sense since you said it was a woman and I presume you're gay. So, is she hot?"

"Definitely."

"You going for respect or 'I want to jump your bones'?" Preston asked.

"Well, we kinda have an Internet friendship. We've been corresponding for five years now," Jasmine explained.

"That's a long time to have that kind of friendship. You said this was a contest or something? Are you sure about that? I mean, contests don't usually entail spending the whole weekend with a celebrity. Maybe she wants something and the contest was just a ruse."

Jasmine scrunched up her face. "Do you think that's possible?"

"You ever met her in person before?"

"Yes, once. It was five years ago."

"So, she got a good look at you, right?" he asked.

Jasmine nodded.

"Yeah, I definitely think it's possible. Look, you're drop-dead gorgeous, and if I wasn't gay myself, I probably would have tried to hit on you. I think it's a fair assumption that she might hunger for you as much as you're lusting after her."

Jasmine blushed. "Hmmm. I suppose it's possible she rigged the contest. I'm a beta reader for her, and she knew I'd probably be the first one to post a review once she'd tossed out that challenge. I still need some advice on how to greet her though. I'm about ready to piss my pants here. How can I dazzle this woman right from the start?"

"If you've been friends for five years, how come you haven't tried to hook up before now?"

"She was happily married."

"Was?"

"Her wife died three years ago, and she hasn't really come out of hibernation until now."

"Hmmm…that puts a whole new spin on things," Preston stated.

"Oh God, I am so pathetic. I'm asking a complete stranger how to go about impressing a woman I've only met once, who still mourns her dead wife and lives two thousand miles away in some tiny town in Washington," Jasmine blurted.

"Again, breathe. I'm not a complete stranger now. Girlfriend, now that you know my first name, we'll be besties for life. Okay, listen closely 'cause I'm giving up my best stuff here. Greet her with a hug and hang on just a few seconds longer than normal. Hand her the expensive chocolate and say, 'Life is too short for cheap chocolate.'"

"What? I don't have any chocolate, and that's the best you got? Won't that 'life's too short' thingy remind her of her wife? I don't want to make her any more melancholy than she already is, and trust me, she's not the same woman I met five years ago. I think a part of her died with her wife."

Preston slapped his hand across his chest. "Oh, that is so sad and tragic. Don't worry about the chocolate. I was supposed to bring my boyfriend back some Christopher Elbow artisanal chocolate. They make it right there in Kansas City, Missouri." He waved his hand. "Anyway, he's getting a little pudgy, so he definitely doesn't need any chocolate. You've just given me a great excuse for why I'm not bringing any back for him and I won't have to say anything about his expanding waistline. He's a little sensitive about that."

"That's awful nice of you to offer, but are you sure about that line? It's kind of odd. You got anything else in your arsenal?"

Preston brought his index finger to his cheek and tilted his head. "Hmmmm, okay, how about, 'I've got a feeling we're not in Kansas anymore, but we sure don't need to see the wizard to give you a makeover.' Get it, because we just came from Kansas?"

Jasmine frowned. "Maybe the third time is a charm. One more, please."

"All right. Classic line coming right now. 'You had me at hello.'"

"I think I should stick with the chocolates. At least it's creative and doesn't come from a movie. First, you butcher a quote from *The Wizard of Oz*, which by the way I'm not surprised. I know I'm calling out a rude stereotype, but I'm betting you might have memorized everything Judy Garland said. Then you quote something from *Jerry Maguire*, which is probably the most overused line in the heterosexual world, but doesn't work all that well with lesbians. So, by process of elimination, I'll go with door number one." Jasmine held out her hands. "Gimme the beautiful chocolates, please."

"On one condition," Preston hedged.

Jasmine arched her eyebrow. "Okay, what is it?"

"Call me and tell me every little detail about the weekend. I am such a romantic, and I want to hear all about how you looked into each other's eyes and realized you were madly in love with one another. The weekend progresses and finally your writer friend can move on because she's lucky enough to find love again. I told you we'd become besties, so now I'm holding you to it. Besides, you'll be doing me a huge favor by getting rid of the extra tire maker."

"'Extra tire maker'?" Jasmine scrunched up her face.

"Yeah, that chocolate is sure to put an extra tire around Bruce's waist."

Jasmine chuckled. "You know that's mean, don't you? You shouldn't be saying those things about your boyfriend."

Preston waved his hand. "Oh, he knows I love him."

Jasmine hadn't realized how close they were to landing, and when the plane bumped along on the asphalt as it touched down, the beautiful winged creatures in her stomach began their constant flutter again. She grabbed her stomach and groaned.

Preston pointed to the pocket in front of her. "Barf bag. Don't forget."

"I'm not airsick, you goof, just nervous," Jasmine assured him.

"Oh good, because I have a terrible gag reflex and always do the sympathy puke."

"Ew, can we talk about something else, please?" Jasmine pleaded.

Preston reached under the seat in front of him and pulled out a medium-sized white box from his flat manpurse. He handed Jasmine the box and held out his hand. "Phone, please."

Jasmine lifted her right cheek and pulled her iPhone from her back pocket. She slapped the phone into Preston's hand. "Wow, that must be a really expensive box of chocolates if payment is my phone."

"That's funny—not. I'm putting my phone number in your contacts, and you better not delete me, because I will track your skinny ass down. Pretty Preston under your *P*'s, dear."

Jasmine listened to the passengers unbuckling their seat belts and clutched the box of chocolates as if it were a life raft. After Preston finished putting his number in her phone, he handed it back, grabbed his bag, kissed her on the cheek, and floated down the aisle.

"Call me," Preston ordered, and then he was gone.

Jasmine let all the other passengers deplane before taking a huge breath, standing up, and retrieving her backpack from the overhead bin.

Chapter Two

Silver stood in the middle of her walk-in closet with her fluffy, white robe wrapped protectively around her body. It wasn't giving her much comfort today as she pondered what she was going to wear to pick Jasmine up from the airport.

"Oh for crying out loud, Silver, it's not like this is a date or anything," she lamented.

"Meow," Socrates answered. He'd been weaving in and out of her legs ever since she'd come out of the shower.

Silver thought that with each meow he was asking her in his little kitty manner what was up, because something was definitely going on and he had to know. He was the cat that usually followed her around whenever she was in a frenzy, and she was definitely in panic mode.

Sinbad pranced into the closet. For such a big cat, he had a considerable amount of finesse.

"Meow," Sinbad joined the chorus.

"So, what would you wear to a non-date where you want to entice the person without letting them know you want to make an impression?" Silver looked down at the kitten and his brother.

She began ruffling through her wardrobe, plucking out a myriad of outfits—everything from casual and sporty to elegant and dressy. With an armful of clothes, she walked out to the master bedroom and gently laid each outfit on the bed.

"Hmmm, maybe I should put back the dressy outfits. She might run for the hills if I show up in a satin blouse and tuxedo pants." Silver grabbed her chin and rubbed it in an unconscious gesture of contemplation. "Maybe I should go with some skinny jeans and a nice button-down, fitted shirt. Jasmine's from Kansas, and I'll bet the Midwest doesn't do fancy."

Silver nodded and set aside her low-rider jeans with a bright green shirt that always had the effect of turning her hazel eyes to a soft green. Naomi had always told her it was one of her favorites.

"Oh God, what am I doing? Naomi, I miss you so much. Why did you have to leave me on this unforgiving planet with three furry children who need me? Now I have two more to take care of. Do you think it's wrong of me to do this—whatever the hell *this* is?"

Silver could imagine Naomi chuckling up in heaven. She'd often caught Silver talking to herself or the cats while she worked out dialogue in a new book. Naomi would sneak up on her and kiss her neck just as the dialogue got interesting. That was the sign that it was good and she approved.

At first, her wife would procrastinate reading any new book, but after Silver published her second novel and her wife had loved it, she told Silver she enjoyed reading something she normally stayed clear of. Scientific journals were more suited to Naomi, and she almost never selected romance or fiction.

Silver shook her head. "Talking to my cats and my

dead wife is not a good sign. Crazy cat lady—that is definitely me."

Silver wanted, no, she needed to move on for her own sanity. She was just having a hard time making the transition. The first step had been writing her most recent novel. It wasn't all rainbows and unicorns, and that had surprised a few readers. They expected light, happy tales of romance, but even though this was far from a lighthearted love story, she'd put her heart and soul into the novel and it was probably her best work. She hadn't had the right inspiration to make it as upbeat as most of her other books. Maybe Jasmine would change that.

Silver stepped back into the master bathroom and grabbed her watch that was charging on the bathroom vanity. When she glanced at the time, her panic doubled.

"Aw, shit. I'll probably have to speed now, and you know how Mommy hates to speed."

Silver scooted into the master bedroom and quickly pulled on her jeans. She didn't have time to find underwear and socks. She'd tossed her bra on the nightstand and grabbed it to put on under the shirt she'd picked out. It was one thing to forgo underwear, but whenever she tried to put on a shirt—even a soft cotton one—it rubbed against her nipples and not in a good way. As she walked out of the bedroom buttoning up her shirt, she frantically looked around for her keys.

"Please don't tell me you used my keys as a hockey puck last night. Son of a gun, where did you bat them? You little shits." She glared at three of her cats sprawled on the kitchen table.

Silver had long ago given up on disciplining them in any way that might stop the behavior. Naomi had been so much better at it.

She ran back into the bedroom and bent to check

under the bed. Nothing. "I don't have time for this."

She spied the bits of paper on her nightstand that she'd haphazardly strewn last night as she'd jotted down several notes for the novel she was working on. After lifting the large envelope with her sloppy handwriting covering every empty space at various angles, she saw the glint of silver.

"There you are. Sorry, Socrates, I guess I was too quick to lay the blame on you."

As Silver dashed out the door, she noticed she'd forgotten to button up the last two buttons on her blouse. She chastised herself. It was always the little things that escaped her notice. Naomi usually caught them for her and would gently remind Silver that she wasn't put together before she walked out of the house. She jumped in her car, screeched out of her driveway, and headed to the airport.

†

Jasmine entered the bustling airport like a woman heading to her own execution. Even though it was too late to turn back now, she debated about running to the airline counter and paying for the next available flight back to Kansas City.

Although she hadn't checked a bag, she'd arranged to meet Silver at baggage claim. Jasmine shuffled down the stairs, avoiding the escalator that frightened her almost as much as the impending weekend.

As a small girl, she'd tripped on the last step and face-planted in front of dozens of people in a large shopping mall. Several of her friends at school had seen the embarrassing display and laughed at her. The memory was burned into her psyche. It wasn't the last time the girls in her class would laugh at her. As Jasmine progressed to junior high and high school, the taunts from the gaggle of popular girls grew more frequent. Her combination of Japanese and Norwegian heritage made the fact she wasn't another Midwestern girl next door painfully obvious. Discovering her preference for girls at fourteen didn't help either.

When Jasmine reached the rotating conveyor belt that unceremoniously plopped the bags onto the carousel, she looked around but didn't see Silver anywhere. She was both disappointed and relieved. That gave her a few more minutes to collect herself. She'd secured her backpack and left her hands free to clutch the fancy box of chocolates. As she was second-guessing herself about the greeting Preston had suggested, she looked up, and there was Silver panting from obviously having just sprinted into the airport.

"Sorry, oh God, I'm so sorry I'm late," Silver said in an explosion of air, trying to catch her breath at the same time she offered her greeting.

Jasmine thrust the box of chocolates at her. "Life is too short for cheap chocolate."

"What?" Silver scrunched up her face.

"I knew that was dumb," she mumbled. Jasmine stood in front of Silver and wondered whether she should try to hug her.

Silver took a step forward and accepted the offered box as a small smile blossomed on her lips.

"Did you bring me chocolate?"

Jasmine nodded, and Silver reached her arms around in an attempt at a hug. With the box of chocolates in one hand and Jasmine's backpack in the way, it was beyond awkward, but Jasmine put her arms around Silver and did as Preston suggested—held on just a few seconds more than was normal for a typical friend hug. At first, Silver stiffened, then she relaxed and seemed to accept Jasmine's attempt to greet her.

"Yoo-hoo, Jasmine, honey," Preston interrupted.

Jasmine groaned as she let go of Silver. She turned to see Preston grabbing the hand of a short, slightly pudgy man with round spectacles approaching her with a wide grin.

"This is my boyfriend, Bruce. Is this Silver?" he asked.

Bruce narrowed his eyes and seemed to have a laser focus on the white box in Silver's hand. "Oh no, tell me you did not give away my box of chocolates."

Preston put his finger to his own mouth. "Shh. I'll get you another."

Jasmine cringed. "Kill me, kill me now, and put me out of my misery," she whispered to herself.

Silver looked perplexed. "Um, hello."

"Jasmine and I are besties now. We met on the plane. I know y'all have a busy weekend planned, but when Jassy here comes back to Seattle, we all simply must get together. I'm dying to get to know a famous lesbian author."

"I'm not famous. I'm not even particularly good," Silver corrected.

"Stop that right now. You know you have a huge following and everyone loves your work because you are a fantastic writer," Jasmine chastised.

"I don't think readers would agree based on feedback from my last novel," Silver argued.

Preston grabbed Jasmine first, pulled her into a hug, and proceeded to kiss the air on each side of her cheeks. After he was finished with Jasmine, he repeated the process with Silver—apparently taking her by surprise, based on her facial reaction. "Tootles, you two." He put his hand up to his ear and mouthed, "Call me," at Jasmine and then dragged Bruce out the door.

"I'm glad you're here, but I have to admit I'm not sure how I feel about your friend." Silver chuckled. "I'm sure he's harmless, but a bull in a china shop comes to mind. That brief interaction exhausted me."

"Confession time. In a moment of insanity, I actually asked a stranger for advice on how to greet you. Preston was sitting next to me, and well, Chocolategate was born. On the upside, he did give me that super-nice box of chocolates to present to you in hopes I might dazzle you with my newfound brilliance. I'm afraid it went over like a lead balloon. That's the last time I'll take advice from a perfect stranger. Although I did kind of grow to like his exuberance and I might just call him for grins after the weekend," Jasmine explained.

Silver laughed, and it was music to Jasmine's ears. "I'll match that confession and raise you one embarrassing revelation. I stood in front of my closet and asked for advice from my furbabies on what to wear to pick you up at the airport. Ridiculous, I know."

"That's twice in less than five minutes I've heard you laugh or chuckle. My work here is done. Of course, I had help from an outrageous queen. I think we all need one of those in our lives. It keeps things light. Lead the way, oh famous lesbian author." Jasmine smiled.

"Oh and for the record, the chocolates did not go over like a lead balloon. The quickest way to a woman's heart is with chocolate, especially expensive chocolate." Silver winked.

"Good to know, yes, very good to know." Jasmine's smile could have lit up downtown Seattle.

Silver wasn't quite sure if she was supposed to hug Jasmine or not, but since they'd been writing back and forth for the past four years and the posts in the last six months had seemed to slide naturally into a closer, more personal space, she took the plunge.

At first, she struggled to navigate around the backpack

and her halfhearted attempt was lame, but then Jasmine seemed to draw her in, and Silver definitely stayed in an embrace longer than two friends would have.

Silver nearly bit her tongue when Preston barged in and rudely interrupted her just as she took in Jasmine's sweet citrus scent—*orange spice*. In that instance when she'd started to take a deep breath before the disruption, she felt a sense of peace. Still, Silver supposed his intrusion broke the ice, and that was a good thing. She'd even laughed—twice. Her laughter spontaneously bubbled from her chest. It felt like a foreign object at first, and then she remembered how often she used to laugh when Naomi was alive. She didn't exactly classify her laughter as a miracle, but it was something new for her. The fact Jasmine had noticed brought the realization to the forefront.

"Do you have another bag we need to wait for?"

"Nope. I packed light, not much baggage at all," Jasmine answered.

"Does this translate to your life as well?" Silver asked.

Jasmine arched her eyebrow. "Hmmm, are you asking me if I'm involved with anyone right at this moment, or whether I have deep-seated emotional issues and will turn into some crazed fan the minute we get to your house?"

Silver shook her head. "Sorry, rewind. That was very inappropriate of me to ask. Can we just forget the last ten seconds ever happened?"

Jasmine smiled. "At this very moment, I am free as a bird, but doesn't everyone have some baggage?"

"I suppose so, but I imagine some have a single carryon, while others bring their matching seven-piece set. I probably fall somewhere in between, but lately might fall into the latter category." Silver shrugged. "Let's get out of here before I step into it any more than I already have. I'd take you to see Pike Place Market, but it's getting late and you're probably tired."

"I'm up for anything, but don't feel like you have to be a tour guide for me. I'm usually content in a quiet setting without a lot of shiny baubles to distract me. Your place sounds lovely and restful," Jasmine assured her.

Silver bravely looped her arm through Jasmine's and led her to the short-term parking area. She'd been able to get a parking space on the same level as baggage claim. They dashed across the street, and Silver unhooked her arm from Jasmine's and retrieved her key from her pocket. She pressed a button on the fob and the lights blinked on a black Volkswagen Passat. After Jasmine slipped her backpack off, Silver grabbed it and put it in the back, where the hatch lay open like a baby bird ready to receive a meal from its mother. She gently set the pack next to her bag of recycling that she'd forgotten to empty earlier in the week.

"Thank you. I could have laid it at my feet, but it's nice to have the extra leg room. How long will it take to get to your place?" Jasmine asked.

"Oh, about an hour and a half. It's just on the other side of the pass. It's a very scenic drive through the mountains that I think you'll enjoy. I never get tired of the beauty." Silver sighed.

Driving through the mountains had been one of Naomi's favorite things to do. They both loved to ski and hike—those were two of the many things that drew them both to the area.

Jasmine climbed into the passenger seat and turned her head in Silver's direction as she slid into the driver's side and buckled up. "Did you just have a nice memory pop into your head?"

Silver looked into Jasmine's ice-blue eyes and saw nothing but compassion. She decided to tell the truth. "Yes, Naomi would always comment about how much she liked driving through the pass on her way to Seattle or coming back from the city. The mountains have a healing effect on me, and they did on her as well."

Silver started the car and took a big breath before putting it in gear.

Jasmine placed her hand on top of Silver's. "It's good to keep remembering the pleasant things. It keeps her in your heart, which is a place that she'll always be."

Silver couldn't help the tear that managed to escape and travel down her cheek. "Memories are all I have left of her, but I've been using them as a crutch. I'll never walk on my own again if I don't find a way to keep my memories without losing myself in the process."

Jasmine brought her hand to Silver's cheek and wiped the tear away. "I'm not even going to try to offer any of these old clichés because I don't know what it's like to walk in your shoes. I hope you know you always have an ear to bend or shoulder to cry on with me."

Silver nodded and turned her head over her shoulder as she backed out of the parking space. She traversed through the winding cement structure until she made it to the highway.

Deep in thought over Jasmine's genuine offer, she almost missed the turnoff to I-90. When she jerked the wheel and crossed quickly over two lanes, she glanced over at Jasmine, who had gripped the "oh shit" bar and was looking wide-eyed at the car directly in front of them.

Silver eased off the gas to avoid hitting it. "Sorry, sorry. I'm not usually a reckless driver. I was daydreaming and almost missed the exit. I swear, most people call me a gramma driver. I tend to go ten miles under the speed limit on the highway. Really, I promise you are safe with me. It used to drive Naomi nuts and she would insist on driving everywhere, stating she wanted to get to our destination in this century."

Jasmine released the bar and smiled. "It's okay. I believe you. I do feel safe with you, but I admit that little maneuver did scare the crap out of me."

"Does it bother you that I talk about Naomi all the time?"

"No, of course not. She was a big part of your life and someone you should never forget. I'm afraid I can't really relate to a love that pure. My on-again, off-again relationship doesn't compare at all. She's been like an addiction to me—an unhealthy one. I suppose I should be flattered someone that accomplished took notice of me. I don't recommend getting involved with your boss though. It makes it uncomfortable during the off-again times." Jasmine sighed.

"Why don't you just get another job?" Silver asked.

"As uncomfortable as it gets when we're off-again, like right now, it's secure and easy. Making a change like that would send me into a frenzy I'm not prepared to handle. It's easier now that I don't work directly for her anymore. Dara offered me a job eighteen years ago when prospects were limited for a young woman with a women's studies degree. I should have pursued business or just about any other degree than that one. I know it's not a major accomplishment or anything, but I worked my way up in the company from a lowly clerk to her administrative assistant. She depended on me to keep her work life organized. Now I'm in the Human Resources department, and that has growth potential," Jasmine explained.

"I could use someone like you to keep me organized. Naomi used to do that for me. She would make all the travel arrangements, set up the book signings, and generally organize my chaotic life. I don't travel anymore. I'm fairly certain you're the only reader who's stuck by me during the lean times when I didn't produce a single thing, not even a short story or novella."

"Is that a job offer?" Jasmine chuckled. "No, don't answer that. If it was for real it might be too tempting, and then you would send me into a state of apoplexy."

As they traveled over the mountain pass, Silver pointed out the various landmarks and explained how the Keechelus Lake provided the lifeblood irrigation to the farmers and residents of upper Kittitas County.

"These last couple of years we haven't had the necessary snowfall, and it created havoc on our forests and farmlands. Last year the forest fires on the east side of the state were very dangerous. Nothing came close to the house, but some of the people I used to work with lost their home. It was heartbreaking. I was in my own state of depression at the time and wasn't a great friend. I should have reached out to them, but I didn't."

"I'm sure they understood," Jasmine replied.

Silver nodded absently. She remained quiet the rest of the way to her house and was thankful Jasmine didn't feel the need to occupy the peaceful space. Her music played in the background and Silver listened as Brandi Carlile belted out "The Story." It was one of Naomi's favorite songs. Silver lamented not being able to enjoy the company of this beautiful, compassionate woman as she continued to think about her dead wife. Would it never end? The grief that completely overtook her former life and changed her forever now clung to her like a bloodsucking leech.

Chapter Three

As they pulled up to Silver's house, Jasmine marveled at the beauty. Large evergreen trees stretched to the heavens as they framed her charming home. Upon closer inspection, she noted weeds in the few visible patches of landscape. The ferns, plants, and variety of trees crowded most of the weeds out, but there were a few places Jasmine thought needed some tender loving care. However, none of those overgrown areas detracted from the glorious view as the mountains provided a picturesque backdrop. Jasmine had the feeling Silver's home was a deep breath of peace for her. She was glad for this one bright spot in Silver's otherwise sad world since her wife had passed.

"Wow, your house is simply breathtaking. How in the world do you get anything done with this view? I would be astral-traveling twenty-four hours a day with this panorama of exquisiteness. We're not in Kansas anymore," Jasmine enthused.

Silver chuckled. "I suppose you don't have mountains in Kansas, huh?"

"Preston told me I should use that line on you when

you picked me up from the airport, but even I knew not to add the second part to it," Jasmine confessed.

"Oh, I have to hear the second part now. You can't leave me hanging."

"Okay, but you have to promise not to laugh too hard, because I confess I did consider it for a brief moment."

Silver crossed her heart with her index finger. "I promise."

"I've got a feeling we're not in Kansas anymore, but we sure don't need to see the wizard to give you a makeover."

"Oh my God, that is horrible."

"I know, right? Aren't you glad I came to my senses? You would have gone screaming into the hills and I'd be stranded at the airport right now."

Silver laughed.

"I'm so glad I can make you laugh. Shall I reveal the third line he suggested?"

"Oh yes, please do. If it's as good as the others, I must know. Inquiring minds, you know."

"You had me at hello," Jasmine revealed.

"Okay, not exactly original, but that one is the least campy."

"So was that greeting better than, 'Life's too short for cheap chocolate'?" Jasmine asked.

"Oh no, that was perfect, especially when you handed me the chocolate, which by the way I am dying to tear into. Let's go into the house and see what treasures lie inside the little white box," Silver directed.

Silver pressed the garage-door opener and the door whirred upward.

Jasmine noted the disarray. A lawn tractor occupied the space on the right. Several coolers were scattered to the left of the tractor, along with a push mower, cans of paint, several bikes, bags of recycling, plants, and other boxes. Several recumbent bicycles, including two trikes, hung on the walls.

Silver put the car in park and walked around to the back to retrieve Jasmine's backpack.

"Don't judge me too harshly for my garage. I've been meaning to clean it out so I can park my car there, but just haven't had the energy to do it." Silver scrunched up her face. "I suppose from an outsider's perspective, this screams, 'Hoarder, hoarder, clutter supporter.' We were both at fault on this. The builder never put in a path to the front door, so we've always just entered the house through the garage. Welcome to my world of craziness. You already know I have five cats, and I hope you're not allergic. My furbabies rule the roost. They'll want to climb all over any new victim vying for attention. I don't know if it's a blessing or a curse that none of them fall into the stereotypic aloof category."

"I love cats. I didn't have five, mind you, but I miss Harold and Maude. Maude got sick six months ago, and I finally had to put her to sleep. It broke my heart when Harold stopped eating and I finally had to let him go as well. I know I waited too long for both, but I just couldn't part with them until it became clear that they wanted me to release them from their pain." A tear slipped out as Jasmine revealed this.

"Oh crap, I forgot. You mentioned that in a PM to me. Sorry, I've been so self-absorbed lately."

"No worries. I can't wait to have a cat climb all over me—or kitten. Kittens are so much fun. When you posted the pictures after you rescued them and I saw their sweet little faces, I got so excited about meeting them."

Jasmine followed Silver into the house, where an enormous black cat and two small kittens were waiting on the other side of the door.

"Back, back, back," Silver directed at her furchildren.

"Be careful, Jasmine, they are little escape artists and they know they aren't allowed outside without supervision."

"Oh my God, the kittens are so adorable." Jasmine scooped up the little gray one.

"That's Socrates. He's a little lover. His sister is the little gray-and-orange tabby. She's going to start crying for attention any minute now."

"Meow," the small tabby interjected.

"Yep, right on cue." Silver put the box of chocolates on the unique kitchen island made of a large block of wood and set the backpack on the floor beside it. She picked up Socrates's sister and kissed her nose. "You big baby, Artemis, you can't stand that Jasmine picked up Socrates first."

The big black cat started weaving in and out of Silver's legs. She gently put Artemis down and picked up the big feline.

"Is that handsome fellow in your arms Mister Freud or Mister Sinbad?"

"This is Sinbad. Freud will come out later, but he's very shy. He doesn't generally greet visitors. Not that I've had any in the past three years, but he never greeted them before...." Silver didn't finish her thought.

"Where's Plato?" Jasmine asked.

"He'll come around before Freud does, but he's a bit on the shy side too. Freud and Plato were feral kittens when I first got them, and they haven't lost that wariness. Both of them are real sweethearts, but they have to get to know strangers before they make their appearance. I suspect they are peering out at you from whatever hiding place they've chosen for today."

Jasmine continued to stroke the kitten, who licked her face and purred loudly. "I'm in love," she blurted out.

Silver whipped her head around to look at Jasmine, and her wide-eyed panic took Jasmine by surprise. "What?"

"With your kitten," Jasmine amended.

"Oh." Silver put down Sinbad and picked up the backpack. "I'll just put this in the spare bedroom."

Silver scurried out of the kitchen, and Jasmine watched her climb the stairs to where she suspected the master and spare bedrooms were located. She wondered what Silver's master bedroom was like but shook her head and told herself to stop thinking about those things. Friends, they were only friends, right?

Jasmine awkwardly waited in the kitchen. She wasn't sure what she was supposed to do. Did Silver expect her to follow her up the stairs? She felt a buzz in her back pocket, put the kitten down on the shiny maple-wood floor, and pulled her cell phone out.

"Hello…. Oh, hi, Dara. We just got to her house…. Don't start, please…. I know, I didn't come here for that…. Oh for God's sake, what do you care anyway...? I have not."

Jasmine looked up as Silver entered the kitchen. "Look, I gotta go. I'll talk to you later…. It's in the file cabinet beside your desk under the board committees section…. I'm sure Barbie can find it for you. She seems to have found everything else for you lately…. Oh, pity. I thought this one would last a bit longer…. Please don't force me to do something neither one of us would want. I don't want to talk to my boss, but I will if you don't start relying on your new assistant and leave me alone…. I'm hanging up now."

Jasmine jabbed at the End button and sighed. She knew she should have let the call go to voicemail and wasn't sure why she'd bothered to answer.

Silver stared at her, and the pointed gaze caused Jasmine to look down to avoid the question in her eyes.

"You okay?" Silver asked.

"Yeah, that was Dara, but I suspect you already

guessed that."

She was glad when Silver changed the subject. "How hungry are you?"

Jasmine shrugged.

"I've planned a home-cooked meal for tomorrow, so how about if we order a pizza? The place I get it from is great, but very slow. Well…that's not really fair because I do live out in the boonies and it takes them longer to deliver to my address. Are you okay with waiting forty-five minutes to an hour?"

"Oh absolutely." Jasmine felt the buzz of the phone in her hand and chose to ignore it when she glanced at the screen and noted it was Dara again.

"I have beer, wine, hard cider, hard lemonade, water, Diet Pepsi, um, I think that's about all."

Jasmine laughed. "I'll take a hard cider. Beer or cider seems to go well with pizza, and I don't really care for beer."

"Me neither, but I didn't know what to stock up on, so I got a wide variety. I'm usually a wine or cider girl myself when I eat pizza. Hard lemonade is nice on a really hot day, but not necessarily with pizza." Silver pulled open the refrigerator and grabbed two ciders. She handed one to Jasmine and pointed to the sliding glass doors.

"Your view in the back is as breathtaking as the front. I think if I lived here, I would never leave the property."

"It's still relatively nice out, so do you want to sit outside while we wait? Do you have a special preference on toppings, or can I surprise you with my favorite?"

"As long as it doesn't have meat, like sausage or pepperoni, I'm good," Jasmine answered.

"I'll call right now. Go on out, I'll be there in a minute," Silver directed.

†

Silver hesitated for a second after placing the call and watched as Jasmine's beautiful face looked at her mountains.

Jasmine was a striking woman. Her black hair fell in one silky shroud over her back. Silver wondered what it would be like to kiss those plump, red lips. Her angular-shaped eyes in combination with the ice-blue color were beyond remarkable. Her pert nose sat perfectly between impossibly high cheekbones. Silver often wondered why Jasmine hadn't pursued a career in modeling. She would have been a shoe-in. The tiny half-moon scar on her chin could easily be air-brushed out of a close-up.

Silver wanted to kiss the scar. She'd always wanted to ask her about it but didn't want to appear rude.

She took a deep breath and pushed open the sliding glass door, noting the dirty glass. She had a fleeting notion that Jasmine wouldn't have noticed this. She seemed preoccupied, and Silver wondered if the call from Dara had rattled her. She was curious about Dara and hoped asking about her on-again, off-again ex wouldn't be a sore subject.

"I think if I lived out here, I would host a barbecue every week. It's just too spectacular not to share with other people," Jasmine broke into Silver's internal dialogue.

"I'm not big on parties. That was Naomi's forte. You know what, I'd like to do something tonight, and I need your help," Silver declared.

"Anything you need," Jasmine answered.

"I'd like tonight to be a Naomi-free zone. For just one night, I don't want to remember anything about her. I don't want to talk about her, think about her, nothing. Instead, I want to learn more about you. If I stumble and revert to my rut, I need you to gently remind me. I haven't been very fair to you when every other minute I talk about Naomi. Deal?" Silver pleaded.

"If that's what you really want, I can do that," Jasmine whispered.

"It is. Tell me about Dara, if it's not too painful to talk about."

Jasmine paused and took a deep breath before responding. "I was twenty-one when we met, and I went gaga over her. She didn't have to work very hard to seduce me. I've always been a sucker for beautiful, successful older women." She pinned Silver with a smoky look.

"Go on, don't tell me that's all I get," Silver teased.

"At the time I wasn't admitting to anyone else that I was attracted to women, and I guess you could say I had a hard time coming to terms with my sexuality. The relationship suffered from my initial waffling, so it's my fault Dara started acting on her roving eye. Our first breakup was because of my inability to be open about my sexuality."

"And…," Silver prodded.

"We'd been seeing each other for about six months and a lawyer for the company started buzzing around. I was flattered by the attention he paid me. He was handsome, rich, and very nice. If there was ever a man I could fall for, it would have been Peter. Dara could tell I was ambivalent about him. A new clerk had started the month before, and Dara noticed her right away. She was a gorgeous woman and hung on Dara's every word. That was the start of a pattern that's followed our relationship for the past eighteen years."

"So did you ever date Peter?"

"On no, I was ambivalent, but I knew deep down that dating a man was never going to do it for me," Jasmine explained.

"So what pattern are you referring to?"

"Something prompts an argument, we fight, Dara finds someone else to warm her bed, and then blames me for whatever caused the argument in the first place. She apologizes and tells me I'm the only one for her after spending a bit of time with the flavor of the month. I take her back because I believe she's right and I'm the one who caused the row. The pattern occurs every couple of years and, on a few occasions, she's stayed with the new woman a year or two. During those times, I've managed to have my own short relationships, but none worth staying away when Dara comes calling again."

"Wow, eighteen years. That's a long time to do this dance. Have you ever thought about going to counseling and dealing with the root issues?"

"I have, but you know, I don't think what we have is really soul-deep love. It's been more of a habit that's hard to break. Five years ago, if she'd asked, I would have married her—not that she ever would have asked, but that all changed when I saw how a real relationship is supposed to work. I saw what I was missing—the passion, the deep love and respect. Ours was never like…oh shit, sorry, I almost broke the rule for tonight."

Silver waved her hand in the air. "No worries, good save in the end."

"When I first met her, she was on the selection committee for the medical records clerk job I applied for. That's what they called it back then. I had zero experience, but every time I looked at Dara, she nodded and smiled at me. It helped. I'm sure she was the reason the hospital offered me the position. Every time she received a promotion, there was a magical opportunity for me and I rose along with her. I never worked directly for her until about five and a half years ago when she hired me as her administrative assistant. The lesbian writers and readers conference wasn't her thing, but she came with me that very first time when I met you. I don't know if you remember her."

"She was the woman nearly welded to your hip," Silver answered.

Jasmine nodded. "Anyway, six months ago I'd had enough of her shit and went to HR. I asked for a transfer after our last fight. It was the first time I actually fought back and gave as good as I got. Human Resources had an opening for an assistant, and they gave me the position. They even kept my salary the same, although the position was about a dollar less than my range. I think they were afraid I would file a sexual harassment lawsuit. Our relationship was the best-kept non-secret in the organization. Everyone knew the CEO was sleeping with her assistant, but not one person said a word."

"So what prompted the last breakup?"

"Dara was looking over my shoulder six months ago when I sent that PM to you."

Silver tilted her head. "What PM?"

"Remember when I asked if you had dipped your toes into the dating pool yet?" Jasmine asked.

"Oh yeah, I remember." Silver slapped her hand to her mouth. "Oh no, I knew better than to respond the way I did."

Jasmine chuckled. "Yeah, Dara was not too amused by your response. When you sent back the question, 'Are you offering?' the fireworks started."

"Oh, God, I am so sorry. I never intended that to cause problems. That was very inappropriate of me. I can talk to her if you want. Maybe you two can patch things up."

"Don't worry—it was the prodding I needed to get off my butt and end the destructive cycle. We said some nasty things to one another that can't be taken back. This time it's over and there's no turning back now."

Jasmine took a sip of her cider. "I don't want to return to that. I need to move on. Dara uses our fights as an excuse to do what she really wants. She's like that dog in the animated movie *Up*, you know the one who keeps saying, 'Squirrel,' every time he's distracted by a new, shiny object? Beautiful women are Dara's new, shiny objects. Sometimes it takes longer than other times for her to realize that beneath all that glitter is dull, cheap metal."

"I just have a hard time imaging any shiny, new object being brighter than you. Dara is a fool. Are you positive the relationship can't be saved? What could you have possibly said to one another that couldn't be marked off as words you didn't mean in the heat of an argument?"

Jasmine laughed. "I told her she was a pathetic, middle-aged cougar that couldn't keep a woman satisfied even with an instruction manual to the elusive G-spot and that I'd been faking orgasms for years."

"Ouch."

"Oh, she got me back by saying I was a lowly secretary too dumb to have a real career. She followed that with something like, 'You're so pitiful pining after a woman who isn't likely to realize you even exist.'"

"Harsh. So, do you have a love interest? Tell me all about it. I need to live vicariously through someone, so it might as well be you."

Jasmine tipped her bottle of cider. "This was really good. Do you mind if I have one more? I promise not to get drunk and say inappropriate things."

Ding-dong.

"Saved by the bell. We'll take up this topic after we satisfy our hunger. That was the fastest time they've ever delivered, but don't worry, I won't forget what we were talking about earlier." Silver winked.

Chapter Four

The middle-aged woman held the tumbler of expensive scotch in a white-knuckled death grip so tight that if she had supernatural strength, she would have crushed it. She looked at the picture of Jasmine and Silver smiling for the camera at the writer's conference five years ago. She'd been stalking them both on their Facebook pages ever since. She barely saw the shadow of herself in the background of that picture. She'd gone to the conference as a lark.

That was when it all started. The conference where they'd met. It was irritating when she hadn't remembered her from the writer's convention. She had sensed her love was ready for a new beginning, but then that blasted contest interfered with her plans. It didn't matter now though because she was getting closer to making her move, preparing the soil, and was confident it would work out for them.

The nasty pictures in her head wouldn't go away. The woman imagined Jasmine and Silver sprawled on a massive bed screwing like little bunnies. They were together now, and that was unacceptable.

She read on Jasmine's Facebook page about how excited she was to have won the contest and to spend time with her favorite author. Silver had announced the winner of that stupid contest a month ago, and now the two of them were together, doing God knows what while she was helpless to stop anything.

She rubbed her finger around the rim of the glass and then in a fit of anger slammed the tumbler on the table before sweeping it into her fireplace. The leftover alcohol flashed as the combustible liquid hit the flames.

"Perhaps I'll take another vacation to Seattle. I've heard it's beautiful there this time of the year."

The ominous nature of the remark seemed to hover in the air above her. She'd hidden her malady well over the years. Not even her closest friends or lovers realized how unbalanced she was.

As a respected professional, she'd fooled everyone. The slow progression of the tumor in her brain had eaten away at her sanity when five years ago, the poison began to take root, and her obsession grew exponentially. It was a miracle no one had noticed.

She glanced at the broken glass scattered around the bricks of her fireplace. She set her laptop on the coffee table in front of her, and her chair creaked as she emerged to pick up the pieces of glass.

As she grabbed a large, jagged piece, the sharp edge sliced her flesh and the blood pooled on her finger. She looked curiously at the cut, wondering if it was deep enough to go to urgent care and get stiches. Her thoughts took her to what seeing the traitor's blood spilled on the floor might be like. Did she have carpet, tile, or wood floors? Tile or wood would be easier to clean.

The grin spread across her face as she imagined her competition dead with her vacant, wide eyes open and staring into space. She didn't have a choice anymore. She needed to eliminate the woman, and then she could woo the other and finally have her heart's desire. She had no doubt that once that obstacle was gone, everything would work out.

†

Silver leaned back in the patio chair and groaned. "I always eat too much of their pizza. I know its name, Pumba, is odd, but that's one of the finest combination of ingredients I've ever come across. I always overindulge."

Jasmine patted her stomach. "I'd have to agree with you. I like all the ingredients, but basil pesto sauce, fresh garlic, feta, Kalamata olives, artichoke hearts, and tomatoes all rolled together was perfection in a pie. I don't think I can move. Just toss me a pillow and I'll just fall asleep out here looking at the stars with your beautiful mountains embracing me as I dream. I can now die a happy woman."

Silver frowned. "Don't say that."

Jasmine winced. "Oh God, sorry. I didn't mean it like that."

"I know, I'm too sensitive. Hey, can I show you something? I'd like your take on it," Silver asked.

Jasmine was glad Silver had abruptly changed the subject. She didn't want their evening to take a depressing turn or for her to have to remind Silver about the deal she'd agreed to earlier. "Sure."

"Wait here, I'll get my laptop."

Jasmine blew out a breath and crossed her ankles.

A few minutes later, Silver came back to the porch carrying her laptop. "About five years, ago I accepted a friend request from this woman who claimed she'd met me at the writer's conference and loved my work. The only person I really remember at that conference was you because we took that picture in front of my publisher's booth. I remember being flattered that anyone would want my autograph and a picture."

"Okay," Jasmine hedged.

"Since then, I get an odd PM from her every once in a while. She was also a beta reader for me and honestly provided good feedback. I didn't send her my last book though; I only sent that to you, and I'm not sure why. Normally they are benign, but this last one kind of crossed the line into creepy." Silver handed Jasmine the laptop. "What do you make of her latest message? I'm not sure why this message struck me as odd, but it gave me the heebie-jeebies."

Jasmine looked at the text in the small rectangular box on the screen.

I'm coming to Washington. See you soon. I hope you look forward to the visit as much as I do.

"What do you know about this woman?" Jasmine asked.

"Not much. Like I said, the private messages were infrequent. They've always been a little odd, but I just assumed they were jokes or innocent flirtations. They were things like, 'Did you write that last book with me in mind?' Or 'Wow, you nailed me with your description of Sasha.' Remember, Sasha was one of my characters in my third book. I would write back something like 'LOL' and pass it off as a joke. At first, I think she posted on my wall because we had something in common."

"What did you have in common?"

"Well, you know, before I made any real money at writing, I worked in healthcare. That was the job that paid the bills. I remembered when you told me that you worked for a hospital. I suppose there are a lot of lesbians who work in that field because it's a predominantly female occupation.

Apparently, she does as well. Her Facebook name is Nurse Executive. She could be a chief nursing officer somewhere or maybe even a CEO. The hospital I used to work for had a nurse as their top executive."

"You know what's so strange about this? Dara was a nurse executive before her promotion to CEO. What a weird coincidence. I know she's not really a huge fan of yours, especially after seeing that message six months ago, although I did make her read all your books. I'm not really an expert on things like this, but I think you might have a stalker. It could be dangerous, so if I were you, I'd show this to the police. Let them decide if it's something you should be worried about."

"It's probably nothing, but it did unnerve me," Silver admitted.

Jasmine noted the worried look on her face. "If you want I can go with you to the police."

"Thanks, I appreciate the offer, but I don't want to waste our time together with a boring trip to the police department. I want to show you my beautiful state."

Jasmine grinned at her. "So, are you too full to break into Preston's box of delectable chocolates? I just can't imagine what treasures are waiting for us."

"Holy cow, I've been having such a good time, I completely forgot about that. Let me tell you that is a cataclysmic feat because I never forget about chocolate. Normally, I would have had half the box eaten by now. I am never too full for chocolate, so we're breaking into that bad boy right now."

Silver set the laptop on the patio table, jumped up, and raced into the house. Thirty seconds later, she returned with the white box in her hands, and a huge smile blossomed on her face. She lifted the lid and peered inside.

"Oh, Jasmine, these are almost too beautiful to eat.

Almost being the operative word. Wow, there are some unusual flavors. Yum, there's lavender, spiced apple, key lime pie, passion-fruit, bananas Foster, Venezuelan dark, rosemary, champagne..."

Jasmine was delighted to see Silver so overjoyed with the gift. She would definitely have to call Preston and thank him for his generous gesture.

"Whatever you don't want, just toss my way," Jasmine said.

"I should really let you pick first. You are the guest of honor, but I can for sure give up this raspberry one. I don't care much for raspberries."

Silver walked over and tilted the box as Jasmine peered inside.

"Oh, these are beautiful. Which one is the raspberry chocolate?"

Silver pointed to the square with round, red circles in the middle of the decadent treat.

Jasmine removed the artistic creation and popped it in her mouth at the same time Silver selected the oval-shaped, lavender candy.

"Oh holy hell, this is the most scrumptious thing I think I've ever tasted. I might have to move to Kansas City to be near the factory," Silver gushed.

"This one is sinfully good as well," Jasmine mumbled while chewing the dessert. "Can I try another?"

Silver hugged the box. "Mine." She laughed. "Just kidding. Here. I'll bet the key lime pie will get your juices flowing."

Jasmine blushed.

"Oh my God, I didn't… never mind… I'll just stop right there before I dig a deeper hole." Silver chuckled and handed Jasmine the lime-colored piece shaped in a decorative swirl.

"Don't offer me any more or I'll tackle you and shove the rest in my mouth just like Lucy and Ethel when they got behind in the chocolate factory on the *I Love Lucy* show."

Silver doubled over in laughter. "I just got a visual of you doing that. *I Love Lucy* is one of the funniest television shows ever made, and that scene is classic."

"Seriously, I think I'm done now, because if I have one more piece of candy I will blow up like that blueberry girl in *Willy Wonka and the Chocolate Factory*."

"You mean Violet?" Silver asked.

"Okay, I am seriously impressed you remember that character's name." Jasmine giggled.

"It's either getting extremely late and we're getting slap-happy or we've had too much to drink." Silver held up her bottle. "Care for another?"

"Sure, why not. I'm on a mini vacation, but if you try to wake me before nine a.m., I'll scratch your eyes out and that would be a pity since they're so beautiful." Jasmine slapped her hand across her mouth. "Aw crap. I said that out loud, didn't I?"

Silver smiled. "You sure did, and now you can't take it back. It's been a very long time since a gorgeous woman complimented me. Thank you."

"That's only because you've been living like a hermit for the past three years. Oh God, shoot me, shoot me right now. I am so sorry. You've had a damn good reason for locking yourself away. Can you just hand me a bottle of Jack Daniels and I'll drink myself into a quiet stupor? I'm not always this insensitive. When I'm nervous, stupid words flow out of my mouth like a raging river. I promised not to get drunk and say anything inappropriate, but I've only kept half my promise—I swear I'm not drunk," Jasmine blurted.

Silver chuckled. "It's okay. For what it's worth, I've thoroughly enjoyed myself tonight. The few times we've slipped and danced the edges of that depressing topic that I made you promise to avoid, you've caught yourself. I'm grateful for the company of someone that doesn't have fur covering one hundred percent of their body. My cats have great listening skills, but *meow* is the only word in their vocabulary."

Jasmine watched as Silver went back into the house to retrieve another cider. It would be her third for the evening. She was already feeling good and made a promise to herself this would be the final one. Slightly tipsy was acceptable. Falling-down drunk was not. She needed a little bit of liquid courage because just being in the presence of Silver was nerve-wracking. She was far too enamored with the famous author for her own good, and she knew it. The fact Silver was every bit as nice in person as she was when interacting with her readers on social media wasn't helping Jasmine keep her feelings in check. Falling for her would be so easy.

Silver was smiling when she stepped onto the back patio. She handed Jasmine an open bottle of cider.

"You know, I'm not a very good host. I never asked if you wanted a glass. I just assumed you were a heathen like me and drink straight from the bottle. I guess it's too late now to correct my oversight," Silver confessed.

Jasmine twirled her hand in the air. "You should know by now that I am a heathen—a big old lesbian heathen. You know, there's actually a Facebook group called Lesbian Heathens. They asked me to join. I did. I fit right in."

"You're pulling my leg."

"No. I'm serious, and since you aren't a member, I don't believe for one second you're a heathen."

Silver grabbed the laptop she'd set on the patio table earlier. "I'm asking to join right now. How did I miss a group that's right up my alley?"

"Exactly how many groups do you belong to?"

Jasmine asked.

"Oh, I don't know, maybe ten, but I haven't been very active lately. I used to mess around several hours a night on Facebook. It was fun. There are some hysterical people out there posting every night on the various groups. I have to admit—I've missed the action."

"You still answer my private messages. Don't you keep in touch with the other fans?" Jasmine asked.

Silver shook her head. "No, not really. I haven't put out a book in a while, so there wasn't really a burning need to keep posting things. I used to stay active mostly as a means of promoting myself—it used to be the only way anyone learned about my work at first. Then it became a bit of an addiction. I suppose the fact I've just realized how much I've missed the interaction is a step in the right direction. I can't really say why you're the only one I've kept in touch with."

"Well, I'm certainly glad you did. I'd like to think we're friends. I know being Facebook friends is a bit artificial, but I've come to value our friendship. Sure, it would have been a whole lot better if we'd lived in the same city. I could have been more of a support. I would have dropped everything, you know, to… uh…." Jasmine caught herself again.

Silver grabbed her hand. "I know you would have, and I loved getting your supportive messages. It's what kept me semi-sane these last few years. Your gentle prodding is the sole reason I started writing again. Thank you for that. Maybe my next book will be a little less depressing."

"I loved your book. It was different from your previous work, but the writing was outstanding and it created a depth of emotion I don't normally feel when I read lesfic. I crave that from time to time—so you did good."

"Thank you," Silver whispered.

Jasmine sensed Silver needed a few moments of quiet to collect her thoughts. The pause in conversation allowed for companionable silence, and Jasmine relaxed into the feeling. It was nice to sit and share the same space without filling the air with awkward conversation. Except for those few moments when Jasmine felt like she'd stepped into a pile of steaming poo, she felt good about how easy it was to talk with Silver.

Jasmine had been so preoccupied with their previous conversation she failed to realize how dark it was outside and the twinkling stars began to dance across the sky, until she saw the full moon provide just enough light to frame Silver's beautiful face. Jasmine studied her profile and wondered how Silver managed to avoid the crow's-feet most women in their forties developed. Her skin was still smooth and youthful.

Jasmine wanted to run her fingers across that gorgeous face and touch the smoothness of Silver's skin. She imagined placing her fingers on Silver's full lips and with a feather light touch tracing the outline before capturing her mouth with her own.

Jasmine thought she was a horrible human being for having those feelings. Silver needed a friend, not a sex-crazed fan. She tried to remember what her mother used to say to her. *"Feelings aren't good or bad, Jasmine, they just are, and no matter how hard we might try, we can never stop ourselves from having them."*

Her mother's words had been the balm for Jasmine's confusion about her sexuality when she first realized her attraction to women. When Jasmine finally confessed those feelings, she'd been surprised at her mother's nonchalant reaction. Her father wasn't as understanding and needed a few years to get used to the idea.

"You know I haven't forgotten about your argument with Dara over a secret love interest. Care to share?" Silver asked, breaking Jasmine from her reverie.

"Dara was just being a bitch."

"So you don't have someone you're pining after?"

"Oh, I didn't say that, but that's a topic for another day. I plan on cramming in a full day tomorrow and I'm getting too old to stay up late. You don't mind if I turn in soon, do you?"

"Of course not. Like I said," Silver pointed to herself, "heathen. I should have known you would be tired after your long flight. Let me show you to the guest bedroom and bath. I'll probably forget something, so please feel free to let me know if you need anything. My bedroom is just down the hall."

Chapter Five

Jasmine tossed and turned in the bed as she reviewed the highlights of the evening. Sometimes she thought Silver was flirting. It was subtle, but she didn't think she was completely off base. She latched on to Silver referring to her as gorgeous and focused on the statement Silver had made about Dara being a fool. Yet when she really dissected the whole night, Silver had treated her more like a friend and asked about her ability to patch things up with Dara. That certainly didn't add up to flirting or receptiveness to taking the next step beyond friendship.

After the call from Dara, Jasmine had stuck the phone in her back pocket and felt the vibrations on at least five separate occasions. She hadn't bothered to look at it until she had settled in the guest bedroom. There were six voice messages and three texts—all from Dara. She decided to ignore all of them. She wasn't Dara's assistant anymore and she had no obligation to return her calls or texts. Somehow being with Silver this evening had given her the strength to avoid her destructive pattern of running back to Dara every time she called.

Before she'd crawled in bed, she plugged in her phone and set it on the nightstand. It buzzed three more times before she eventually closed her eyes and fell into a fitful sleep.

†

Something was tickling Jasmine's nose. She startled awake when a rough tongue swiped her chin. Jasmine pried her eyes open and peered at the tiny, gray kitten purring loudly while his soft, furry body stretched across her chest. She pulled her hand from under the covers and stroked his silky fur as he continued to give her a bath.

Jasmine remembered Silver's parting words last night and grinned as she imagined an entirely different meaning, which had led to some interesting dreams starring Silver as the leading lady.

Silver had handed her a fluffy, green towel. "If you'd like a visitor tonight, just leave the door cracked open; otherwise shut the door, or you'll most likely have an unwelcome guest crawl in bed with you."

Jasmine knew she was referring to one of the cats or kittens, but it was fun to imagine Silver as the visitor. She missed her cats, and waking up to the purring kitten was nice.

She stretched, but the kitten remained glued to her chest. "Well, aren't you an affectionate little guy. I'm sorry I can't remember your name, Sinbad, Socrates, Plato. I'll have to ask Silver."

When Jasmine heard Silver downstairs grinding coffee and what she suspected was the clanking of pots or pans, she rolled over to check her phone. "Seven thirty. Oh yeah, that's right, Silver is an early riser."

The other kitten began crying outside her door as the

gray kitten started to pounce on her feet. "Well come on in here, you little baby."

She wiggled her toes, and the kitten pounced at the same time the other flying furball jumped on the bed. The two began playing and biting each other, and then the little gray guy started chasing his tail on the bed. Soon they were hurtling after each other around the bedroom and Jasmine figured it was time to get up. She smiled when she heard Silver humming downstairs. The smell of coffee and something else she couldn't quite put her finger on permeated the air as her stomach growled.

Jasmine stepped into the guest bathroom and ran her fingers through her hair. She quickly brushed her teeth and took one last look in the mirror to make sure she was semi-presentable. She'd never worn a lot of makeup anyway, so she didn't feel the need to, as her mother used to say, "put on her face."

She briefly considered putting on a bra underneath the T-shirt she'd worn to bed with her loose exercise shorts. She wasn't overly endowed though, so she figured it would be okay to forgo that piece of clothing.

Jasmine galloped down the stairs, eager to greet the day and spend it with Silver. This was sure to rank right up there as one of the best vacations she'd ever taken—even if it was only for an extended weekend.

†

Silver concentrated on evenly placing the blueberries on the batter already starting to bubble in the center of the frying pan. She knew the few special ingredients she added to the Snoqualmie Falls pancake mix were a big hit. When Naomi had invited the members of the Rainbow Riders group to their house for a weekend bike ride, she always asked Silver to make her famous pancakes. They would receive rave reviews, so she hoped Jasmine enjoyed them this morning. She took a sip of her french press coffee and waited until just the right moment to flip the pancake.

"Morning."

Silver jumped and turned around, taking in the adorable sight of Jasmine rubbing her eyes. Silver suspected it was still a little early for Jasmine. She was wearing shorts and a T-shirt, and Silver had to keep from sliding her eyes up and down Jasmine's body. By the looks of it, Jasmine was in great shape. Her stomach was flat, and her nicely shaped legs had just the right amount of muscle tone. Silver hoped Jasmine would like her idea to explore the neighborhood on bikes. Looking at her beautiful body, she didn't think Jasmine would have any trouble keeping up with her.

"Hey there. Gosh, I'm really sorry I woke you. I wanted to make all the pancakes first and then let you wake up at a reasonable hour on your own. Do you want some coffee, or are you a tea person?" Silver asked.

"Coffee, please. I can get my own. I see you have some left in the press over there." Jasmine picked up the empty mug on the island. "I assume this one's for me. Bonus points for the french vanilla creamer. I know this stuff is probably horrible for you because the remnants in the mug look like leftover paint, but God I love it."

"Oh me too. I do have regular cream, if you'd prefer the more natural, but not necessarily healthier version."

"Nope, I'll take the artificial paint, please," Jasmine joked.

Silver turned back around to focus on her cooking and flipped the perfect round pancake.

"Crap."

"What?" Jasmine was beside her in two seconds. "Did you burn yourself?"

"No, but the pancake did not escape that fate." Silver sighed. She should have been watching what she was doing instead of ogling her guest. She was acting like some ridiculous adolescent with her first crush. Yes, Jasmine was a beautiful woman, but Silver felt incredibly guilty simply acknowledging that fact—never mind letting her eyes rove up and down Jasmine's body. It was as if they had a mind of their own and wouldn't listen to her brain as it kept yelling, *This is all wrong, stop it, you pervert. She's a friend, that's all.*

Silver scooped up the burned pancake and angrily tossed it in the garbage. She dipped the measuring cup into the bowl of batter and poured a new cake into the pan, then once again carefully placed each blueberry on top.

"What are you doing, making some kind of design?" Jasmine peered over her shoulder and was standing dangerously close. Silver could smell her minty-fresh breath and felt the warm air on her neck. She fought the urge to spin around and kiss her senseless.

"No, I just like an even amount of blueberry interwoven into the batter. This is my signature breakfast dish, so don't make fun of my technique."

Jasmine took a step back. "Never. I would never make fun of your technique. Blueberry pancakes are my favorite. I'm not dumb enough to rile the chef and take a chance that I'll be denied a delicious breakfast. Mamma didn't raise no fools."

"Go on and sit down on the couch and enjoy your coffee. These will be done in a little bit, and then we can talk about my idea for what we can do to keep us out of trouble today." Silver glanced over her shoulder and caught Jasmine's pout.

"Aw, that's no fun. I'm thousands of miles away from home, so I was looking forward to some rabble-rousing."

Jasmine leaned on the counter but didn't make a move to relax on the couch. Silver assumed she wanted to continue their banter.

"Somehow you don't seem the type. I'll bet you got straight A's in school and always followed every rule," Silver declared.

"Nuh-uh. My dad is all too happy to tell anyone who will listen about the goody-goody class president who pulled the fire alarm in junior high and got suspended until she went to the fire station and listened to the required lecture. The fire chief carefully explained how irresponsible it was to pull the fire alarm when there's no fire. You know, it causes them to send valuable resources to the location and they might actually be needed somewhere else," Jasmine parroted.

"No way. You pulled the fire alarm. Why on earth would you do that? You don't seem like the type."

"In my defense, I wasn't trying to cause problems. I was showing my little sister how they needed to replace that little piece of glass or else the alarm wouldn't work. She didn't believe me. I had to prove her wrong. Unfortunately, I was the one woefully misinformed. They thought my little sister did it and yanked her into the principal's office the next day."

"And," Silver prompted.

"Well, this is where the story turns into the family classic. My sister did her thing, and when the principal asked if she pulled the alarm, she vigorously denied it. The principal in his wisdom said, 'Well, if you didn't pull the alarm and you and your sister were the only two there, then your sister must have done it.' I think he was trying to smoke her out, because surely the class president and winner of the prestigious citizenship award didn't do this heinous thing."

"So what did your sister say next?" Silver asked.

"That's the classic part. She said, 'I guess it sorta

looks that way.'" Jasmine chuckled. "She never did exactly rat me out, and when the principal called me in and asked, I dissolved into a basket of tears and promptly admitted my mistake."

"Your reputation remains untarnished. If that's the worst, you cannot put *troublemaker* on your résumé. That is reserved for those of us who deserve the title."

"I suppose you are one of those that claim that mischief-maker label," Jasmine stated.

"Oh I definitely am. I gave my mom fits. I was kissing cheerleaders under the bleachers and defiantly tossing that in the teachers and my parents' faces. They wanted to practice kissing; I obliged."

"That doesn't sound so bad to me," Jasmine stated.

"One was the principal's daughter, and the other was the preacher's daughter. I might have copped a feel or two as well. They didn't seem to mind, but when the principal noticed his daughter's bra was undone, well let's just say he wasn't very pleased. It didn't help when they found the pack of cigarettes, the flask with peppermint schnapps, and my one hitter hidden in my jacket pockets. I had one of those big army coats with all the nifty compartments. I thought I was hot stuff. The lecture I endured wasn't from an upstanding fire chief—my mom yelled at me for three days." Silver removed the pancake and placed it on top of the tall stack warming in the oven.

Jasmine's eyes got wide. "Um, Silver. Who else is coming for breakfast? Surely you don't think the two of us can eat all of those." She pointed at the oven.

Silver glanced down at pile of pancakes and started to laugh. "I guess I just got in the groove and forgot I was only cooking for two. Normally, I'd be preparing pancakes for a dozen people. Maybe we can wrap a few up and take them with us. We might need the extra carbs today for what I have planned."

"You're going to make me get sweaty, aren't you?"

"Are you opposed to sweat and activity?"

"Depends on what causes it." Jasmine wriggled her eyebrows.

Silver opened a drawer and selected two potholders and a hot plate with an orca design on it. She carefully removed the plate with the large stack of pancakes tilting precariously like the Leaning Tower of Pisa. Two plates, forks and knives, butter, and both maple and blackberry syrup were already on the block of wood that was the kitchen island. She chose three large pancakes and placed them on one of the plates and put two on the other.

Handing Jasmine the plate with three cakes, she pointed at the condiments. "I hope butter and syrup are what you like on your pancakes. I have homemade jam or marmalade if that's your preference. Would you like something else to drink besides coffee? I have orange, grapefruit, and grape juice."

Jasmine giggled. "Would you think less of me if I selected the grape juice? Unless it's anything besides Welch's; I have my standards."

Silver frowned. "Sorry, it's an organic brand."

"Oh my God. I'm kidding. What did you do, buy out the store with every possible breakfast item?"

"I wasn't sure what you might prefer," Silver admitted.

"I'm not picky. You could have tossed a box of cereal at me, or nothing. Sometimes I just have coffee in the morning." Jasmine put her hand up. "I know breakfast is the most important meal of the day."

Silver opened the stainless-steel refrigerator, pulled out the grape and grapefruit juices, and set them on the counter. She poured the dark purple liquid into a clear mason jar and handed it to Jasmine.

Jasmine had just finished pouring the blackberry syrup on her pancakes. Silver noticed she hadn't slathered them with butter, like she normally would on her own.

After Jasmine accepted the grape juice, she took her fork and added another pancake to Silver's stack.

"I'm not letting you make me look like a pig. If I get three, so do you. Since I love pancakes, I'm going to eat every last morsel, and I expect you to do the same. You've lost weight—you could use a few more calories," Jasmine admonished.

"Okay, okay. Go ahead to the table and I'll be right there after I pour myself some juice."

Jasmine grabbed her plate and her glass of juice, and then hesitated as she stared at her coffee. "I need three hands."

Silver was slicing two large chunks of butter and shaking her hand so they would land on top of the enhanced stack.

"I promise I won't spit in it to claim it as my own. I have my own cup. I'll bring it to you. Go on," Silver directed.

Jasmine smiled. "That's some very fine brew. I was tempted to spit in yours, you know—just so I could have a few more swallows."

"I do have more. This isn't World War Two rationing. I can make some more right now." Silver walked to the stove and picked up the teapot to fill it with water.

"Stop right there. Put the teapot down and step away from the sink."

Silver glanced over her shoulder and saw Jasmine turn her hand into a mock gun and point it in her direction.

"I was kidding. Get your cute butt over to the table and join me. I hate eating alone," Jasmine ordered.

Silver picked up Jasmine's coffee cup, set it next to her, and then placed her own cup at the place setting across from Jasmine. She walked back to the island, poured a glass of grapefruit juice, and grabbed her own plate with the generous globs of butter melting on top.

Jasmine had her hands folded in her lap, and Silver suspected she was waiting patiently for her to join her before digging in.

Silver sat down and waved her hand. "*Mangia, mangia.*"

"Huh?"

"Sorry, that's 'eat' in Italian. My grandfather used to say it to us on Sunday mornings when he would cook breakfast for the whole family."

Jasmine used her fork to cut a large piece and shoved it in her mouth. "Mmmm, this is sinfully good. I don't think I've ever tasted a better pancake than this. I know there is some secret. Care to share?"

"Sure, as soon as you tell me all about your secret love interest."

Jasmine quickly loaded her mouth with another large forkful and gestured to indicate she couldn't speak.

"Okay, I'll take the hint and let you off the hook. Since you've avoided or changed the subject three times now, I suspect this is something you are bound and determined not to reveal. I guess we all have our secrets. Vanilla."

Jasmine rapidly chewed her food. "Vanilla? Is that the special ingredient?"

"Yep."

"Hmmm, so simple, yet so effective. Good idea. I'll have to try it the next time I make pancakes."

"Yes, but don't use those awful Krusteaz or Bisquick mixes. Snoqualmie Falls is by far the best."

"Good to know. So, what are the special plans you

have mapped out for us today?" Jasmine asked.

"Do you cycle?"

"Well, other than the face plant at age six when I first started learning, I've only had a couple of close encounters of the pavement kind. Those darn clip-in pedals are downright scary sometimes. I'd be moving along at a good pace, and then bam, a change in the pavement. I couldn't get out fast enough to stop from toppling over. There was this one time when I first started learning how to click in and click out that I slowed down and as I came to a stop, I just tipped over. It was like a slow-motion accident. My friends thought it was particularly funny." Jasmine blushed.

Silver was delighted to learn Jasmine wasn't a casual cyclist. Anyone who'd equipped her bike with clip-on pedals was a relatively serious biker. She wondered what Jasmine would think of her recumbent bikes. She wondered again about the scar on Jasmine's chin.

"Is that how you got that little half-moon scar on your chin?" Silver asked.

Jasmine rubbed her scar. "Oh no, that was a much earlier bicycle accident. Kids have no fear, and when I was first learning to ride a bike without training wheels, well, let's just say it didn't go so well. Obviously, that never stopped me from my love of cycling. I didn't think too much of my fall at the time until my mom saw the blood pouring from my face and freaked out. I held my sleeve up to the cut and told her, 'I'm okay, Mom, it's just a little boo-boo.' Instead of having a plastic surgeon sew me up, the doctor in the emergency department sutured the cut, and my mom still won't forgive herself for not being assertive enough to ask for the plastic surgeon. Oops, TMI. I guess. 'No' would have been a better answer."

"Oh no. I enjoyed your lengthy response. Do you think a thirty to fifty mile ride would be too far for you?"

"No, not at all. I do the Kansas City Bike for the Brain ride every year and choose the seventy-two mile route. I've been training for the past two months. I love long rides; I just wish my butt wouldn't get so sore. The chafing isn't very fun. Too bad I don't have anyone to put the balm in those strategic locations to avoid the inevitable saddle sores."

"Don't worry, I have the perfect solution for you," Silver responded.

Jasmine raised her eyebrow. "Not that the thought isn't appealing to me, but…."

"No, not that. I don't have any balm for you, but I do have the kind of bike that is so comfortable, saddle sores are a thing of the past."

"Oh yeah, right. I saw your recumbent cycles when we came in last night. I've often envied those on the ride who cruised by, looking like they're on a Barcalounger versus a bike. They're never willing to trade me," Jasmine joked.

"That's because we call your kind of racing bike an upwrong versus an upright bike. Once you ride a recumbent, you'll never want to put your butt back into your racing bike again. Speed is overrated. I might be considerably slower climbing a hill, but on the flats I can clip along at a pretty good pace."

Jasmine frowned. "I don't have my bike cleats with me."

"What size shoe do you wear?" Silver asked.

"I'm usually a seven, why?"

"I have some shoes Naomi used to wear that should fit you—unless you think that's kinda creepy wearing a dead woman's shoes."

Jasmine got quiet for a minute, and Silver thought that maybe she'd made her uncomfortable.

"Silver, you know I'm not angling to replace Naomi or anything. I'm quite sure I'd never be able to figuratively fill her shoes, but I would love to go biking with you, and if you're not bothered by it, then I don't think it's creepy. Thanks."

"I know. I'm not looking for someone to fill Naomi's shoes," Silver whispered and a lone tear snuck out.

Jasmine grasped her hand. "God, I'm such an idiot. I've made you sad again and all I want to do is make you smile and laugh."

"You do make me smile and laugh. I just can't help missing her sometimes. Truthfully, she never really enjoyed cycling as much as me. I think she only rode to make me happy. She always preferred hiking. Hiking was too slow for me. We compromised a lot."

"Hey, eat up, because I can't wait to try out one of those newfangled contraptions you have in your garage. Can I ride one of those trikes? They look like a total kick in the pants."

"Oh they are. They're like little racing machines. I prefer them to their two-wheeled cousins." Silver grinned.

"I can't wait."

Chapter Six

Dara had tried to contact Jasmine since last night when she'd hung up on her. She knew Jasmine slept in when she was on vacation, but it was nearing nine in the morning—Pacific Coast time.

She was worried. In their eighteen-year relationship, Jasmine had always caved in after the second or third call. Roses, dinner, and a truckload of apologies guaranteed Dara would worm her way back into Jasmine's bed.

Dara kept making those stupid mistakes with women nearly half her age—well not quite, but very close. Her latest fling was twenty-five and she'd just turned forty-five.

Jasmine was coming up on the big four-oh. Maybe she was going through some midlife crisis, as Dara had certainly done when she turned forty. She'd used that as an excuse when she'd stepped out with the new director of community relations, a sultry redhead. It hadn't lasted long. The affairs never did.

Jasmine was the love of her life, and Dara hadn't figured out yet why she kept screwing things up. Jasmine was the most beautiful woman she'd ever laid eyes on, and the fact Jasmine hadn't realized her attractiveness was a constant puzzle to Dara, but she was grateful nonetheless. Jasmine didn't have a lot of self-confidence, and that resulted in her remaining in the on-again, off-again dance they'd engaged in for the last eighteen years. Of course Jasmine's beauty wasn't the only thing that kept Dara interested, even though it was a requirement for any potential partner. Dara was admittedly on the shallow side when it came to her choice in lovers—she never argued that point. However, Jasmine was also kindhearted and loyal, traits that were hard to come by when accompanied by stunning good looks. At least that had been Dara's experience.

It was Saturday and she knew she shouldn't bother Korrine, the chief nursing officer, but she'd proven herself an excellent listener and had become a confidante over the last several months. Korrine had wisely advised her to choose a dowdy, middle-aged person to support her administrative needs. When Jasmine transferred over to human resources after her last indiscretion, Dara had decided to take a different tack for clerical support. Unfortunately, that had only occurred when the first replacement hadn't worked out. It didn't hurt that human resources had strongly recommended against the young, attractive, inexperienced woman who was her initial first choice, after the disastrous young woman with whom she'd had a brief affair. Korrine being both a lesbian and a huge fan of Silver Lining was a bonus, because Dara could pump her for more information about the attractive author.

Korrine wasn't anything to look at, but she was a good friend—Dara's only friend, really. One night Dara was working late and feeling sorry for herself. She hadn't wanted to go home to an empty house, so on a whim she'd invited Korrine out for a drink after work. One drink turned into four and Dara was confessing her love woes before she was able to censor herself.

Dara declared that she thought Jasmine was secretly in love with Silver Lining and blamed this for her recent split-up with Jasmine. Korrine mentioned she was an avid fan and Facebook friend of the author. She didn't think anything would come of Jasmine's crush because she'd been following Silver for years on Facebook and so would know if a new relationship blossomed in the author's life. Dara wasn't so sure about that, especially with this recent contest. It was all just a bit too contrived for her.

Korrine had grumbled that the contest was rigged since Jasmine was Silver's only beta for her most recent novel. She'd been the second one to post a review, but by then it was too late. Dara knew then that Korrine would be the one to help her keep tabs on what was happening with the attractive author who had captured Jasmine's eye five years ago.

Dara picked up her phone and pushed the button on the screen to select the nursing administrator's number. "Hello, Korrine, Dara here. I was wondering if you would like to have lunch today?... Wonderful… I'll meet you at the bistro… How about noon? Okay, see you then."

Dara ended the call and smiled. If Korrine was one of Silver's close Facebook fiends, she might even know where in Washington Silver lived. Dara had a lot of vacation time saved up. A trip to the Pacific Northwest wasn't out of the realm of possibility. She needed to nip whatever was happening between her love and the author in the bud before anything had a chance to develop between the two. *Why the hell did the bitch's wife have to die and ruin everything?*

†

Korrine was sitting at a table with her hands folded

neatly in front of her staring into space, not necessarily focusing on anyone or anything. Dara watched her for a few minutes. She was a little odd, but excellent at her job. The other nursing directors loved her. The nursing division had never been stronger, and that reflected positively on Dara.

She wasn't exactly ugly, just nothing special. Her mousy-brown hair hung limply to her shoulders. Her milky-brown eyes were set too far apart for anyone to consider attractive and always seemed slightly unfocused. Dara always had a vision of a chipmunk when she looked at Korrine's rounded cheeks. The only feature a prospective lover might find appealing was her full lips. Unfortunately, that was the only attribute that could entice anyone to take a second look. Normally her stern colleague wasn't the type of woman who would stand out in a bar or a crowd.

Dara had revealed a bit too much about her personal life to the dour nurse executive but hadn't learned a single thing about the intensely private woman. She hadn't even learned if Korrine had anyone special in her life. She only knew that the austere woman was an avid reader and loved Silver Lining's work.

Dara walked up to the table and took a seat across from her. "Thanks for meeting me for lunch."

Korrine looked up, blinked her unfocused eyes, and stared without saying a word. It was slightly disconcerting. After about twenty seconds, which felt a little too long for Dara to consider the interaction normal, Korrine answered, "Of course. You must be terribly concerned about what might occur between Silver and Jasmine while she's visiting her at her home."

Dara narrowed her eyes. "Did Silver post something on Facebook that would lead you to believe their relationship has evolved beyond friendship?"

"No, but I saw the way that Jasmine looked at Silver at

the conference," Korrine stated without emotion. "Of course Silver didn't return the adoration. She was married and Silver is not the type of person to cheat on her wife."

Dara thought it was odd how Korrine relayed this piece of information, without any inflection in her voice, but decided to find out if somehow she knew where the elusive author lived.

"Korrine, you've been a fan of Silver Lining for years, right?"

"Yes, I have. I was one of the first fans to ever contact her and let her know how much I enjoyed her debut book. She was very pleased that I sent her that first email. She let me know how much she appreciated it. We've stayed close ever since. I wanted to be there for her when her wife died, but she pulled herself into a shell. The poor thing was grieving, but I think she's ready to move on now. Jasmine shouldn't take advantage of her and try to worm her way in just because she's finally ready to get back out there again."

"So, do you know where Silver lives?" Dara asked.

"Yes, I do. She lives in Roslyn, a very small town in Washington State. There aren't too many famous authors named Silver Lining with a dead wife whose name was Naomi. With a few well-placed questions, when I traveled to Washington, I was able to track her down. Of course, she wasn't ready to interact with anyone yet, so I didn't approach her. I've always wanted to visit her hometown. Washington is such a beautiful place, you know. My sister and brother-in-law live about forty-five minutes from Roslyn. I've been planning another visit to my sister, and maybe I can connect with her then."

Okay, that was kind of creepy. Dara had what she needed. Korrine knew the location of the author, and that was what she'd come to lunch to try to find out. It was time she paid Silver a visit. Jasmine was far too impressionable, and powerful women seemed to be her weakness. She knew that from first-hand experience because it had been so easy to seduce the young woman eighteen years ago. Jasmine hadn't changed that much since. She was still incredibly innocent and naïve. All Silver would have to do is pay her a few compliments and Jasmine would respond to the attention—opening her petals like a rose in bloom. She'd have to wait for Jasmine to return home, and then she would make the trip and have a nice long conversation with the author. Dara knew exactly how to handle those flaky artist types.

"Do you think you can give me her address or phone number if you have it?" Dara asked.

Korrine narrowed her eyes. "Why?"

"Well, you know how I've explained that Jasmine is far too naïve for her own good. I'm afraid she'll make a fool of herself and I don't want Silver feeding her fantasies. You know I still care about Jasmine, and I would hate to see her hurt," Dara cautiously explained.

"I don't think Silver would respond to her overtures, but I suppose everyone is human and Silver might be tempted by her beauty. When were you planning to pay her a visit?"

"Oh I don't know. I should probably wait until Jasmine returns. I don't want her to think I'm stalking her. I only have her best interests at heart," Dara claimed.

"Yes, you're a good woman. I could talk to Silver too. We're good friends, and I believe she needs a more stable woman in her life. Jasmine is a bit flighty. She keeps breaking up with you because of some fantasy potential with Silver. I'd planned to visit sometime in the next few months anyway. I was just waiting for the right time."

Dara wondered if Korrine was imagining her own fantasy relationship with the author. From what she knew, Silver hadn't had close relationships with any of her fans, besides Jasmine, since her wife's death. That fact definitely stuck in Dara's craw because it had prompted the last fight and ultimate breakup. She shrugged. Who was she to burst someone's fantasy bubble? Maybe Korrine would be able to help her situation. Certainly, it couldn't do any harm. Two separate visits discouraging any budding relationship would have double the impact. "That sounds like a good idea. I appreciate your help. If you could just give me the information, we can both make sure a mistake isn't made by either of them," Dara said.

Chapter Seven

Jasmine stared at her reflection in the mirror. She was wearing Naomi's bike shorts, shirt, socks, and would soon don her shoes. She'd meant what she said about not wanting to step into Naomi's shoes.

Yes, she was attracted to Silver. Everything about the woman was pulling her in like a strong magnet. Silver was kind, witty, intelligent, and beautiful. Who wouldn't fall for that? Her vulnerability was the one thing that kept Jasmine from confessing her attraction—oh, and the ghost in the middle of the room. Naomi's presence was everywhere.

Jasmine frowned. She didn't want to remind Silver of her dead wife, but she didn't have the proper clothing for a bike ride and had to accept the outfit provided. She had to admit that it fit like a glove. She vaguely remembered Naomi from the conference and noted they were both about the same size. If only Silver were able to see her as a woman separate and distinct from the love of her life and not a reminder of her lost love.

Jasmine sighed and walked down the stairs, mentally preparing for the day. When she saw Silver, looking out the sliding glass doors apparently deep in thought with her own bike attire hugging every glorious curve, her breath hitched. She needed to school her expression and hope that Silver hadn't heard her reaction.

Silver turned around, and when her pupils slightly dilated, Jasmine entertained the notion that maybe Silver found her equally attractive. Jasmine blushed and looked down as she tugged on the bottom of the bike shorts that left nothing to the imagination.

"I'm glad they fit you. You would have been uncomfortable in jeans and a T-shirt. Comfort is key when going on a long bike ride," Silver remarked.

"Thanks. Are you sure it's okay to wear this? I admit I feel a little strange wearing Naomi's clothes."

"I'd give you something of mine, but I don't think it would fit. It would probably swim on you. Honestly, it's fine. It doesn't take much to send me down memory lane, so you don't have to worry that you're the cause of it. I probably should have given away her things several years ago, but I just couldn't bring myself to do that. Somehow, I think she's smiling down on us and happy that someone is getting good use out of her bike gear. She was big on recycling and never let me toss anything aside haphazardly. She grew up poor and never wanted to throw anything away." Silver smiled.

Jasmine thought Silver's smile seemed genuine. It wasn't sad, maybe nostalgic—that was progress. She hoped someday Silver might want to move forward, even if it wasn't with her. Someone deserved to feel her love.

"I'm ready to see your beautiful countryside now. You'll go easy on me, won't you?" Jasmine teased.

"Somehow, I don't think you'll have a problem keeping up. In fact, I'll bet the only reason you won't leave me in the dust is that you won't know where you're going. I'm not going to give you the GPS gadget because then I've got nothing to keep you beside me," Silver said.

Jasmine thought that if Silver ever seriously meant that comment, she'd stay by her side forever and thank her lucky stars this wonderful woman wanted it that way.

"I'm not used to riding a trike. I'll bet I use a completely different set of muscles, so I doubt it'll be easy to keep up with you, but lead the way because I'm going to give it my best effort."

†

Silver kept sneaking glances at Jasmine as Jasmine made climbing the big hill look effortless. Silver was panting by the time she reached the crest.

"Holy cow, how much cycling do you do? I thought I was in good shape, but you are kicking my butt all over this pavement. Do you ever sweat?" Silver asked.

"I am sweating, I just have a knack at hiding my exhaustion." Jasmine chuckled. "I'm desperately trying to impress you. It must be working, because I've managed to completely bamboozle you."

"I am impressed. You act like you've been on a trike all your life."

"I seriously covet one of these. When I get back to Kansas, I'm forking out whatever dough is necessary to get me one of these newfangled contraptions. They are a total blast to ride. Thank you so much for showing me the error of my ways with the upwrong bike."

"Oh don't do that. I'm happy to give you the trike you're riding. I was just waiting for the perfect person to gift it to. I needed to make sure it was someone who would truly appreciate her attributes. Clara loves admiration, and I don't want just anyone to own her."

"You name your bikes?" Jasmine asked.

"You don't?" Silver retorted.

"Um, no. Should I?"

"Of course you should." She laughed.

"How about you leave the bike here and perhaps I can visit again and shower her with love?" Jasmine tentatively suggested.

"That's a grand idea. I now have something that will entice you to come back to my little slice of heaven."

"There are numerous enticements. I don't think you have to worry," Jasmine declared.

Silver was having such a good time. The sun was shining brightly, caressing her body with warmth. Jasmine was proving to be a great biking companion, and she sincerely seemed to enjoy the ride. They were almost at the midway point and Silver was starting to get hungry. The pancakes hadn't lasted long, and after twenty-five miles, she needed more fuel.

"Um, Silver, not that I'm tired or anything, but do you know when we'll take a rest? I'd like to fuel up before I hit a wall."

"Were you reading my mind?" Silver chuckled.

"Oh thank God, you're on the same wavelength. I thought you were like one of those Energizer Bunnies, where you keep going and going and going. I desperately need to feed the beast if I'm going to make it back. I saw you making those wonderful sandwiches, and my mouth is literally salivating right now in anticipation."

"In about a mile there is a great picnic place by the river. Can you make it?" Silver asked.

"Sure, no problem. As long as you aren't one of those people who exaggerate distances to keep your bike partner going, I think I'll survive."

"Nope, it is definitely only…" Silver looked down at her GPS "…less than a mile now."

They cycled in silence for a few minutes, and then Silver turned into a gravel lot adjacent to a small, grassy park with several empty picnic tables. She was thankful they were the only two people in the park. She'd often chosen this recreational trail area because not too many people knew of its existence. It wasn't uncommon for her to occupy the picnic spot alone with no other distractions except for the birds and squirrels. She would toss little pieces of her lunch to them, even though she knew she shouldn't. They were so adorable. She imagined that the same ones came to greet her each time she biked to this spot. Eventually they'd come close enough to take the tasty morsels from her hand, and that always pleased her.

The river lazily meandered along the park only a few hundred feet away. On occasion, she would see a Great Blue Heron hunting for trout that peppered the famous waterway. Silver hoped Jasmine would catch this sight while they relaxed with their lunch.

Their bike cleats landed on the gravel, and the combination crunching and clicking sound sent the birds flying. Finally, the metal on their shoes tapped on the soft, green grass and the earth absorbed the noise. After a few minutes, the birds returned to the picnic area chirping, tweeting, and singing their songs as they perched on the branches.

Silver placed the bike bag on the weathered wood table and began pulling out the sandwiches, chips, oranges, and chocolate chip cookies she'd packed earlier. She decided to save the apples and cheese for later in the day when they would need another snack for the return ride home. The water bottles were almost empty, so she walked back to her bike to retrieve the spares she'd stored in her other bag. They might need to stop along the way to refill them or purchase an energy drink. Dehydration often snuck up on her, so she had to keep reminding herself to drink. Naomi used to make sure she drank every few miles, and Silver smiled as she noted that Jasmine had periodically reminded her to take a drink during their ride.

In many ways, Jasmine and Naomi were a lot alike, yet in others, they were very different. Naomi was more confident and sometimes downright stubborn. Jasmine seemed unsure of herself at times and extremely malleable.

Silver walked back to the picnic table and, as her shoes pinged along the gravel, the birds took flight again only to return as she sat down and plunked the drinks on the weathered wood.

A brave squirrel approached and stood up on its hinds legs.

"Oh look, Silver, isn't he cute. God, he's so close. Can I give him a little piece?" Jasmine looked up in wonder.

"How do you know it's a he? Did you see his little junk?" Silver teased.

"I don't know. Isn't it funny that I always refer to wildlife as male?"

Silver pinched off a small piece of bread. "I'm sure if there were rangers around, they would chastise us for feeding the little guy, but I think that's Franklin, and I'm betting he was waiting in the wings for my bike to pull up."

Silver tossed the morsel to the furry rodent and smiled when he snatched it up and scurried away.

"So I take it I won't tip the balance of nature if another one comes begging and I toss him a nugget?"

"No, I don't think so. Franklin is always the first to beg, and then his friends come calling. Don't worry, you will have plenty of opportunities to feed the little beggars. I did bring some extra bread for them, so that's the last piece I'll offer up of my sandwich."

"Do you name everything? First your bikes and now

the squirrel." Jasmine beamed.

"Of course I do. You don't think they deserve proper names?" Silver asked.

"Well I guess so, but I'd probably run out of names. By the way, how do you come up with names for everything and for the new characters in your books?"

"A book of baby names."

"Seriously?"

Silver crossed her heart. "Yes, seriously. One year a colleague at work gave me the book, and I've been using it ever since. I'd exhausted the names of all the people I work with, my family and friends, and was having a hard time thinking up new names. I flipped the book open and it was like magic. It's on my coffee table at home. Sometimes I get ideas from my readers as well. On occasion one of them will joke about liking the story, but hate that I've used their name for one of the evil characters."

"I don't think I've ever seen Naomi or Jasmine in any of your books," Jasmine noted.

"Naomi adamantly refused to have her name memorialized in any of my books, except for in the dedication. She put up with so much when I got in the writing groove that it was the least I could do—even though I would have never used her name for one of the nasty characters."

"And Jasmine, why not use my name? Is it so horrible a choice?"

"No, not at all. I've been saving it for a very special character. I started the book a year ago but got stuck on where I wanted to take the story, so I never finished. The character Jasmine is very special—a lot like her namesake."

"Oh."

Jasmine's sudden silence told Silver all she needed to know. Her honesty was definitely not a welcome trait if it caused embarrassment and discomfort. She wondered if Jasmine thought she was trying to force her into Naomi's shoes both literally and figuratively.

"Look, Jasmine. I'm sorry if what I said made you feel uncomfortable. I'm not trying to suggest anything, or ..." Silver was at a loss for words. She didn't know what she was trying to say.

"Silver, what do you expect or want from me? Whatever it is, you've got it and I'd do anything to put a smile on your face," Jasmine declared.

"Oh God, I don't really know what I want. Things are confusing for me right now. Do we have to define anything?" Silver asked.

"No, we don't. If it's any consolation, I think you're special too, and I have for a long time. I've only just come to terms with my feelings, but I'll take whatever you're ready for, no more, no less. If we are destined for only a great friendship, that's okay with me."

"I'm so close to being ready for more, but I'm just not there yet. The worst part is I don't know if I will ever be ready to take the plunge again. I wish I could. Believe me, you have no idea how much I wish for that."

Silver wanted to say that at this particular moment she felt the fervor of their attraction for each other so intensely that taking the plunge into an icy pool was an appropriate metaphor. That was likely the only thing that would quell the heat for a short time. Unfortunately, she felt as if she'd dipped her toes in the shallow end and it was too chilly. The shock of the dive into the sweet coolness would be too scary at the moment.

Jasmine stood up and scooted next to Silver. She took her hand and kissed her cheek. "It's okay, I understand."

It was such a sweet gesture, and Silver wanted to turn her face to feel the passion spread throughout her body as soft lips met hers for the first time. Every time Naomi kissed her, it was like that. They'd never lost their craving for each other. Yet, it was those sweet moments, when they shared the same space that she longed for—the times when they barely connected with each other as their hands clasped together or Naomi's arm or leg made contact in the middle of the night.

"It's getting late and we still have about twenty-five miles left before I cook that dinner I promised. I hope you like fresh seafood."

Jasmine grabbed the sandwich and before taking a big bite declared, "I love it. It will be a special treat. Kansas isn't exactly a hotbed of quality seafood."

"No, but you do have the best chocolate I've ever had," Silver stated.

"Chocolate can be easily shipped, seafood not so much. I think your location has the better amenities."

"I don't disagree," Silver acknowledged.

Chapter Eight

The Fourth of July holiday was just around the corner. That would be the perfect time to make the trip to the Northwest. Enough time had passed and Silver might entertain the idea of a new relationship. She couldn't let that happen. She would have to confront Silver before it was too late.

Her headaches were becoming more debilitating. The pills she'd pilfered from the unit were starting to cause concern. She was worried about the comprehensive investigation into the missing drugs. Management was always privy to this type of sensitive information because the senior leaders presumed a staff nurse was stealing the medication and not an esteemed leader in the organization.

One of the clerical staff had asked her if she was okay today. She looked down at her wrinkled suit and wondered if she'd worn this one two days in a row, but she couldn't remember. She made her morning selection from the pile of clothes in the corner of her room. She really needed to take them to the cleaners or at least press them before putting them back on her body.

Everyone assumed she seemed distracted because she was working too much lately. When she informed the assistant that she'd be taking a few more days off around the holiday, the assistant had responded that it was a good idea because it *looked like she could use a vacation*.

She was thankful she worked in an industry that was predominantly women because they were such caring sorts. She could always count on nurturing support from most of the nurses. There were a few nurses who could be absolute bitches and it wasn't as if she allowed anyone to get too close to her, but nurses tended to protect their own. In the past, she'd had close nurse friends, but that hadn't exactly worked out the way she'd wanted it to.

Her personal life was a bit in an uproar right now, but she would fix that soon. Jasmine and Silver weren't meant for each other. She was disturbed by the overly friendly banter between the two on the Facebook posts she could view. She could only imagine what kind of interaction occurred in private messages. She would nip that in the bud when she went to visit the author in July. She didn't think this could wait until September when she hoped that Silver would attend the Gay Romance Northwest Meet-Up in Seattle. Silver hadn't attended for three years, but with her new book out, she was sure to promote it at an event so close to home.

The woman decided to send Silver another message. Manners were something she had in spades. A person never showed up for a visit without ensuring the time was convenient. She needed to confirm that Silver had fair warning. She considered whether the use of Facebook was an appropriate vehicle for this type of communication and shrugged. Picking up her cell phone, and using her anonymous Pinger text account, she typed the short note. Electronic communication made conversation so convenient these days and yet so anonymous.

She was looking forward to her visit. Roslyn didn't have a hotel or motel, but that resort, Suncadia, would be the perfect place to spend the holiday. She'd read all about it in a travel magazine.

†

Jasmine needed some distance from Silver. She'd insisted that friendship was enough, but who was she kidding? Jasmine couldn't fool herself anymore. She wasn't just attracted to Silver—she was falling in love. Her feelings ran much deeper than what she'd ever had with Dara. When she'd first met Silver at the conference, she was starstruck, but after sending messages back and forth, she felt like she'd gotten to know the person behind the mask—especially over the last six months. The recent twenty-four hours had only solidified her burgeoning feelings.

Jasmine let the warm water of the shower cleanse her body and wash away the tears. Naomi was an ever-present wedge that kept anything from developing between them. She wasn't angry about that reality, but it hurt nonetheless. She'd noted Silver's appraising looks and thought about the possibility of their relationship evolving into something more than a friendship, but the odds were against them.

Naomi wasn't the only obstacle. Long-distance relationships rarely worked out. Dara wasn't the type of person who gave up easily, creating another obstruction to add to the increasing mountain of complications.

Jasmine knew she needed to cut her losses and convince herself that having Silver as a good friend was enough, but this would take as much effort as Silver was putting into starting over again without Naomi in her life. Jasmine wasn't sure she would be any more successful than

Silver had been with moving on from her personal tragedy. She needed a game plan, but for right now she would employ all her efforts into hiding her true feelings and offering Silver whatever support she needed as a friend—only a friend.

After her shower, Jasmine dressed quickly and looked into the mirror. "Happy face, put on a happy face for Silver." Her red-rimmed eyes told another story. "Crud, she's going to know I've been crying."

Jasmine hoped Silver wouldn't say anything because she didn't want to lie, but she certainly couldn't reveal the truth. She started opening drawers and peeking in the bathroom cabinets looking for eye drops.

"Bingo. Thank God you keep this in the guest bedroom."

Leaning her head back, Jasmine squeezed the small bottle until several drops coated her eyes. Blinking rapidly, she glanced at her reflection in the mirror. She frowned when she didn't see an immediate improvement.

"Maybe by the time I walk downstairs, some higher power will take pity on me and perform a miracle on my eyes."

†

Silver looked up from slicing vegetables for the salad. Jasmine looked so naturally beautiful in a simple pair of jeans and a pullover jersey. She noted Jasmine's bright blue eyes had a red tint and wondered about the reason. Had she caused that? *Oh, Silver, how egotistical of you.*

Silver wondered if a call from Dara had made Jasmine cry. She didn't know if she should broach the topic or not. Jasmine had been there for her as she talked freely about Naomi, but something in Jasmine's posture indicated she wasn't too keen on exploring the reasons for her obvious despondency.

To Silver, the smile plastered on Jasmine's face seemed forced. "Hey, what can I do to help?"

"Nothing. Remember, the contest advertised a home-cooked meal. I'm doing the cooking and you're doing the relaxing. I hope you don't mind that I sort of cheated and bought some already-prepared crab cakes from Whole Foods. However, in my defense, I did prepare the roasted red pepper sauce, asparagus, and homemade balsamic dressing," Silver confessed.

"I feel uncomfortable just lazing around while you slave in the kitchen."

Silver laughed. "I hardly call this 'slaving in the kitchen.' After I make the salad, I'll turn on the grill and then take a quick shower while it's heating up. If you don't mind, can I show you my latest project? I'd like to get your opinion on it. I stayed up late last night writing the first couple of chapters. This is the book I tried to start about a year ago. The characters were screaming in my ears, and I had to get up and put pen to paper—or more accurately fingers on computer keys. One of the main characters is named Jasmine."

"Sure, I'd love to see your latest project. Although, I always hate reading the first chapter and then not being able to read what happens next. The waiting always tests my patience—or lack thereof."

Silver walked into the living room and opened the lid to her laptop sitting on the coffee table. She motioned for Jasmine to join her as she sat on the couch. She typed in her password and opened the document titled *Second Time Around.*

Silver noted how Jasmine left at least a foot of distance between them when she sat on the couch. She had to turn the laptop in Jasmine's direction because she was sitting too far away to look over her shoulder.

"Wow, you already have six thousand words written. Did you get any sleep last night?" Jasmine asked. "You must be exhausted, Silver. You should head to bed early tonight. I have my trusty Kindle to entertain me. You don't need to worry about forcing yourself to stay awake on my account."

"When I get in a groove, I can go for days without sleep. After you leave, I'll probably crash, but I'm doing fine. Actually I'm better than fine. The bike ride today was glorious, and this visit is just what the doctor ordered. I haven't felt so alive in a long time, and I credit you for my current euphoria. I'm going to turn on the grill now and then take my shower. Thanks for reading this and giving me your honest assessment."

Silver stood and opened the sliding glass door to the back patio. After lighting the grill, she took one last glance at Jasmine, whose lips moved as she focused on the laptop with an intense look of concentration. Silver smiled as she made her way up the stairs to the master bathroom. It was adorable how Jasmine nearly read out loud. She mouthed the words as if they would come alive for her.

Silver did not harbor any pretense that Jasmine was her muse and inspiration for her current work in progress. The book hit very close to home. It was about a woman who'd lost her wife to a sudden illness and took a chance at love again. Naomi hadn't died because of an illness. She'd lost her life when she contracted an infection after routine surgery. The main character wasn't a writer, but a singer who fell in love with an avid fan. The similarities were hard to miss. If only Silver were able to let herself fall for Jasmine. Oh, criminy, she wasn't fooling anyone, including herself. She had already started down that slippery slope, but something kept getting in the way of allowing her to fully express or act on her feelings. That something was a ghost.

She wasn't ready to let go of her memories of Naomi.

†

Jasmine started to read the words on the screen. She heard a ding, and she couldn't help clicking on the Facebook page that was open on the screen behind the document. It was wrong to pry, she knew that, but she convinced herself that the odd message Silver had shown her earlier was important and worth following up on. Once she clicked on the page, the private message popped up. It was right there in black and white.

I've made arrangements to visit on the Fourth of July. Details to come later.

At first Jasmine was irritated. The message sounded like it came from someone Silver might be seeing—romantically. She discarded that notion as ridiculous. Silver had given every indication that she wasn't ready to dip her toes in the dating pool yet. This had to be from her stalker friend.

The message came from Nurse Executive. Bingo. The private note was from the same person who'd sent the previous creepy message. Jasmine wasn't sure if she should tell Silver right away about the new message or let her discover it on her own. If she told her about the odd communication, Silver would know she'd violated her privacy, but if she didn't, Silver might not see the message until she went on Facebook. It was a dilemma for Jasmine, but honesty and openness no matter the consequences always won out. She would confess her sins as soon as Silver came back down.

Jasmine closed down Silver's Facebook page and went back to reading the story. She wondered if Silver was sending her a subtle message. If only that were true, but

Silver had been abundantly clear she wasn't ready to move on yet.

Jasmine heard Silver's light footfalls as she descended from upstairs and rounded the corner. She looked up from the screen and smiled.

"I'm not quite finished reading your new novel, and I'm almost afraid to ask any questions about it," Jasmine confessed.

"I suppose you picked up on the parallels," Silver remarked.

"Um, yeah, they are kind of obvious."

"I suppose they are."

Jasmine turned her eyes toward the vibrating phone on the back counter, where Silver had plugged in her phone, tablet, and MP3 player. She'd also tossed her keys and wallet in the same location. *Saved by the buzz.*

Jasmine didn't like the frown that nearly marred Silver's beautiful face as she looked at her phone. She suspected it was bad news or something disturbing.

"Something wrong?" Jasmine asked.

"I just got the strangest text message from an unknown number," Silver answered.

Jasmine stood up and walked over to where Silver was intently looking at her phone.

"Let me see."

Silver handed her phone to Jasmine, and it was her turn to grimace.

Don't do anything rash. I'm coming to visit soon.

"What do you think?" Silver asked.

Jasmine took a big breath. "Okay, I was going to come clean anyway. When you were taking your shower, your laptop dinged and I clicked on your Facebook page to see what the message was. I'm sorry. It was completely asinine and insensitive of me to do that. I let my curiosity get the better of me after you showed me that other strange post. Anyway, it's a similar message. What do you know about this Nurse Executive person, and how did they get your cell phone number?"

Jasmine didn't want to believe Silver had given out her cell phone number to another fan. Silver had never offered her that information. Jasmine wanted to believe she was special, and if another fan had the number and she didn't, that definitely relegated her to nothing distinctive. That would break her heart all over again, and she didn't think she could control the tears at that point.

"That is a really good question. My cell phone isn't under my pen name. It's under my real name, and no one has that number but my family, my publisher, and…. Oh crap, every business requires a phone number. I hate that I'm required to give my cell phone number every time I open a bank account or any other account. What's odd is that I think you're the only reader that knows my real name. Of course my publisher and editors know it, but they would never reveal it to anyone." Silver pursed her lips.

"I think it's time you involved the police. The Fourth of July is just around the corner, and the specificity of the messages is disturbing. I'm really sorry again for trampling all over your privacy."

Silver smiled. "Normally I'd be angry about that, but for reasons I don't completely understand, I don't mind that you peeked. I don't want to close myself off to you. Right about now, I need a good friend, and you seem to be offering to fill that role. I'm just selfish enough to take it."

"That's not selfish at all. I care about you, Silver, and I want to be there for you in whatever capacity you need. By the way, I've always wanted to know. Does it bother you that I don't call you Helen? I know that's your name, but you'll always be Silver to me. It suits you."

"Naomi thought it suited me too. No, it doesn't bother me at all. I have a crazy idea. Oh never mind." Silver waived her hand.

"What? Come on. I'm sure it's not that farfetched. Remember, we're friends and I'm the kind of person that does just about anything for their good friends. I don't have too many, so I shower the ones I have with love and support," Jasmine declared.

"You might just regret what you just revealed. Um…." Silver shuffled her feet and wouldn't make eye contact. "I've been mulling over something since the middle of the night. I was going to ask if you were interested in coming back to spend the long Fourth of July weekend with me. I know you rarely take vacation, and, well…I think you've enjoyed your time here…. I know it's a long way to come, but, um, I was hoping that…."

"I'd love to. Besides, I can't let you hang out alone with some crazy fan promising to visit. I hope I'm the only crazy fan you want busting up your solitude."

"I'll of course pay for your tickets again. Can you take a few days off and make it a full week or more?" Silver asked.

"I can and I will, but I'm paying for my own vacation. I'm not destitute, you know." Jasmine's tone came out sharper than she intended, and Silver cringed.

"God, I'm sorry. I didn't mean to offend you. It's just that I'm asking as a favor because I don't want to be alone. My family all decided to take a cruise to Europe during the holiday. I couldn't bear to be around thousands of people, so I declined. Pathetic, huh?"

Jasmine reached for Silver and touched her arm. "No, I'm the one who should be sorry. Sometimes my stupid pride leaks out. I don't feel like I have a very important job and it makes me overly sensitive."

"Oh, Jasmine, don't sell yourself short. I think supporting the executives and working in human resources is far more important than you think. People are always the most valuable resource in a company, and if you don't have a great Human Resources department, a lot can go terribly wrong. Behind every successful executive is their assistant making sure their life is organized enough to allow them the time to get their work done. I would kill for an assistant like you."

Jasmine laughed. "It wouldn't take much to entice me to work for you."

"I'll remember you said that, and you never know, a new job offer might be on the horizon. I can be very persuasive when I want something. I might steal your company's greatest asset right out from under their noses," Silver teased.

"My mama told me to always keep my options open." Jasmine winked.

Jasmine was giddy with anticipation. All of a sudden, she had plans for the Fourth and had the privilege of seeing Silver again in less than three weeks. This was a dream come true and she wondered if Silver just needed more time. Jasmine would give her all the time she needed if it led to more than a friendship. Silver was worth it. She was willing to occupy the hole left by Naomi, even it if meant that a large part of Silver's heart would always belong to her dead wife. It was a price she was willing to pay for the chance to be with Silver. As these thoughts swirled around in Jasmine's head, she cleared from her mind the stalker and the their previous conversation about needing to bring the police in to evaluate the threat level.

"You must be starving by now. Let me just pop the asparagus and crab cakes on the grill and it'll be ready in a jiffy. Would you care for some wine? I have a very nice

Sauvignon blanc that I hear will go well with what we're having tonight," Silver offered.

"I'm not really a wine snob, so any white wine is fine with me. At least I'm cultured enough to know a Sauvignon blanc is a white wine. Dara taught me a few things about wines, but I'm more the kind of gal who either likes something or doesn't. I can't really distinguish any nuances in the wines I drink. I can open the bottle and pour the wine while you slave over the grill." Jasmine grinned.

"Deal." Silver opened a closet door in the kitchen and selected a bottle of wine. Jasmine stood and waited patiently for Silver to hand it to her.

Silver laughed. "Um… that's the wine cellar. I like to be unconventional. Why build a wine cellar when I have a perfectly good closet that stays cool? Naomi always wanted to buy a wine refrigerator, but we never quite got around to it."

Silver retrieved the corkscrew and handed it and the bottle to Jasmine. She opened the enormous stainless-steel refrigerator and pulled out a pan. Four mouthwatering crab cakes sat on top of a piece of foil alongside a Tupperware container that Jasmine suspected had the marinated asparagus.

Through their correspondence in the last year, Jasmine had learned one of Silver's favorite things to fix was grilled asparagus. She would liberally coat the thin stalks in her homemade dressing and then toss them on the grill. Jasmine was looking forward to tasting the specially prepared vegetable.

Silver balanced the meal on her forearm as she slid the patio door open.

Jasmine sneaked glances at Silver while she methodically placed the cakes and asparagus on the grill. Her smile made Jasmine's heart skip a beat. Sometimes Silver would have a faraway look in her eyes, but she also smiled and laughed a great deal more than Jasmine thought possible. She hoped she was the cause of Silver's intermittent moments of happiness. Jasmine shook her head and returned to her task at hand.

She knew there was probably a trick to opening a bottle of wine without getting pieces of the cork inside, but she'd not mastered that skill. Dara never let her open wine after the one time she'd started to pull the cork out before having the necessary leverage. When she hadn't secured the two-step lever to the lip, bits of the cork started coming out. Her second big mistake was not putting the screw exactly in the center. Dara had ended up trying to salvage her botched attempt and let her know how incompetent she was at the same time.

Jasmine glanced nervously outside before sneaking over to Silver's laptop and typing, *how do you correctly open a bottle of wine* into Google. She giggled when an option for a video popped up.

"Thank God for Google. She's my other best friend," Jasmine murmured.

The video instructed her to take the screw at an angle so the point went straight into the middle. This time Jasmine made sure she screwed the auger in far enough to use the first step to pull the cork up just a little bit until she could grab the lip with the second step and pull the cork completely out. When she heard the pop, she nearly danced around the kitchen.

Jasmine closed out of Google to hide the evidence of her insecurity. She brought the opened bottle back into the kitchen and set it down on the counter while she looked for the wineglasses. As she pivoted, she spied a glass-enclosed cabinet that displayed fine china and other glassware. She selected two small wineglasses and poured until they were three-quarters full.

Leaning against the counter, she waited for Silver to return with what she knew would be a fabulous meal.

Silver popped her head inside and asked, "In or out?"

"Excuse me?" Jasmine wrinkled her brow.

"Do you want to eat inside or outside?" Silver asked.

"Oh, it doesn't matter. I'm easy," she answered.

Silver smirked. "Hmmm, you're easy, huh? I'll have to store that little tidbit for later. I propose we eat outside. It's a beautiful night and it won't get too cool until later in the evening. Come on out with the wine, and I'll get the salad and roasted red pepper sauce for the crab cakes."

"Yum, roasted red pepper sauce. That sounds scrumptious."

Silver walked inside and pointed to the patio. "Go ahead out and I'll be right there."

Jasmine noted that the cookie sheet with the crab cakes covered with foil and the Tupperware container of asparagus were sitting next to the grill. She grabbed the food and set it on the beautiful stone patio table. The sun was still shining, and the light breeze created the perfect temperature. She sat patiently waiting for her host.

Silver was juggling two large bowls and a bottle of cider as she tried unsuccessfully to open the sliding glass door, so Jasmine jumped up to help. "Here, let me take one of those bowls. That doesn't look like apple cider to me."

"Thanks, you can take the red pepper sauce." Silver handed her the smaller bowl. "No, I use the old cider containers to mix my special balsamic dressings." Silver set the dressing and salad down on the table. "I just need to go back in and get the plates, utensils, and napkins, and then we'll be set. Thanks for putting the stuff from the grill on the table."

"Sure, no problem. Do you need any help bringing

anything else outside?" Jasmine asked.

"Nope, I got it."

Jasmine sat at the table, lifted a corner of the foil, and sniffed. "God, that smells heavenly."

Silver was smiling when she walked over with the plates and utensils in her hands. She set everything in front of Jasmine. "Go ahead, dig in. I see you've already peeked."

Jasmine lifted one of the crab cakes from the sheet with the tongs lying next to the delicacy and set it on Silver's plate, then selected one for her own plate. "Can I just use these tongs to serve the asparagus?"

"Oh crud, I knew I was forgetting something. Sure, if you don't mind. There's another set in the salad and I did remember a large spoon for the sauce, but I used the same tongs to grill both the crab cakes and asparagus."

After Jasmine finished serving up the crab cakes and asparagus and Silver dished out the salad and poured the red pepper sauce, Jasmine lifted her glass of wine. "To the gorgeous chef and new beginnings. I've never had crab before, so I'm looking forward to trying something new."

"Thank you, and I am so delighted I can introduce a new food to you."

Jasmine noticed Silver didn't make a comment about the new beginnings, and she wasn't sure if that was a good or bad thing.

Chapter Nine

Silver knew she was giving Jasmine mixed messages. One minute she was telling her that she wasn't ready for anything more than a friendship and quite possibly would never be prepared to move on. The next minute she was inviting her to spend the Fourth of July holiday in Roslyn with her—just the two of them again.

Silver had wanted the dinner to be special, and it was. She'd pulled out all her best cooking tricks to prepare a meal that was easy but distinctive. As they ate and talked, the time flew by, and before Silver realized, the sun was starting to set. She hadn't wanted the evening to end, so she suggested they take two of the lawn chairs out to the fire pit and she'd started a fire.

Silver kept filling the wineglasses and they continued their conversation. She tried not to feel guilty for having one of the best nights since her wife died. This was as close to a date as she'd come since the tragedy. Oh, who was she kidding—an outside observer would categorize this as their third date. Jasmine had arrived a little over twenty-four hours ago and already they'd had dinner together and a glorious bike outing complete with a romantic picnic lunch.

As Jasmine leaned back in her chair, with the fire as a backlight, the soft glow spotlighted her beauty. Silver couldn't remember the last time she'd desperately wanted to take someone in her arms and place a gentle kiss on her lips. She knew she was staring intently, but she couldn't help herself.

Jasmine turned and met Silver's intense gaze. "Dollar for your thoughts. My niece reminded me the other day that inflation has had an impact on that saying. Nothing can be bought for a penny these days."

Silver laughed. "I could tell you, but then I'd have to kill you or myself."

"Oh, that good, huh? I swear I'll keep your secret so you don't have to kill anyone," Jasmine assured her.

"I'll probably regret being so open and honest with you, but you're like a confession magnet. Too bad women can't be priests—you'd make a stellar priest. Everyone would flock to you for confession. I must admit to being thankful that you aren't a priest or a nun because I'm having very inappropriate thoughts about you right now."

"Please go on, confess all your sins. You'll feel so much better, and I won't even assign any Hail Marys," Jasmine teased. She looked directly at Silver and shifted in her chair.

Silver wasn't sure if she was nervous or eager to hear her response.

"I was thinking I'm giving you a lot of mixed messages and that isn't very fair to you. I'm sorry," Silver whispered.

"I'm not going to lie to you and say I don't dream about taking our relationship in a different direction, but I'm a big girl and I know the deal. I'll suffer the consequences as long as I get to occupy your orbit. I'll admit it isn't easy to hold back, but I'd rather do that than ruin our friendship and eliminate all possibility that we could get to that place sometime in the future. I'm an optimist," Jasmine replied.

"I'm honestly still struggling with an incredible amount of guilt over the fact I'm wildly attracted to you and feel like I'm trampling all over Naomi's grave. I know I can't help my feelings, but it sure feels like crap right now. This is a moral dilemma I haven't quite got a handle on just yet. I wish there was some kind of higher power that could put the solution in my head. Perhaps it's time to see my therapist again. She did help me work through some of my initial grief and depression right after Naomi died."

"I don't know if there is a higher power or not, but I do believe the universe will ensure life works out as it is intended. It's never good to force anything or to hold back because you think that's what you *should* do. Whenever we *should* all over ourselves, it's like another *s-h* word that creates a big stink. You are far too lovely to start smelling bad."

"Okay, wow, that was a disgusting visual. I think I come with too much baggage," Silver lamented.

"Au contraire. As we talked about before, everyone comes with baggage, but if you're lucky you find someone who can help you unpack."

"I did have that someone. The question is can I allow another person in to unpack my new, stuffed-to-the-brim suitcase? I ought to write down these little metaphors and use them in my current project," Silver remarked.

"I sure hope so, Silver. You already know I'd volunteer in a nanosecond. You just say the word and I'll become your master unpacker."

"You're very sweet, Jasmine, and you'll be the first one I go to if and when I'm ready."

"One more thing to consider that my grandma once

said to me, 'Expectations are like a creeping, noxious, vine and have the bad manners to strangle the life and love out of people leaving a husk of regret and torment'." Jasmine laughed. "I think she might have read that on a fortune cookie or she made it up. She was a wily old woman. Be kind to yourself, Silver, and don't burden yourself with too many expectations."

"You are a wise woman, Jasmine. It's one of the things I love about you."

Silver couldn't believe she'd tossed this out so naturally. Was Jasmine burrowing into her heart? She was fond of her, but love? Was it even possible for lightning to strike twice? Could she allow herself to fall in love again? She'd started writing that new manuscript about second chances and that rare type of love happening to her main character twice in her life. Did the book parallel what was happening in her life? This might take some serious soul-searching and good old-fashioned therapy to figure out.

Jasmine smiled, and Silver was grateful she hadn't responded to her last comment.

†

Jasmine lay awake in her bed thinking about her evening with Silver. She knew Silver was struggling with her feelings, but she couldn't help feeling giddy that Silver's internal debate was occurring. Jasmine wondered if she would be able to help Silver unpack the large suitcase filled with guilt over having feelings for another woman.

Jasmine needed to look at her own bag filled with her insecurities. At the top of the list was her doubts about Silver loving her in equal measure to Naomi. The question of whether it mattered filled the smaller carryon bag propped next to its larger cousin—she was tempted to accept that lesser prize. Did that make her just plain pathetic? Maybe Dara was right and she was pining after someone who would never be obtainable. She feared she would always be second fiddle.

Tomorrow was their last day together, and then she had a flight out later that evening. She wondered what the day would bring. The fact she would be returning in a few short weeks brightened her mood. Silver had asked her—that had to count for something.

Jasmine heard Silver shuffling around outside her door and noted her insomnia was probably the culprit. Jasmine didn't usually have a hard time sleeping, but being so close to the woman she was falling for left her wide awake. She debated peeking outside the bedroom door and offering to keep Silver company.

A sliver of light cast a shadow inside the room because she'd left the door cracked hoping one of the kittens would visit again. She sat up and saw a streak of fur before a large cat jumped on the bed.

"Well hello, handsome," she murmured.

The large black cat pushed his head up against her hand as she stroked his soft fur. Jasmine lifted her head when she heard the light tap on her door.

"Yes?" she called out.

"Everything okay in there? Is Sinbad bothering you?" Silver asked.

"Not at all. Hey, why don't you come in? I'm awake and I heard you rustling around out there. I suppose that means you can't sleep. Well, neither can I. We can share our insomnia. Misery loves company, you know."

Silver pushed the door open and hesitated in the doorway before coming inside.

Jasmine thought she looked positively adorable in her light flannel pajamas. She scooted over and patted the spot next to her. "Come on in, I promise I won't bite."

Jasmine had to bite back, *Unless you want me to,* which was on the tip of her tongue. She must have revealed something in her expression, because Silver grinned at her.

"I'm having a hard time sleeping tonight, even though I'm exhausted from last night's flurry of writing. I've had insomnia for a long time now, but at least I've been able to get a few hours of sleep each night. Lately, it's been a struggle to even manage that."

Jasmine pushed the covers back farther. "Look, I know this might be a completely inappropriate suggestion, but why don't you try falling asleep next to me? I've been told I have magic fingers."

Silver arched her eyebrow.

"Wait, I didn't mean that in the way it came out. What I intended to say is that I'm always able to put someone to sleep with a relaxing head rub. Let me do that for you. I promise not to cross the line," Jasmine amended.

She wanted to add, Not that I don't want to, and just say the word—I'll trample all over the edge.

"I haven't slept in the same bed with someone else since…."

"It's okay. Really, it's only sleeping that I'm suggesting. Honestly, the warmth of another body will help me sleep better too."

Silver climbed into the bed beside Jasmine and curled into her waiting arms.

As Jasmine began to stroke Silver's head, she could feel the warm wetness of her tears soak through the soft cotton of her T-shirt. She continued to rub Silver's head until she felt the rhythmic air as Silver breathed in and out. Sleep finally overtook Silver's exhausted body. Jasmine wanted to hold Silver every night for the rest of her life. Nothing had ever felt so right to her. Tonight, nothing was between them, not even Naomi's ghost.

Jasmine felt the lull toward dreamland shortly after Silver had surrendered to sleep and relaxed, her head snuggled against Jasmine's shoulder. Jasmine's last thought was profound relief that Silver could finally get the rest she so desperately needed.

Chapter Ten

Dara sat in her living room sipping her specialty coffee, wondering what Jasmine was doing. *She's probably still asleep, and I hope she's alone.*

She debated making another phone call to Jasmine even though she hadn't answered any of her voice mails or texts. Thankfully, she was coming home tonight, and Dara hoped she would see Jasmine at work tomorrow. She'd cautiously asked around and learned Jasmine was taking a long weekend, and when she didn't see her on Friday, she wondered if the long weekend included Monday as well. Jasmine had posted on her Facebook page that she would be returning home on Sunday evening after her visit with Silver.

It was ten in the morning, which made it eight in Washington. Dara scowled, remembering Silver was an early riser, just like Jasmine. Dara didn't usually get up before nine thirty on the weekends. It was a point of contention between the two.

Jasmine always wanted to start the day early and enjoy the outdoors, regardless of the weather. Dara preferred a more robust nightlife. Even though she was in her forties, she still went clubbing and danced the night away. Watching all the young lesbians sway to the music was always a turn-on for her. Jasmine would reluctantly go, but her acquiescence to do what Dara wanted had lessened about a year ago. Dara felt like Jasmine hadn't even cared whether she picked someone up or not. That was the beginning of the end, and soon after Dara had viewed the flirtatious banter between Jasmine and Silver on Facebook.

Her roving eye had not been the cause of this last breakup. She hadn't been innocent on that front but managed to keep it from Jasmine. Her transgression with the twenty something health information clerk ended quickly and she was sure Jasmine hadn't even heard about it, but still Jasmine steadfastly refused to reconcile and had driven home the point when she'd asked for a transfer. The subtly veiled threat human resources tactfully presented to Dara had kept her from pursuing the matter further. She'd decided to give Jasmine a little time and space, but then she'd learned about the blasted contest.

It was time to take a more active stance. Dara couldn't resist making another call to Jasmine. Maybe on this occasion she would answer. She also considered sending a short message to the author.

†

Korrine stared at her computer screen. Nothing. Not one single post on either person's Facebook page since late Thursday evening. She frowned and paced in her spacious kitchen, mumbling to herself.

"That emptyheaded beauty queen has all the breaks." She pinched the bridge of her nose and continued her diatribe, "I've been a loyal fan. Silver values my opinion above all others. Jasmine wiggles her ass and they all fall at her feet."

A sharp bark diverted her attention to her backyard. She looked out the window and watched as her beautiful husky-wolf mix chased her tail and ran around in circles. As if sensing someone watching her, she stopped in mid-play and tilted her head as she looked at her master.

"Woof."

Korrine opened the back door and called out, "Silver, come."

The dog bounded over and licked her hand.

"You are so beautiful, just like your namesake. Silver will be so happy to meet you. You're not like her mangy cats. Sneaky little things. I don't trust them at all. They aren't like dogs—no loyalty or obedience. I must have submission from the ones I love."

Korrine walked over to her couch and sat down, placing her coffee on the table as she patted her thigh. "Come, sit."

The fluffy dog dutifully sat beside her owner.

Korrine absently stroked the soft fur. She picked up her coffee and gulped it down before placing the cup back on the table and picking up her phone. She checked her Facebook page, keyed a few posts, sent several private messages, and then leaned back on the couch as a satisfied grin occupied her face.

†

Silver opened her eyes and realized she was drooling all over Jasmine's T-shirt. Embarrassed, she rolled over and wondered what time it was. Today was the last day with Jasmine, and even though they didn't have the whole day because she needed to drive her back to the airport tonight, Silver wanted to make the most of their time together.

Jasmine stirred when Silver moved away. Quickly she wiped her mouth and thought, *Ew, that's not the kind of wet spot people appreciate waking up to.*

"Morning," Jasmine groggily said. She smiled that sexy little smile, and Silver's heartbeat increased.

"Good morning. Um… I'm just going to admit to drooling all over you. Sorry."

"Oh, I never mind when beautiful women drool all over me." Jasmine chucked.

"I left a wet spot on your T-shirt," Silver admitted.

"You have no idea how many possible retorts to that I could make, but I better leave it alone. How did you sleep?" Jasmine turned her body to face Silver.

"Never better. Thank you for last night."

"It was truly my pleasure. I know you're an early riser and so am I, so let's get the day started. You know I was only joking about scratching your eyes out if you woke me up too early the other night. I want to take full advantage of the last day of my visit. I'm up for anything," Jasmine enthused.

"Would you be interested in going to Seattle? We can spend the day there at Pike Place Market, the Experience Music Project, or the Pacific Science Center if you'd like."

"That would be great. I've never been to any of those places and I've always wanted to check out the market. That seems fun. We can take my bags, and then you can drop me off at the airport afterward."

"That was exactly my thought," Silver added.

"In case I haven't told you yet, I've really had a wonderful time. I can't thank you enough for opening up your home and planning such fun activities. This is the best weekend I've had in a long time. I wish Kansas had as much to offer. It's not that I'm discouraging a visit or anything, because you are always welcome to pop in and I'll do my best to show you what we do have, but I don't think it will come close to comparing with Washington."

"Oh, I don't know, those chocolates were heavenly. I'd say Kansas has a lot to offer. You're there, after all." Silver rolled her body out of bed. "How about if we take quick showers and head out? We can grab some breakfast on the way."

"Sounds perfect. I'll pack my bags and can be ready in less than an hour."

"No rush. I think it's still early." Before Silver exited the room, she looked back and saw Jasmine stretch lazily in bed. Her T-shirt rose up, and Silver got a glimpse of her flat abdomen. A tingle in her stomach told her she wasn't immune to the beautiful woman. No matter what level of guilt she felt regarding her attraction, her body wasn't about to listen to her head.

Jasmine bounded from the bed after Silver left. She touched the wet spot on her T-shirt and smiled. It wasn't exactly the wet spot she'd hoped for, but it felt good to have Silver so close and relaxed enough to drool on her. It was such an ordinary, endearing, and completely normal thing to occur between two people who cared for each other.

Jasmine decided to pack her bag before getting ready so that all she had to do after her shower was grab it and head downstairs. She rolled all her clothes carefully and placed them in the carryon bag, keeping a pair of jeans and a short-sleeved shirt out to change into after drying her hair. She would toss her bath items on top after she finished using them.

She walked into the bathroom and began her morning routine. She always started with brushing her teeth before walking into the shower. The buzz on the counter where her phone was charging broke Jasmine from her musings and morning routine. She suspected it was Dara again and didn't really want to check, but it seemed like Dara wasn't going stop trying to open the lines of communication.

Jasmine sighed as she picked up the buzzing phone. She glanced at the screen and noted two text messages, but one of them wasn't from Dara. Jasmine shivered when she read it.

Stay away.

Jasmine wasn't sure what the message meant, but she felt like it was a threat and wondered if the police would link it to the messages Silver had received in the last few days. She debated showing the message to Silver but discarded that idea. Silver had enough on her plate without her adding to the pile.

Jasmine deleted the message and reluctantly read Dara's text.

Please call me when you get back. Can we get together and talk?

Jasmine didn't really want to answer Dara, but she thought she at least owed her the courtesy. They hadn't talked since the big fight, and she supposed Dara deserved a civil closure to their relationship. She would bite the bullet and arrange to meet with Dara so she could make her position clear. She'd finally found the courage to move on, and nothing was going to get in the way of Jasmine making the right decision about what she needed in her life. Dara was never going to be the type of person she would grow old with.

Okay, I'll call, she texted back.

Jasmine hoped it wouldn't get ugly. She turned around and moved the lever on the shower to between the hot and cold markers. As she waited for the water to warm up, she remembered how good having Silver in her arms last night felt, and she was giddy with anticipation for not only the last day of the visit, but the upcoming Fourth of July vacation.

†

Silver felt refreshed and ready to start the day. She'd hurried through her shower so she could make some coffee before they left for Seattle. When she entered the kitchen, she heard her phone ding and scrunched up her face, wondering who would send a text message this early on a Sunday morning.

Silver gasped as she read the message.

Stay away from Jasmine. I'm coming to see you soon.

Startled, she looked at the number and it wasn't one that she recognized. She wondered if the message had come from Nurse Executive. Silver was always polite when she received a private message or email from her, thanking her for her support and the positive reviews. She'd expressed her genuine sorrow when Nurse Executive had talked about her struggles with depression and trying to find the right partner. Silver was now questioning whether this was a smart move on her part. Other fans she conversed with were a lot safer since most were married or happily partnered unlike Nurse Executive. Yet, when she first received a message from the reader, Silver was also happily married.

Silver sat heavily on the kitchen stool. She didn't want to ruin the day by showing this latest text to Jasmine. Even though her worry over the situation was ratcheting up, she had plenty of time to take this to the police. So far, the communications weren't exactly threatening, just a little creepy. Then again, she supposed that "stay away from Jasmine" was a sort of threat, or at least a reasonable person might perceive it as one.

Silver shook her head and was careful not to delete the message so she had proof to show to the police when she did get around to bringing this to their attention. The whistle of the teapot took her attention away from her concerns, and Silver conveniently drove the disturbing thoughts from her mind as she poured the hot water into the french press and moved on to her plans for the day.

No matter how many times Silver visited Seattle, she never tired of the market. It had so many great places to eat, and she wouldn't mind picking up some fresh foods or other specialty items to restock her pantry. Naomi used to love going there, and the crowds never bothered her. On occasion, Silver felt uncomfortable in a crowd, but the unique wares at the jam-packed market outweighed her anxiety. Silver imagined Naomi pushing her way to the surface again and engulfing Silver in a wave of guilt and anger.

"Oh, Naomi, I am so angry with you right now. Why did you have to leave me? All my connections at the hospital didn't mean a damn thing, did they?"

Silver thought back to the day after the routine surgery. Naomi had been complaining about stomach pain. After Naomi's appendectomy, neither one of them thought about the potential consequences of this relatively routine surgery. The on-call surgeon had performed the operation when Naomi came to the hospital complaining of nausea and stomach pain. He hadn't been Silver's first choice since several of his surgery cases had gone before peer review, but due to the emergent nature of Naomi's condition, they didn't have an option.

While Naomi was still in recovery, the surgeon had come out to the waiting room and was all smiles. He'd told Silver the surgery went well. The nurse who followed him had a scowl on her face, and Silver had gotten a bad feeling right then. Silver tried to track down the nurse, but she'd scurried away, and Silver didn't get a chance to talk with her until two days later when Naomi spiked a shivering fever and

Silver brought her back to the emergency department. The area around the incision was red and enflamed, and Silver knew right away that she'd acquired an infection.

It had gone downhill from there. The hospitalist had carefully explained that infections in the bloodstream were the most dangerous and often led to the body's inflammatory response called sepsis. In Naomi's case, she developed severe septic shock, and soon after her organs began to shut down. Naomi's mother believed strongly that every sniffle in childhood required a strong dose of antibiotics, so Naomi had unfortunately developed a resistance to every drug they'd tried. When her organs started to die one by one, Silver watched helplessly as her wife died before her eyes. Naomi made her promise not to grieve too long. She knew she was dying.

Heartbroken, Silver hadn't even wanted to accept the settlement the hospital offered, but her older sister had convinced her otherwise. She'd taken an early retirement and spent the first year in intensive grief therapy.

Cocooning herself from the rest of the world, she'd only just started to emerge and she wasn't sure why she'd maintained that tenuous thread with her readers, especially Jasmine. She'd replied to posts and messages intermittently from everyone else who sent well-wishes, including Nurse Executive. They'd all understood, but Jasmine had continued to send her subtle support over the years, even when Silver didn't respond for weeks.

"I know you told me not to pine after you or you'd haunt me from beyond, but I don't know if I can do it. Your face is fading from my memory, and that's just unacceptable. I feel something for the first time since—" Silver cut herself off. She felt ridiculous speaking to the empty room. Maybe she would call her sister tonight after dropping Jasmine off. She always provided much-needed perspective.

The ding of the timer she'd set earlier refocused her attention on the coffee she wanted to pour into the travel mugs. She quickly fixed both of the expensive thermoses and took a small sip. As the hot liquid reached her lips, she pulled back, feeling the slight burn on her tongue. She would have to remember to warn Jasmine about the temperature.

When she heard Jasmine's steps on the staircase, she pushed all thoughts of Naomi aside, determined to enjoy her last day with Jasmine. As Jasmine entered the kitchen, the brilliance of her smile lifted Silver's spirits. Jasmine already had her backpack securely fastened to her body and looked eager to start the day. Her gaze tracked on the travel cup Silver had just placed on the counter.

"Be careful. Don't guzzle the coffee, it's still really hot."

Jasmine picked up the mug and unscrewed the top. "I think I'll just let the cool air do its magic." She blew on the open container, winked, and took a sip. "I don't think I've confessed my impatience before when it comes to the first cup of the day. I smell it and I'm like Pavlov's dog. I've got to make sure a heathy amount hits my system before I'm ready to start the day."

Silver chuckled. "Oh God, I'm the same way. I'm positively stupid until I've had my first cup. Are you ready to go?"

"Yep. Lead the way. I can't wait to explore Seattle."

"We'll hit the bakery on the way out unless you'd like a heartier breakfast."

"No way. A pastry in the morning is just about the most perfect breakfast I know. It's not very healthy, but it's so dang yummy. I'd eat junk all day long every day of the week if it weren't so devastating to my almost-forty-year-old body. I'm starting to sag in places I can barely see in a mirror. Lately I've limited my unhealthy eating habits to the weekends. Today is Sunday, so I'm good. Bring on the sugar and carbs."

"You don't look like you have to worry one bit to me," Silver noted.

"Oh trust me, I do, but I work out nearly every morning for at least ninety minutes so I can eat those bad things. I'm making an exception today, but I haven't missed a single day in over three years. I'm glad we went biking yesterday. I would have felt terribly guilty missing two days in a row."

"I have an elliptical in the room above the garage if you want to take the time to do that before we head to Seattle. I'm sure I could occupy myself writing a bit more on my current project. I don't want to interrupt your routine," Silver offered.

"Nope, I'm good. Besides, I just took a shower, and I get stinky and sweaty when I work out. It would end up creating a two-hour delay. I'm anxious to see the big city, and one day off is definitely not going to kill me."

"All right, let's hit the road." Silver opened the door to the garage and waved Jasmine forward.

Chapter Eleven

Jasmine stood awkwardly in the area in front of the airport security lines. She wasn't sure what to say to Silver, who had an expectant look on her face. She looked so vulnerable and petrified. Jasmine followed her instincts and placed her hand on Silver's cheek. She brushed away a tear and brought her lips to Silver's for just a fraction of a second. It was enough to demonstrate the depth of her feelings without suggesting they take things further than Silver was willing to go.

"I can't even describe how wonderful these past few days have been with you. I'm glad you asked me to come back on the Fourth. No pressure, Silver. Whatever boundaries you define will be okay with me. Believe me when I say I'm not vying for the place in your heart Naomi still occupies. If there's another corner free, I'll take that."

Silver gathered Jasmine in for a hug and gently pulled her fingers through her hair. Jasmine felt as though Silver was breathing in her scent. This time she had no doubt that the hug was too long for mere friends.

"Oh, Jasmine, you deserve a prominent place in

someone's heart, not a small corner. If you'll give me a little more time, maybe you can coexist with Naomi. I'm not exactly sure how that will work, but I'm definitely going to explore that possibility with my therapist and my wise older sister. Don't give up on me just yet."

"Never." Jasmine pulled away. "Can I call you? Skype?"

Silver's smile widened. "Absolutely, please do. It gets very lonely and boring at my place. I think I'm ready to join the rest of the world, so I'd welcome the interruption to my writing. The cats are great, but they don't seem to want to have the same meaningful conversations human beings do. All Sinbad cares about is his treats in the morning and the good-looking stray gray cat he peers at through the front window. The rest of them talk a lot among themselves and only let me know when they're hungry or need some affection."

Jasmine hitched up her backpack to reposition it and turned slowly then made her way toward the security lines. She looked over her shoulder and gave a tiny wave to Silver, who was standing in the middle of the passageway looking particularly forlorn. Jasmine wanted to find a way to take Silver with her. She chuckled to herself as the image of reducing Silver to doll size and placing her in her backpack flashed before her eyes. It was going to be a long three weeks until she saw Silver again. Her heart was already aching. Yep, she had it bad. Only time would tell if they had any kind of future, but thankfully Silver had just opened the door a tiny crack. Jasmine hoped it was wide enough for her to slip through.

Silver watched for another minute as Jasmine progressed in the line. When she turned to leave, a wave of loneliness washed over her. She needed to try to get her crap together in the next three weeks. Jasmine had managed to worm her way into her heart, so it was hard not to consider taking what Jasmine so generously offered. Silver sensed that all she would need to do was say the word and Jasmine would open herself up for a relationship. The distance was the least of Silver's concerns. Jasmine didn't seem to have locked herself into living in Kansas. Silver knew the largest barrier was her ambivalence over allowing herself to love and accept love again.

Silver touched her lips where Jasmine had placed that sweet kiss. She smiled to herself, noting this was the first kiss she'd received in over three years. It felt more right than she wanted to admit to herself.

When Silver climbed into her car, she decided to call her older sister, Meredith, right away. Meredith had moved to Chicago to start her doctoral program at the University of Chicago, and she and her husband had decided to stay. They'd lived there for the past twenty-five years.

Silver put the car in gear and backed out of the space in the garage. "Call Meredith," she directed her hands-free system.

"Helen? Are you okay? You rarely call, so something must be up," Meredith answered after a few rings.

Silver smiled to herself when Meredith called her by her real name. Even Naomi had started to call her Silver, stating that she liked it better than Helen. Since she hadn't had a whole lot of interaction with anyone after Naomi's death, with the exception of Jasmine and a few other readers here and there, her pen name had started to feel more comfortable to her.

"I need your sage advice," Silver announced.

"Okay. I'm happy to provide a little perspective, little sis. Shoot."

"I think I've told you about my devout reader, Jasmine. I don't really think of any of the women that follow my writings as fans because that sounds so egotistical, you know?"

Meredith chuckled. "Leave it to my famous sister to redefine the term *fan*. Yes, she's come up in conversation before. She's the drop-dead-gorgeous woman with the Japanese Norwegian heritage, right? Hey, isn't she the one that won that contest you sponsored? Brilliant idea, by the way."

"Yeah, that's Jasmine. Well…um…she was just here for the weekend and I think I'm starting to have feelings for her, but every time I think I'm ready to move on, Naomi pops into my head and I feel guilty for having those thoughts."

"Oh, hon, feelings aren't good or bad, they just are. You can't help how you feel. You know Naomi wouldn't want you to live out your life alone. What are you really afraid of?"

"I don't want to hurt Jasmine. She is really a special human being, and I just don't know if I have much left to offer anyone."

"Helen, you have one of the biggest hearts of anyone I know. I doubt Jasmine expects you to forget Naomi. I know you have plenty of room in that big heart of yours for another great love. They can coexist there and it doesn't mean you're replacing Naomi—it only means you're letting someone else experience the love I know you have to give to another. I think I need to meet this woman who has captured your heart."

"It's interesting you would put it in those terms. Jasmine said something similar, only she mentioned feeling okay about occupying a tiny corner of my heart. I like the idea of coexistence. Although I have to admit it feels a little like those sister wives in Utah, and that's kinda creepy," Silver groaned.

"It's not anything like that and you know it. Stop putting up that wall of yours and just let nature take its course. Promise me you'll open up your heart again. I don't want to see you continue to lock yourself away. You already have an occupation well suited for a hermit, and I just can't stand to see you spend the rest of your life alone. By the way, how is your latest project coming? I sure hope it's more uplifting than your last book. No offense, sis, but it was a little depressing. Great writing, shitty ending."

"Leave it to you, Meredith, to not pull any punches. I think you'll like my new book. I'll send it to you before I submit it for consideration. This time I'll listen to your feedback. I hope you understand why I couldn't alter the ending of my previous book. It was cathartic for me, and, in a strange way, I think it helped open me up to new possibilities. I needed to get that crap out of my system."

"I do and did understand. I told you that at the time, but you know I don't like books that have unhappy endings. I had to tell you that or you would have known I was lying. I've always given you my honest opinion, and I wasn't going to stop doing that no matter how much pain you were still working through."

"You're right, of course, and I don't ever want you to lie to me. I love you, big sis."

"You sound good, Helen. I want to meet the woman who has put the pep back in your voice. I knew it would happen eventually. I might have to start calling you Silver now, because it seems like you've found that silver lining again," Meredith said.

"Mom," a young male voice called in the background.

"Sounds like Tyler is hailing you." Silver chuckled.

"I should have pinched that kid's head off when I had

the chance. Want a new visitor? I've decided I no longer want to be a mother, so it's either military academy or cool aunt's house."

"You know I'm happy to have Tyler come out for a visit anytime he wants, but I don't think Chris will be too happy about losing his star soccer player."

"Two-for-one deal. I'll send them both your way. Oh shit, gotta go. I swear I'm gonna kill that kid."

"Thanks, sis, talk to you later."

Silver had a lot to think about and only three short weeks to accomplish everything. With Jasmine and where their relationship might be headed on her mind, she pushed any thoughts of her would-be stalker out of her head.

Chapter Twelve

Jasmine was still smiling when she opened the HR office the next morning and went straight to the breakroom to set up the Keurig so it would be ready for her coworkers. She'd already stopped at Starbucks and had gotten her vanilla latte to go.

While she was pouring water into the coffeemaker, she heard the outer door open and moved quickly to greet whoever had come in. Sometimes the night-shift staff came in after the end of their shift and wanted help with benefit or transfer forms. Jasmine was always eager to provide them support before her other officemates started their day. She always felt bad when they had to stay up longer because most of the hospital didn't get going until a little after eight.

Jasmine walked out of the break room and came face-to-face with a scowling Korrine.

Jasmine tried not to let her wince show. "Good morning, Korrine. What can I help you with?" Jasmine asked.

"I dropped off a posting on Friday and it still hasn't been put on the job board. Don't you people know how important it is to post job openings right away? Nurses don't grow on trees, and I don't think you understand how difficult it is for my nurses to work short-staffed while they wait for HR to do their job," Korrine barked.

Pauline, the volunteer director, entered the reception area and scurried back to her office after making eye contact with Jasmine, who gave a slight shake of her head.

"I'm so sorry, Korrine. I was out of the office on Friday. As soon as I get to my desk, it will be the first thing I do."

"I know that, but you'd think you would have passed that task along to someone else if you were going to be gone. Aren't you guys cross-trained?"

Jasmine started to head back to her desk on the other side of the reception area behind the glass enclosure. She knew better than to attempt to defend herself when Korrine got in a snit. She blew out of sigh of relief when she saw Carla, her boss, push open the outside door and enter.

"Good morning, Jasmine. Welcome back. Hi, Korrine, is there anything I can help you with, or is Jasmine taking care of you?" Carla asked.

Korrine smiled. "No thanks, Carla. I'll just straighten it out with Jasmine. I've got a busy day, so hopefully it won't take too long."

"I'm sure Jasmine will take good care of you. I'm running late myself. I'm supposed to be over at the hospital for an early morning meeting." Carla pushed open the door that separated the back offices from the reception area and breezed through.

Jasmine felt like Korrine's eyes were two laser beams as she refocused her attention back on her.

"I promise, Korrine, the posting will be up by no later than eight," Jasmine assured.

"I have no idea how you managed to keep things

straight in administration. I suppose Dara protected your job and tolerated your incompetence. We all know the reasons for that. My, you are a busy little beaver. Are you giving Carla the same personal treatment you gave Dara? I didn't think she swung that way."

Jasmine turned bright red and looked down. She hadn't seen or heard Carla come back into the area and didn't realize she may have overheard Korrine's last comment until she recognized Carla's terse tone.

"Korrine, do you have a minute? I'd like to talk to you about something," Carla clipped.

Korrine turned her head, and Jasmine thought she saw embarrassment flash across her face.

"Um, I have an early morning meeting I really need to get to, and I know you do as well," Korrine answered.

"It can wait—this is important," Carla pushed.

"All right."

Carla opened the door and waved Korrine through. Before she followed Carla, Korrine glared at Jasmine.

Jasmine didn't know what she'd ever done to offend Korrine, but for the past five years, they'd had increasingly unpleasant interactions. She'd had to deal with her more when she worked in the administrative suite, but they were rarely alone, and with others around as witnesses, especially Dara, Korrine had managed to treat her with polite indifference.

Since she'd moved to HR, the interactions were less frequent, but definitely more hostile. The Human Resources department was in a completely separate building from the main hospital, so they enjoyed quite a bit of independence and freedom from the scrutiny of the rest of the senior leaders.

Jasmine liked working in this building and especially enjoyed working for Carla, who was fiercely protective of her staff. She was liberal with her praise and tactful when correcting someone. Jasmine had learned that one of her pet peeves was when a leader, a nurse, or other professional staff person treated the support staff with disrespect. Jasmine liked that Carla truly believed every single staff member made a difference. She would often lecture that no one person was more important than any other to the overall success of the organization.

Jasmine sat in her chair and tried not to let the dressing down get to her. She wouldn't give Korrine the satisfaction of seeing her become upset. She busied herself by booting up her computer and checking her inbox. She sifted through the papers until she found the posting Korrine had referenced. It wouldn't take her long to type the information into the applicant tracking program.

Jasmine heard the door leading into Pauline's office open, and ten seconds later, Pauline walked up to her desk, offering a blueberry muffin. She set the breakfast treat on the ledge of the glass partition.

"You okay?" Pauline asked.

Jasmine smiled brightly. "Absolutely. Did you have a good weekend?"

"Who or what crawled up her butt this morning? I heard how she talked to you. Did Carla hear it as well?"

Jasmine shrugged. "Maybe the very last sentence, but I don't think she heard the whole exchange."

"I can tell her exactly what that witch said to you. I can also tell her about all the other times she's been rude. I don't get it. She's nice as pie to everyone else. You don't deserve the way she treats you. You're the nicest one in this office and a heck of a lot better than the last assistant we had. We hit the jackpot when you transferred to HR. If Korrine chases you away, I'm going to be really pissed. I'll bet Dara would be interested in how she treats you, but don't count

Carla out. She's like a mama bear with her cubs when someone abuses her staff," Pauline said.

"I don't think she meant to abuse me. She was just upset about the delay with her posting, and I don't blame her. It is difficult to recruit nurses, and they have to work short-staffed while we try to find those replacements for them. The quicker we get the postings up, the better chance we have to fill the position in a reasonable amount of time. I should have anticipated that the posting would be submitted on Friday because I knew Alisha resigned on Thursday. It was my fault," Jasmine admitted.

"Are you freakin' kidding me? You weren't even here on Friday. How the heck were you supposed to do the posting?"

Jasmine was uncomfortable with the conversation. She never wanted to speak poorly of one of the senior leaders, even if they weren't respectful to her. She was happy when she heard Korrine and Carla exit the back-office area.

†

Korrine was frustrated and angry. She hadn't intended for Carla to overhear her conversation with Jasmine. It seemed like every corner she turned, Jasmine was making her life miserable. *How is that little bitch able to snow everyone with her sweet, innocent act?*

Korrine chastised herself for crossing the line. She knew she could get away with treating Jasmine with rude indifference or making subtle demeaning comments, but this time she'd been more direct and was caught in the act. She was dreading the confrontation with Carla, who could create problems for her.

Carla motioned for her to sit in the chair across from her desk. Korrine noted she hadn't offered her a seat at her conference table, and the message was clear. This would be a serious conversation, and Carla wanted her power as the chief human resources officer respected.

"Korrine, let me get right to the point because I know you appreciate when people are direct and don't beat around the bush. I don't know the nature of the conversation prior to when I entered the reception area, but what I heard does concern me. It isn't like you to treat employees the way you treated Jasmine. The insinuation you made is not only disrespectful to her, but you included me in that disrespect. Jasmine has been a stellar employee for me, and frankly, a superstar. I wish we had a hundred like her. Can you tell me what prompted the comment? I'm trying to understand your perspective and what provoked this interchange," Carla asked.

"You're absolutely correct, Carla, the comment was uncalled for. I'm feeling stressed about the short staffing on our critical care unit, and I'm afraid I took out my frustration on Jasmine. When I learned our posting hadn't gone up yet, I came loaded for bear, and since Jasmine does the postings, she was my target. You know how difficult it is to replace our specialty nurses," Korrine explained.

"I do understand your frustration and I wouldn't want to face the staff to let them know they'll be working short-staffed until we find a replacement for Alisha, but I was the one who made the decision not to post the position on Friday and wait until Jasmine came back on Monday. I guess I didn't realize how much a day would matter. If you have reason to be upset with anyone, you should be irritated with me. I own that decision, not Jasmine. I'd appreciate it if you would apologize to Jasmine and make amends to her. Hopefully, we can forget this indiscretion ever occurred. I do want to make it clear that it will never be acceptable to treat Jasmine or any other support person in the same or similar fashion again. As a senior leader, it is up to us to present a professional image and adhere to our values. We must be the role models for teamwork and respect. The employees expect more from us, not less," Carla advised.

"Yes, of course."

Korrine was seething inside, but she managed to remove all evidence of any anger from her face. Smiling at Carla, she stood, signaling that she was prepared to follow Carla's subtle directive. She was going to have to apologize to Jasmine and that would nearly kill her, but she was convinced Carla would follow her out and make sure the apology occurred. She needed to think more about what Carla had shared with her, because it certainly did not match her impression of the beautiful woman.

"I'll just follow you out and perhaps we can walk back over to the hospital together. I apologize for making you late for your meeting, but I thought resolving this was more important."

As Korrine left Carla's office she saw Pauline leaning against the outside of the reception desk, and she wondered if she'd overheard any of the conversation. Pauline in her estimation tended to stick her nose where it didn't belong. Jasmine looked up, and Korrine smiled as she registered the fear on her face.

†

Although Jasmine was grateful for the interruption to her conversation with Pauline, which she believed was entering dangerous waters, Korrine intimidated her, and she couldn't help her reaction. She slumped a little and probably cringed when Korrine approached the desk.

Korrine glanced at Pauline. "Good morning, Pauline. I'm sorry I didn't get a chance to say hello earlier when you came into the office. I'm sure I looked like a woman on a mission." She turned her head and made eye contact with Jasmine. "Jasmine, I'm very sorry for my earlier behavior. I've been feeling stressed about the key opening on the unit and took my frustration out on you. That was clearly unacceptable. Thank you for your prompt attention to the matter this morning. I appreciate your extra effort to get the posting done right away."

"It's okay, I understand," Jasmine replied.

After Korrine and Carla had left the office, Pauline whispered, "See, I told you Carla would make sure Korrine doesn't give you crap anymore. So…how was your trip to Seattle? I would have been in heaven getting a chance to meet Silver Lining. She's dreamy. You are one lucky dog. I must admit to Facebook stalking her. She's kind of aloof though. I bet it was awkward. You probably shouldn't get your hopes up." Pauline's gunmetal-gray eyes flashed with an emotion that Jasmine couldn't quite put her finger on.

"Oh no, she's really nice. Of course she's still grieving over her wife. I can't imagine how hard that would be. She invited me to come back and visit on the Fourth. I'm going to ask Carla if I can take a week off. I haven't had a real vacation in ten years. Do you think that would be a problem?"

Pauline frowned and then quickly smiled. She thought that was odd.

"Are you sure you want to spend your vacation time there after just getting back? I hope you aren't getting yourself involved in something that's going to end up hurting you," Pauline warned.

"I know, I keep telling myself the same thing. So do you think Carla will approve it so soon after I just took a day off?"

Pauline shrugged. "Hey, listen, I'm sorry, but I have to

meet with a prospective volunteer in a few minutes. I'm glad you're back; the office is just not the same without you. We should go out sometime."

"Sure, that would be fun, but maybe after things settle for me a bit. Thanks, Pauline."

Jasmine was always a little uncomfortable around Pauline. Lately her invitations to lunch and dinner had become more frequent. She didn't want to socialize with the people she worked with. She'd gotten involved with Dara, and that hadn't gone so well. It was better to remain friendly and open at work without carrying on any of those friendships outside of business hours. She would keep politely giving a quasi-acceptance to Pauline's invitations but remain vague about specific dates and times. Besides, people often tossed out generic invitations without really meaning them.

Her real concern was that she'd heard Pauline was bisexual, and she didn't want to give her the wrong impression. Pauline was always extremely friendly, but that didn't mean a whole lot. Through the years, many people had been artificially nice to her because they thought it might give them an in to the powerful senior leaders, or they assumed Jasmine knew more than she actually did regarding any big, impending changes at the hospital.

Right before she'd transferred from administration, Dara had announced that the hospital was in serious talks about an affiliation with a large health system about an hour's drive from their organization. Two years prior, they'd gobbled up a hospital in their area, and that wasn't anything close to an affiliation; it was a takeover plain and simple.

Jasmine and everyone in the whole organization were still reeling from that announcement, and they weren't under any false notions that these talks would result in anything different. Their tiny hospital with the equally small clinic was clearly the next on the health system's list of acquisitions. Dara hadn't revealed anything to her at home, or at work, but Jasmine's coworkers suspected otherwise. Leaders and employees she barely knew had chatted her up every chance they got until she transferred to human resources.

Jasmine couldn't understand why they thought she would have access to confidential information on the affiliation now that she worked in HR. Jasmine and the HR department didn't know anything more than everyone else. Nothing was coming out of Dara's office until she was ready to reveal her plans, and she was keeping her cards close to her vest.

Jasmine transferring to HR wasn't the smartest career move because it was common knowledge that the hospital overstaffed the department according to industry standards, but working with Dara every day had become unbearable, and she had to get out for the sake of her sanity.

The potential affiliation was at least a year off, and that gave her enough time to look for another position. It was scary, but she would do what she had to do. Maybe they would offer a severance if she lost her job. Since she was the last one hired in the department, she was low woman on the totem pole. In a layoff, she would be the first to go because seniority, not competence always prevailed in the mostly union-represented hospital.

Change was hard on everyone, but sometimes transformation was good. Jasmine fantasized about Silver asking her to move to Washington and become her personal assistant. That would be a welcome change—one she would eagerly embrace if only it were an option.

Jasmine had tried to calm some of the employees who'd confided in her about feeling concerned about their jobs. She empathized most with the single mothers.

Healthcare was changing and everyone knew that. The small hospitals were closing at an alarming rate, and, although it never made sense to Jasmine, the employees the big conglomerates typically laid off weren't the ones with the highest salaries—they were the housekeepers, dietary workers, and office assistants.

She wasn't concerned about herself—she'd make it some way—but she was worried about those with limited options. She'd met with a few of them on her own time to help them with their résumés, and she'd taken the time to become knowledgeable about unemployment benefits, subsidized health insurance, and every other form of assistance the state had to offer in an effort to be of more help.

Jasmine shook her head and glanced at her watch. It was seven forty-five, and she quickly turned her focus back to her computer. Her fingers flew over the keys as she entered the job description into the special program they used for employment postings. Within five minutes she'd completed the task and pressed the Upload button, which would put the information out on the website for prospective candidates to view.

Jasmine was relieved she'd completed that task on time as promised and moved on to her inbox. The vibration from her cellphone interrupted her train of thought, and she picked up her phone. Normally she stored it inside her desk drawer so she wouldn't be distracted while working, but since the day had started with a touch of drama, she'd forgotten to put it away.

When a second buzz followed closely after the first, her curiosity got the better of her. She glanced at her phone and read the two text messages.

I was thinking of you and thought I would send a quick text to tell you to have a nice day at work—Silver.

I want details call me as soon as you get home from work. You were supposed to call last night—Preston.

Both messages made her smile. She couldn't help liking the young, effervescent man. She'd text him later, but Silver deserved a quick response right this minute.

Always thinking of you and wishing you a wonderful day. Can I call tonight when I have more time to talk?

The phone immediately buzzed again. *I look forward to it.*

Chapter Thirteen

Silver paced the kitchen and picked up her phone for the tenth time in less than an hour. Jasmine said she'd call and, even though Kansas was two hours ahead of Washington, Silver was impatient and anxious to talk with her.

Silver had been up since four that morning but didn't think Jasmine would appreciate a text at six, so she'd waited patiently until it was eight in the morning in Kansas. Now she was waiting again, but she didn't think anyone, including her cats, would classify her current behavior as anywhere near patient.

The kittens were chasing each other around the kitchen, while Sinbad wove in and out of her legs in his usual desperate attempt to get Silver to pay attention to him. She wasn't sure where Freud and Plato were—probably sleeping on her bed. They were grumpy old men and tended to stay out of the melee—especially when they sensed stress from their mama.

Silver looked down at Sinbad and decided to scoop him up in her arms. Maybe he would be able to distract her for a few minutes. It was only three and Jasmine probably wasn't even home from work yet. She remembered Jasmine worked from seven thirty to four, but she wasn't sure how long Jasmine's commute to and from work was.

Silver walked into her living room, sat down on the couch and then settled Sinbad on her lap. He stretched his paws up to her shoulders, giving his version of a kitty hug, before curling back on her stomach.

"What do you think, Sinbad? Should I give her a call? Maybe we got our wires crossed and she's waiting for me to call her."

Sindbad closed his eyes and failed to respond.

"No advice for Mama, huh? Well, I could call Aunty Meredith, but I can't keep bugging her every time I feel unsure about something. I should wait a few minutes, huh? I need to stop being so impatient."

Sindbad started purring as Silver stroked his silky fur.

"I know Jasmine is interested, but there are so many hurdles. First, there's my guilt, then there's Jasmine's recent breakup after an eighteen-year relationship, and finally we live thousands of miles apart. Oh God, this is surely doomed before it even has a chance to begin. What the heck was I thinking inviting her to spend her vacation here in three weeks? I'm not usually that impulsive, but God, she's so perfect. She's beautiful, kind, funny, and we just click. I can't just toss that away. Can I?"

"Meow."

"Is that a yes or a no?"

When her smartphone rang, Silver nearly sent Sinbad clear across the room as she jumped up to snatch it from the counter before it could go to voice mail. She punched the Answer button and breathlessly said, "Hello."

†

Jasmine raced home from work eager to call Silver as soon as she walked in the door. She didn't want to call while on the road because she would be too distracted to pay attention to traffic. Even though her commute was only fifteen minutes, she had to drive through a busy section of town to get back to the condominium she'd purchased four months ago. She was thankful the closing had gone so quickly because living in a motel with weekly rates after she left Dara wasn't very safe—even in Kansas. Her family thought it was a rash decision and cautioned her about purchasing the condominium instead of renting it, but Jasmine wanted something she owned all by herself. It was the first step toward complete independence, and she needed that.

Carla had kept her a few minutes to explain a special project she wanted her to start on right away. Normally Jasmine didn't mind staying late, and Carla never took advantage of her staff. Apparently, Dara wanted each department to create their own scorecard with relevant data on the functions they performed. She expected the first presentation by the end of the week, and Carla needed Jasmine to pull the statistics on vacancy rates, hiring yield ratios, average number of days to fill a position, and internal fill rates.

Since Jasmine had shown an aptitude for data extraction, Carla wanted to tap into her talents. Jasmine was delighted to help and encouraged that Carla wanted her expertise, but of all the times to lay out the details of the project, tonight was the most inconvenient because Jasmine desperately wanted to make good on her promise to call Silver.

At lunch, she'd texted Preston and told him not to expect a call from her until later in the evening and that she promised to give him an update after she talked with Silver. Preston would be a good person to bounce ideas off, because he was an outsider. She didn't feel comfortable talking with anyone at work because she wasn't sure what would get back to Dara. Preston was safe, and even though the chocolate was sort of cheesy, it didn't flop as much as she'd thought it would. At least it had been a unique opening line. Preston seemed like a good guy, and she could use a friend who had no connection to Dara. Through the years, all of their friends had been Dara's friends and she didn't have anyone she could confide in after they'd split up. The last six months, while freeing, had also been hard because she'd felt completely isolated. Preston was an unlikely friend and confidant, but beggars couldn't be choosy.

Jasmine shifted her thoughts to Dara, who had been her only friend for so long, and that was definitely not a healthy thing. She was thankful Dara had been busy all day with meetings on the impending affiliation. Although she'd reluctantly agreed to coffee, she was relieved Dara hadn't come by human resources to finalize any specific plans. She didn't want to be sidetracked by unpleasant thoughts about her failed relationship before her call to Silver.

Jasmine swung into the parking lot at the condominium and quickly grabbed her small pack containing her wallet and keys. She slammed the car door and hurried to the front door, unlocked it, and hung her bag on the back of one of the kitchen stools. She plucked the phone from the hanging bag, selected Silver's preprogrammed number, and groaned as she noted the time. It was nearly four-thirty in Washington.

When Silver answered on the third ring, Jasmine breathed a sigh of relief.

"Hi. I was really glad to get your text this morning. It brightened my day."

Jasmine could almost see the smile on Silver's face as she answered. "I'm glad I brightened your day. I know I shouldn't probably tell you this over the phone, but sometimes I'm a lot braver when I don't see the other person's reaction to what I'm saying. I'm particularly bold when I write my feelings down, but in this case I want to get it out there right away…."

"Okay...."

A huge pit developed in Jasmine's stomach, and she could almost feel it starting to grow into a tree with multiple branches. Silver took a deep breath on the other end of the phone.

"I've been pacing my house for more than an hour waiting on your call and have spent half the night and the entire day ruminating over what I would say to you the next time we talked." Jasmine heard the crinkle of paper in the background. "I wrote it down. Can I read it to you?"

"Of course," Jasmine replied.

Jasmine knew her response was automatic and clearly did not reveal the dread she felt. She began second-guessing herself, which included a fair amount of chastising.

Maybe she shouldn't have kissed her on the lips—even though it was a chaste kiss. Phone calls were a notoriously poor way to communicate. Perhaps she should suggest that they Skype instead, or maybe suggesting a call was an entirely wrong thing to do. She wondered if she'd laid her feelings out in a way that pressured Silver. All these thoughts rolled around in her head in the seconds before Silver began her speech. It felt like a speech to Jasmine, but maybe that was the only way she could get it all out.

"I never thought I would have to face my golden years alone. I met Naomi when I was young, and we felt invincible. We were convinced we would be sitting side by side in hers-and-hers rockers. My whole world tilted on its axis when she died, and I never thought I'd have feelings for anyone else again. I've been in a dark tunnel for the past three years. About six months ago as I looked down that bleak tunnel, I saw a smidgeon of light. I took my first step toward the light. After this weekend it feels like there's a whole lot more light in my tunnel and I'm making my way to the opening."

The paper rustled again and Jasmine suspected Silver was now speaking on her own without the crutch of the words she'd written down.

"I don't have other words for where I would like to go with this. Saying I'd like to date you, Jasmine, seems so sophomoric. I've never dated before. Naomi and I just evolved into a couple. It happened organically with us. I know there are a boatload of hurdles for us, but I'd like to try, and at forty-five I have absolutely no idea what I'm doing when it comes to dating. I'm also not very good at sharing. If today's version of dating means we both see other people, I don't think I can do that. I can barely admit to myself that I want to give a relationship a try without feeling terribly guilty that I'm somehow trampling over my memory of Naomi. I just know that if I don't take this chance with you, I'll probably regret it for the rest of my pitiful life."

When Silver inhaled deeply, Jasmine knew that was her cue to step in. Sharing what she'd just revealed had been a huge risk for Silver, and Jasmine wanted to put her at ease.

"Silver, everything you've said is music to my ears. I was so afraid when you first started that you were about to tell me it wasn't a good idea for me to visit or for us to remain friends. No matter what, I hope we will always remain friends. I don't think I've made it a secret that I'd be open to more, much more. In case that wasn't clear in all the loud signals I've been giving, I hope it is now. I don't really know what you mean by dating. I'd love to spend more time with you and show you how I feel. Is that what dating means to you?" Jasmine asked.

"Yes, that's a pretty accurate definition, but the *I'm not good at sharing* part means I'm the monogamous sort, and once I commit to seeing a person, I don't feel the need to spend time with others in that special, intimate sort of way. I'm not really talking about sex. Oh crap, this is so hard to explain," Silver mumbled.

"No, I get it—no kissing other women, except maybe on the cheeks or a quick peck, but definitely no tongue, right? It's good to define the kissing boundaries," Jasmine teased.

"You know, um…three weeks is a long time. Would you be up for a visit? I've got time on my hands, being an independent writer and all. I'd love to see that chocolate factory. I think I'm craving more fancy chocolates."

"Did you eat that whole box?" Jasmine asked in surprise.

Silver chuckled. "No, but you could pretend to not be so shocked or disturbed that I want to see you so soon after you've left. I'm feeling a bit vulnerable here," she admitted.

"Whew, God, I thought I was the only one to wear my heart on my sleeve. It's good to know I'm in superb company. For the record, I'd love to show you my little corner of the world."

"How about this coming weekend?" Silver asked.

"Really? That soon?"

"Too soon. Sorry, I'm an idiot."

"No, not too soon at all. I'm just excited that you're able to do that. Oh, the luxuries of the rich and famous."

Silver's nervous chuckle hung in the air.

"Relax, Silver, I want this to work as much if not more than you do, and I can't wait for you to fly to Kansas. I'm not sure we have as much to offer as Seattle, but I'll sure give it my best shot. Do you know when you'll arrive?" Jasmine asked.

"Would Friday night work? I can get a rental car and find my way to you if that helps."

"No way, I want to meet you at the airport. Name the time and I'll be there with bells on my toes," Jasmine exclaimed.

"I'll have to let you know. I wasn't sure you would be open to a visit so soon. I haven't made the flight arrangements yet."

"That works for me."

"Okay, full disclosure. I'm not very good over the phone. Maybe Skype calls or private message communication would be better, but I'm willing to give it a try," Silver admitted.

Jasmine smiled and settled in her recliner. "I'm really glad you said that. I hate the phone. I'm not sure about Skype because I haven't ever tried it, but I am definitely okay with private messages or texts. I get to formulate my responses and try not to sound like an idiot. Of course, with you being the writer, you have a distinct advantage."

"Whew. I can't imagine you ever sounding like an idiot, but I'm glad you share my hesitation with the phone. So…with that confession out of the way, I'll let you go and maybe send a PM later."

"Good night, Silver, sweet dreams. I'll be doing the happy dance after I get off the phone. Just saying…."

"Skype in the future, definitely Skype, because I want to see that happy dance. Good night, Jasmine." Silver chuckled.

Jasmine pushed the End button, and the smile on her face would have provided enough light to fool anyone into thinking it was the middle of the day. She was intelligent enough to realize there was still a lot to overcome, but Silver had opened the door, and she was going to skip right through it.

†

Silver twirled around in her living room and pumped her fist in the air. If anyone had been looking in the window, they might have been surprised by the attractive, middle-aged woman dancing like a teenager. She looked down at the little, gray kitten whose furry head was looking up at her with what Silver imagined was curiosity over what his mama was doing. She set her smartphone on the coffee table, scooped Socrates into her arms, and placed a kiss on his furry head. He responded by purring loudly. Socrates enjoyed when Silver held him close like a baby, unlike Artemis who would squirm in her arms the minute she picked her up.

"Socrates, did you hear? I'm going to Kansas City. Oh crud, I need to get Sally to come by and kittysit. I don't really care how much it costs at this late date to get airline tickets. It will be worth it. I'm dating again. Can you believe it, Socrates?"

Silver squeezed the kitten, and he responded with a weak "Meow."

"Oh sorry, little punkin', Mama is just happy."

Silver gently put the little fur ball on the maple wood floor and danced around some more before looking around for her tablet. She needed to google flights to Kansas City and make the arrangements so she could let Jasmine know the details.

She grabbed her tablet and settled in her favorite chair. As she typed in *flights from Seattle to Kansas City*, she frowned at her choices. It was going to be a painfully long day. She scanned the screen and noted there weren't any available nonstop flights that had her arriving in the early evening. She was so deliriously happy though that her frown didn't last long as she imagined the reunion with Jasmine in the airport.

"Well, it looks like Mama will need to leave early in the morning and not arrive until early evening. I should bring my laptop and try to advance my story a little more. I'll probably have a lot of downtime." Silver leaned over and stroked Socrates as he placed one of his tiny paws on her leg in what she surmised was an attempt to get her attention.

"Hmm. I wonder when I should schedule the return flight home. I don't want to overstay my welcome. I can always find my way back to the airport on my own. I hope it will be okay with Jasmine if I arrange for a Monday flight back. I'd rather not cut the weekend short. Yeah, that's what I'll do."

"Meow."

"I'm so glad you agree." Silver clicked her screen a few times. "I wish you had the ability to retrieve the credit card for me," she remarked to the gray kitten.

Socrates continued to try to get her attention, finally jumping up on the arm of the chair. Silver patted his head, stood, and walked over to retrieve the credit card in her wallet. Socrates remained on the chair and watched her until she returned to her favorite chair in the living room and typed in the number on the keypad.

"Done." She leaned back and grinned. "I should probably forward this information to Jasmine with a clarification that I intend to find my way back to the airport on Monday. I don't want to stress her out. I imagine she has less flexibility with work than I do, and I don't want to get her in trouble with her boss."

Silver crinkled her nose. "Socrates, I think I've been living alone way too long. I'm having conversations with my cats on a regular basis now. At least I don't expect titillating answers back from you." She reached over and fluffed Socrates's fur. "You are an extremely good listener."

Taking that as a cue to snuggle with Silver, Socrates stretched his paws and nonchalantly eased his body onto her lap, nudging the tablet with his head.

Before Silver set the device on the floor, she forwarded the information to Jasmine via a text message. "Okay, you big baby, I get the hint. It's cuddle time." As she continued to pet him, his purr increased in volume.

Chapter Fourteen

The woman stared at the screen on her laptop and brought her fist down on the table, causing the mug to rattle and the milky, brown liquid to spill over. The words *it's complicated* mocked her as she looked at Jasmine's Facebook page. The status had changed in the last twenty-four hours, and she raged over the update.

She wasn't sure whether she would be able to wait to visit Silver. The Fourth was a long way off, and there was no telling what might happen between now and then. Silver's allure was difficult to ignore, even for a woman still grieving her dead wife.

She had to acknowledge there were clues leading her to believe that perhaps the grieving period was ending, and it was simply not acceptable in her estimation. She could not allow Jasmine and Silver to consummate their relationship. No, that would not do at all.

Hearing a bark outside brought her attention to the large, fluffy dog sniffing around. Dogs were loyal. Cats were not. No wonder Jasmine preferred cats. She wasn't loyal and it was time for that to change. If she didn't interject herself into the situation, the train would start down the tracks, and then she would never manage to stop it.

She picked up her phone and sent a quick text message. It was time to stop messing around. She was a woman of action who always prevailed in the end.

†

Jasmine was beaming. She decided to check Facebook and her personal email to see if Silver had sent a private message to her. So far, most of their communication had been through Facebook. She wondered if that would continue now that they had each other's phone number.

On a whim, she had changed her status to *it's complicated*. She'd always laughed at that option, but it certainly fit her current circumstances. Jasmine wasn't sure why she'd done it, but she supposed she wanted to signal that something had changed without putting too much pressure on Silver. Her excitement over Silver's confession got the better of her.

She smiled when she saw the friend request from Preston and quickly accepted. He would be fun to correspond with, and she'd find out how he found her Facebook account when she called him.

Jasmine was still on cloud nine when the first text pinged on her smartphone. She picked up the phone and glanced at the message. Silver had attached her flight arrangements with a quick note that she intended to make her own way back to the airport on Monday.

Her smile ended when the next text came through. It was almost as if her happy balloon suddenly lost all of its air. She dreaded responding to the message, but she'd promised.

Jasmine had a legitimate reason to limit her availability to during the week. That would make this coffee date easier on her. She could suggest a time on Tuesday or Wednesday and keep the conversation to fifteen minutes or less. She wasn't sure how Dara would respond to that suggestion, but that was how it was going to be, and if Dara didn't like it, then Jasmine would tell her take it or leave it.

She quickly typed her response.

10a on Tuesday or Wednesday would work.

I'd rather have some more time. How about dinner instead? Dara responded.

Nope. Take it or leave it. Public place. Café?

We need more than a 15 min conversation. How about on Saturday?

I have plans on Saturday.

Lunch at a public place and you can combine your breaks.

Jasmine caved. *Okay, fine.*

Dara was always very good at negotiating for what she wanted.

I'll come by at noon tomorrow.

Jasmine didn't bother to confirm. She suspected Dara already knew she'd gotten her way. At least she'd displayed a small amount of backbone when she'd insisted on lunch and didn't back down from issuing an ultimatum, which she'd never managed to do with Dara in the past. Maybe Silver was a good influence on her, giving her the courage to set the necessary boundaries.

Tossing the phone on the counter, her mood tempered, Jasmine decided to call Preston after grabbing a Mike's Hard Lemonade. She needed some outside perspective.

She groaned when she heard the ding on the counter as she was grabbing the adult beverage. When she picked up the phone and noticed who had left a text message, she burst out laughing.

Tapping my fine Italian loafers on the wood floor

waiting to hear from you. Dish, girlfriend. Pretty Preston.

Two seconds later the phone pinged again before Jasmine had a chance to call.

Don't ever call me PP, unless you put big in front of it. Big PP. LOL.

Jasmine was still laughing as she scrolled through her contacts and selected Preston, which he'd entered all in caps.

"About time," Preston answered.

"Patience isn't your strong suit, is it?"

"No, it certainly is not. So how did my chocolates go over? Did you get lucky? I Facebook stalked you and Silver and noticed you changed your status. What the hell is so complicated about it? My God, you lesbians are either making things more difficult than needed or moving in after one night of passion. I take it you're not moving in together, so that must mean you didn't get any," Preston chastised.

"You know, Preston, unlike our gay brothers, us *lesbians* do believe there is more to a relationship than sex," Jasmine defended.

"Oh, posh. You need to take the bull by the horns and show her some fancy tongue work, or fingers, or dildos, or whatever." Preston began cackling.

Jasmine could hear Bruce in the background yelling, "Stop being so crude, Preston."

"I called her tonight and she's coming for a visit this weekend. She wants to start dating," Jasmine whispered.

Preston screeched into the phone, and Jasmine jerked it away from her ear before he could do irreparable damage.

"Now we're talking. Lesbians don't date really—they just start relationships, move in together, and get married. You must be special if she's coming to see you so soon and wants to start dating, which by the way is code for 'let's be exclusive and fuck each other's brains out,'" Preston advised.

"Preston, stop, you'll scare the poor woman," Bruce

yelled.

"I don't think Silver is quite ready for that. She's still a little tentative about things. She told me she still feels guilty, like she's walking all over her dead wife's memory. Do you think I'm heading down heartbreak lane?" Jasmine asked.

"Tell me more and I'll let you know what I think," Preston prompted.

"Well, she did say she doesn't like to share and that she thought she would regret not taking this step. I took that as a good sign. Oh, and she invited me back to her place on the Fourth and asked me to take a full vacation so we would have more time. She even offered to pay. What do you think?"

"I think that sounds very promising. The real question I have to ask is do you think she's worth the risk?"

"Oh yes. She is definitely worth the risk. Spending this weekend with her solidified my feelings. She is everything I could hope for in a partner. Before I spent time with her, she was on this big pedestal. I suppose she's still up there for me, but in a completely different way. She wasn't some untouchable famous author. Instead she was this warm, loving, intelligent, beautiful, and vulnerable woman who I could easily fall in love with," Jasmine admitted.

"Oh, girlfriend, I think you are well on your way. It sounds like it's worth the risk. No guts, no glory. The only true missed shot is the one you never take. Why not go out on a limb because that's where the sweetest fruit lives. Oh, and one more, getting into hot water keeps you clean. I have a million of these sayings. I'm a motivational speaker, you know," Preston gushed.

"Really, Preston, that's what you do for a living and you couldn't give me a better line than 'life's too short for cheap chocolate'? By the way, how did you Facebook stalk me? I never gave you my last name." Jasmine was beginning to wonder about Preston and she hoped she wasn't spilling her guts to some crazy person. How pathetic was she to ask the advice of a virtual stranger? He'd seemed harmless on the plane.

"Easy smeasy. I looked up Silver Lining first and then went to her friends list. There aren't that many Jasmines, you know. You really should make your profile private if you want to protect stuff like your dating status."

"Good to know. Yeah, Dara always told me I was too trusting on Facebook. I always accept friend requests without checking people out first. It seems so mean to decline. It takes me back to high school and not getting accepted into the cool clique. I don't want to do that to someone else."

"Yeah I know, I sent a friend request and you accepted right away. I coulda been some pervy straight guy," Preston warned.

"I knew it was you. Preston is not exactly a common name either."

"I suppose so, but you should be more careful about that. I'll bet Silver is cautious, considering she's a famous author and all."

"Not cautious enough. She's getting some strange messages, and I think she might have a stalker."

"Really? That's sounds intriguing. Are you worried? Is she nervous about it?" Preston asked.

"Yeah, I guess I kinda am. I told her she should go to the police. I don't think she's taking it very seriously, but there are some crazy people out there. Look what happened to Jodie Foster."

"Yeah, you lesbians sure attract some psychos."

"At the time no one knew Jodie Foster was a lesbian, so I don't think we corner the market on stalkers. I think it comes with the territory of famous people."

"We're getting off track. I know you didn't just call

me to talk about Facebook and stalkers. What other advice can Professor Preston give you?"

"You've been to Kansas City. Where should I take her? This isn't exactly a hotbed of excitement."

"I'd say Crowne Center or Nelson-Atkins Museum of Art are your best bets. Unless you both want to revisit your childhood and go to the Worlds of Fun amusement park or the Oceans of Fun water park. Personally, I think a journey back to childhood now and again is good for the soul."

Jasmine was twirling her hair as she talked to Preston. The idea of splashing around in the water and seeing Silver in a bathing suit had a tremendous amount of appeal to her.

"You know, Preston, I think that's an excellent idea. I'm going to take her to the water park. I haven't been there in years. Dara never wanted to go because it was, and I quote, 'a ridiculous way to spend the day as an adult.' She didn't think water parks were for mature couples, and because she never entertained the idea of having kids, anything remotely geared toward families was completely out of the question."

"Who's Dara?"

"My ex."

"Oooh, sounds like there is a juicy story there. Give," Preston enthused.

"I'd prefer to avoid that particular topic. It's bad enough I agreed to have lunch with her tomorrow."

"What is it with you lesbians? When everybody else breaks up, that's it, kaput—we want nothing more to do with our exes. You lesbians stay bosom buddies, no matter what."

Jasmine sighed. "She's the CEO of the healthcare organization I work for. We're not exactly best friends, and I've managed to keep my distance over the last six months, except for when I've had to interact with her for work. I think it's better to move on and remain positive about your past relationships. It takes far too much energy to hate someone or stay angry, and I just don't think that's healthy."

"Oh, girlfriend, I love your attitude. I need more positive lesbians in my life. When you come to Seattle for the Fourth, can you and Silver set aside some time? Bruce and I would love to have you over for dinner. I am a fabulous cook, if I do say so myself."

"True," Bruce yelled out.

"You have your own personal cheering section. I'll ask Silver, but no guarantees and please don't scare her away. I have to tread lightly. She's still so vulnerable and fragile right now."

"I will be the epitome of subtlety," Preston assured.

"Listen, I gotta go. I want to do some preparations for the upcoming weekend. I promise I'll call afterward. I'll also let you know about the Fourth. Thanks, Preston. Oddly, it's been good to talk with you. I guess I don't have too many people I can lay my innards out to," Jasmine confessed.

"I'm here for you. Call anytime. Ciao."

"Bye."

†

Silver was still beaming after she'd sent the flight information to Jasmine. The phone conversation had gone much better than she'd thought it would. At one point she wondered how Jasmine would react to her reading what she'd written, but she seemed to be on the same page and the first tentative steps toward a possible relationship had begun.

She had to stop herself from sending another text. She didn't want to move too quickly, even though it would have been nice to Skype Jasmine after sending the information. She wanted to see her face and try to determine if Jasmine was as excited as she was to jump into it. That's how it felt to

Silver—diving into a pool and not knowing how deep or how cold the water was, but she was so hot she was willing to take the chance.

Silver swiveled back and forth in her chair, daydreaming about the upcoming weekend. She became excited when she heard the buzz, indicating a new text message. She leaned over the arm of the chair to retrieve her tablet and disturbed Socrates who'd fallen asleep.

He let her know his displeasure over the interruption to his peaceful nap. "Meow!"

"Sorry, Socrates, but Mama needs to read this."

When she opened the tablet and read the text, her whole body tensed.

Jasmine is not right for you. Stay away.

This text rattled Silver because it wasn't a private message to her Facebook account—this had come to her personal cell phone through her tablet. She wasn't sure if the same person was sending both the texts and private messages, but this time she didn't think she could ignore the escalation—if they were from the same source.

Silver briefly wondered if this message came from Dara and the private messages were from someone else. They weren't exactly threatening, but more along the lines of creepy.

She doubted the police could do anything about it tonight, especially in her small town, so she set the tablet back on the floor and decided to deal with it tomorrow. She was probably making a bigger issue out of this than needed. She was sure it was nothing to worry about.

Shoving her apprehension down deep, she decided to call her sister and give her an update. Meredith would be proud of her—she was sure of that.

She jumped up, grabbed her phone off the kitchen counter, and accessed the number for her sister. She wanted to tell her all about her brave move to reenter the world of romance.

"Hey, sis, guess what I did?"

Chapter Fifteen

Dara was looking forward to her lunch date with Jasmine. She hoped it wasn't too late to repair her relationship. When she'd seen the status change on Jasmine's Facebook, she'd been concerned. It was time to return that runaway horse back to the barn.

She'd carefully selected her outfit this morning. The kelly-green shirt with her black, pin-striped pants was Jasmine's favorite. Jasmine had given her the shirt for Christmas two years ago and told her it brought out the color of her eyes. The pants fit Dara well and showed off her ass—the one she worked hard to keep in shape by using her treadmill every morning.

Striding confidently into the Human Resources office, Dara presented Jasmine with a brilliant smile. "Are you ready to head out?"

Jasmine grabbed her bag and nodded. The neutral expression gave no indication to Dara about how the date might go.

Dara opened all the doors for Jasmine and waited until she folded into the passenger seat of her new Tesla before she gently closed the door and hurried to the driver's side.

Before backing out of the parking space in front of the administrative suite, Dara turned to Jasmine. "Is Joe's okay?"

Jasmine shrugged. "It's kind of far. I really do need to be back in an hour."

"I'm sure they won't mind if you're a few minutes late. I can call Carla to clear it with her if you'd like."

"No, please don't do that, let's just go," Jasmine pleaded.

"Okay." Dara reached across the console and touched Jasmine's hand. She didn't let herself worry when Jasmine pulled away from her touch. Dara began to prepare herself to say the right words to get Jasmine to be reasonable.

She decided to bide her time. Getting into a serious discussion with Jasmine while she was driving would serve no useful purpose. Dara needed to study her facial expressions to gauge where to go with her arguments. Jasmine was an open book. She didn't have the ability to mask her emotions—it was what made it so easy to manipulate her.

The ten minute drive was eerily quiet as Dara navigated through the Kansas City traffic. She tried to temper her aggravation over the unusual number of cars on the road, which she saw as a bad omen. She compared it to the number of obstacles Jasmine might toss on the table.

She was not prepared to accept no for an answer. She'd been shocked when Jasmine had found her own condominium and made good on the threat to move out and transfer to another department where Dara couldn't "choke me with your toxic tentacles." Dara cringed as she remembered Jasmine raising her voice as she spoke those words. It was completely out of character for her sweet and obedient girlfriend.

When they arrived at the restaurant, Jasmine jumped

out of the car before Dara had a chance to open the passenger-side door for her. At least she had waited while Dara retrieved her purse from the backseat. They walked into the famous barbecue place together. Jasmine had yet to bless her with one of her brilliant smiles. Things weren't exactly going as planned, and Dara had one shot to plead her case. She thought giving Jasmine space for six months would allow her plenty of time to come to her senses, but that bitch author had gotten in the middle of things and now she was quickly losing control.

†

Jasmine kept chanting to herself that it was only one hour. She only had to survive this farce of a lunch date for sixty minutes. Piece of cake, she could do it. When Dara had tried to hold her hand in the car, as if nothing had changed between them, she'd nearly said something. Instead, she'd made her position clear on that, and fortunately, Dara hadn't pushed things.

Jasmine took a seat across from Dara and started to glance at the menu—anything to avoid direct eye contact with Dara. It didn't matter that she knew the menu by heart. When Dara started to speak, she slowly lowered the menu. Being rude wasn't in her nature.

"You aren't having your usual?" Dara asked.

Jasmine shrugged. "Yeah, I suppose. I do like their pulled chicken sandwich. I guess you're getting the pulled pork."

Dara smiled. "I am a creature of habit."

"Yes, you are. I never could break you of your habit of chasing the new, shiny bauble," Jasmine bitterly replied.

She thought she saw genuine regret in Dara's eyes.

"I guess I deserved that jab. Isn't there some way we

can get beyond that? I've spent these last six months doing a lot of soul-searching, and yes, I've made a lot of mistakes, but when two people split up, it's never completely one-sided. I started losing you five years ago. I'm not making excuses, but trying to help you understand my horrid behavior."

"I'm not sure I really want to rehash that, Dara, but what the heck, I might as well ask what you mean by losing me five years ago."

"We went to the writer's conference, you met Silver, and you were entranced by her. Before that, you read books and occasionally went on Facebook, but after, it was as if you were obsessed. You never wanted to join me when our friends invited us out. I know I should have talked to you rather than seek comfort in another's arms, and I'll own that."

Jasmine took a big breath. "Dara, I was never comfortable going out and meeting with *your* friends. If you were only honest with yourself, you would admit I never fit into your group. God, Dara, they're the most pretentious group of lesbians on the planet. LA lesbians have nothing on the Kansas City lesbian socialites."

"That's not true. They were always enamored with you."

"Generally it's not in my nature to be so crude, but I can't think of any other way to put this…wanting to sleep with me is not the same as respecting me as a person. You know how much I hate pretentious people, and they've cornered the market," Jasmine explained.

"What are you talking about? They always gushed about how lucky I was to have you as my girlfriend."

"I think you conveniently forgot when Connie asked me what I did for a living, and I told her I was your administrative assistant, the smirk on her face revealed the whole story. See, that's just it, Dara, I was only ever good enough to be a mistress or girlfriend, but never sophisticated enough to be your wife. Not one of your friends is a secretary, housekeeper, CNA, plumber, truck driver, or even police officer. Lesbians in those occupations would never make it into your tight circle of friends. I want real friends, genuine friends."

"You've got to be kidding. You'd want us to hang around with a bunch of diesel dykes? I'm the CEO of the county health system. Of course I have more in common with physicians, lawyers, and executives. Perhaps some of my friends come across as pretentious, but I don't really believe they are looking down their nose at anyone. They simply don't have anything in common with individuals in the occupations you cited. I don't think I'm being pretentious by surrounding myself with people I can find a common ground for discussions. You aren't being fair. You know I repeatedly speak to our CNAs and housekeepers about what an important role they play in the success of the hospital."

"I'm a lowly HR assistant and I'll never be anything more. I'll only ever be your trophy girlfriend. I'll never even ascend to become your trophy wife. Your friends don't respect me. They don't even pretend to involve me in serious discussions about anything, regardless of whether I have an intelligent opinion on the topic or not. They dismiss me as arm candy—a dumb blonde who isn't even blonde."

"You underestimate yourself. You have a college degree, and I know you would be able to join in those conversations, but for whatever reason you've chosen not to participate. What about your famous author friend? I'll bet she's more pretentious than my friends apparently are. I can't see her hanging out with a bunch of hardcore dykes," Dara insisted.

"See, that's where you're wrong. She doesn't even

recognize her fame. Her humility shines through in everything she says and does."

"Typical. You put her up on a pedestal without really knowing a lot about her. I hope you're careful, Jasmine, because when she comes crashing down from that impossible height, I pray she doesn't crush you in the aftermath of destruction," Dara mocked. "I love you and am willing to do whatever it takes to get you back. If I'd known how important it was for us to get married, I would have proposed to you by now. You never mentioned that to me."

"How could I? When marriage became legal, you scoffed at the very idea. I wasn't about to broach the subject after hearing you rant about why it wasn't necessary to have a damn piece of paper to prove your love," Jasmine argued.

"I miss you. I want you to stop all this foolishness and move back in with me. We'll start all over again, and I promise it'll be different. Eighteen years is a long time to be together to just throw it all away. We can get married if that's what you want," Dara offered.

Jasmine slapped her hand against her heart. "Oh be still my heart. That was just about the most romantic proposal I'll ever hear, but I think I'll have to politely decline."

Dara leaned forward, and Jasmine was surprised to see the unshed tears in her eyes. Since Dara was all about control, Jasmine rarely saw her choked up.

"Please, Jasmine, can you just take some time to think about us trying to repair our relationship? I admit it was a stupid idea to offer marriage before working things out. I suppose I'll just have to prove to you how invested I am in making us work."

"There is no *us* anymore. Can't you see that we don't fit? You need a different kind of woman to complete you. It's taken me far too many years to realize that, but I understand it now. I don't want to lose the last bit of respect I have for you, so please don't continue to push. In time, maybe we can find our way back to a civil friendship. Although I honestly believe I'm not the type of person to remain in your inner circle of friends, and I'm okay with that."

"I won't continue to push right now, but I think you're wrong and I'm not giving up. I'll allow you all the time you need if that's what it takes. For now, let's have a nice lunch and not talk about this anymore. I don't want to upset you, and I can see that's what I'll be doing if I continue to pursue this. Why don't you tell me how you like your new position?"

Jasmine was relieved Dara had decided to allow her a reprieve. If only she would admit they weren't right for one another, they both could move on. Jasmine didn't want to carry any more baggage to Washington than was necessary—figuratively speaking. She didn't want to blow her one chance with Silver.

Chapter Sixteen

Silver was enjoying what had turned into a ritual each evening. She'd just ended her nightly Skype call with Jasmine, and she was anxious to finish packing. In less than twenty-four hours, she would welcome seeing Jasmine in person versus what she began referring to as "the Memorex version." She supposed Skype was better than a phone call, email, or text message, but nothing replaced the experience of touching or being touched. Although sexual intimacy was an important aspect to most relationships, she wasn't thinking about that kind of interaction. She just missed the simple ability to hold another woman's hand or nestle beside a person while sleeping.

She still hadn't gone to the police about the strange text messages, because she kept pushing them from her mind, not wanting to make a big deal out of something that was probably nothing.

She felt a niggle of concern for Jasmine's safety because two of the odd messages had specifically referred to her. She'd received one more on Tuesday, telling her Jasmine was involved with someone else. Since she hadn't received any more, she decided it wasn't worth involving the authorities. Other than warning Silver to stay away from Jasmine, none of the messages contained any specific threats.

Sally, her regular petsitter, had agreed to watch her cats while she was away, and she could tell her old friend was excited for her. She'd told Silver how proud she was of her bravery. Sally had been watching her cats for at least ten years—ever since she'd conned Silver and Naomi into adopting two feral kittens, Plato and Freud. Anytime Silver needed to go out of town, Sally offered to help. She hadn't needed to use Sally during the last few years, and she was thankful her friend was still willing to help her out in a pinch.

Silver stared at the picture of herself and Naomi, arms wrapped around each other, wind blowing their hair in all directions, with the biggest smiles on their faces. Meredith had taken it on the last Fourth of July Silver had spent with Naomi. Meredith had decided to visit, and the joy of having her sister and nephews stay for the holiday was a precious memory. Silver remembered how windy that day was, and despite the temperature registering in the eighties, they'd worn jackets because of the famous winds on the east side of the Cascade Mountains.

Silver had no idea that less than one year later, her world would fall apart. They'd been joking and laughing about the fact they would probably end up falling asleep before the first big explosion lit up the sky. Meredith told them to strike a pose and she'd taken the candid shot. It turned out so well, Naomi had it framed and placed it on the bedroom dresser shortly after.

Silver knew she would have to make a decision about the picture, but removing it seemed like an acute violation of something. She supposed it might signify a desecration of her memories, but keeping it on the dresser created a whole other type of harm. Jasmine shouldn't have to see that while…. Silver couldn't finish that thought because it, too, felt like a defilement.

Silver wasn't under any illusion that eventually her relationship with Jasmine would evolve to the level of intimacy she craved. It had been far too long since she'd felt the touch of another woman in her most private places. Her bedroom was the likely location of the consummation of their emotions, and she was sure that picture would not be appropriate to display. The irony that this would most likely occur when Jasmine visited in July didn't escape her.

Silver picked up the picture and traced her finger around the outline of Naomi's face. "Oh, Naomi, please tell me you understand. I don't want to continue to be a shell of a human being."

She gently put the picture back in the center of the dresser and opened the drawers to select a few of her undergarments, socks, shorts, and tank tops. The Midwest was notoriously hot and humid in June. Jasmine had advised her to bring her bathing suit, and she hesitated as she selected the more revealing turquoise one that at one point fit her nicely. She wasn't sure if her middle-aged body would be an embarrassment, so she quickly tossed it inside her bag as the saying *out of sight, out of mind* popped into her head. She'd decide later whether she would wear it in public.

After she'd packed her bag, she sat heavily on the end of her bed and absently played with Plato, who kept batting at the shoelaces on her sneakers. She'd placed the shoes on the bed as she contemplated whether she would wear them and save room, or pack them and wear her casual slip-ons.

By the time she finished and decided to pack her gym shoes, it was nearly ten. She grabbed her tablet and decided to lose herself in a good romance before falling asleep. She needed something to take her mind off the stress of the upcoming weekend where she'd have to follow through on the brave declaration she'd made to Jasmine. A new chapter in her life was beginning, and she wasn't quite sure where the story would end, but she rather liked the start of this new episode.

"If only real life turned out like these lesbian romances, huh, Plato?"

"Meow."

"I know. No guts, no glory, but the more apt saying for me is, no guts, no story." She chuckled. "Get it, Plato, because I'm a writer? Oh my God, I need to go to sleep. I am far too punchy for my own good."

When her phone buzzed on her nightstand and she glanced at the screen, she couldn't help the smile that enveloped her face.

Can't wait to see you tomorrow. Sweet dreams.

Ditto.

Chapter Seventeen

Jasmine was oblivious to the dark sedan in the opposite corner of the parking lot. The complex, while not large, did have over thirty units and the owner of the car went to great lengths to choose a location that provided relative obscurity. The woman knew just by studying her movements and facial expressions that neither Jasmine nor Silver noticed anything amiss in Jasmine's quiet neighborhood.

Part of her was irked at the utter focus they had on one another, but she was also relieved that her stakeout went unnoticed. She decided this might work in her favor. It was disgusting how they fawned all over each other. Not everyone would recognize the intensity of their interactions because the two women weren't touching each other, but their eyes told the true story. There was smoldering desire in the looks that danced across the driveway. She saw it all through the tiny lens.

She pressed the button on her telephoto lens, and the

shutter clicked in rapid succession like an automatic weapon. She would study the photos later in excruciating detail. What she wasn't able to pick up while looking through the viewfinder, she would capture on film and hang in the secret room at her house. The woman could then fantasize that her love intended that look for her and only her—that raw desire and maybe even love she saw from the safe distance of her car. Beneath the shadows of the swaying branches, she imagined herself as a sleek panther stalking her prey. Oh what beautiful prey she was.

She needed to get closer so she could track what they were doing, but peering through the window was risky. That was the downside to living in a condominium complex. "Damn nosy neighbors," she grumbled.

It was almost worth the risk. The woman swiveled her head right to left, canvassing the parking lot for inquisitive interlopers. Everything was quiet. It was a Friday night, and hopefully those enjoying an early weekend celebration were out, while everyone else was safely tucked inside.

She cautiously opened the door, oozed out, and made her way to the window partially hidden by the large red maple tree. The dense foliage was an advantage to her illicit observation of Silver and Jasmine. She needed to know what they were doing behind closed doors and was willing to jeopardize detection. She hoped for everyone's sake things hadn't progressed too far, or she might need to hasten her plans and take drastic action.

†

After a slightly awkward moment in the airport when Jasmine had pulled Silver into her arms for a welcome-to-Kansas hug, she could sense Silver's emotions had settled. Jasmine hadn't expected the initial stiffness at her touch, but was thankful when Silver relaxed and melted into the embrace. To her delight, this hug lasted longer than their first one when she had traveled to Washington. The caress at the end along her arms was a thrilling surprise that sent shivers up and down her body.

The chatter in the car bounced along the surface, remaining decidedly in the small-talk category. They'd talked about their week, collecting additional information that neither had discussed previously in their nightly Skype talks. Silver did not broach the subject of their blossoming relationship, and that was fine with Jasmine, who wasn't sure where that conversation might lead them. Besides, Jasmine wanted to face Silver when they talked about heavier topics.

She needed to see the whites of Silver's eyes as they ventured into virgin territory.

Jasmine felt as if she'd never been so open with anyone about her feelings. In the past, she'd always let Dara lead the way. Dara wasn't the kind of person to slice open her heart and reveal deep emotions. When Silver had read what she'd written on Monday night, the floodgates opened and Jasmine wanted—no, needed to reveal her buried passion.

Before unlocking the door to her condominium, Jasmine turned her head and smiled at Silver. The joy reflected back at her was enough to cause her heart to explode. She couldn't remember ever feeling as happy. She knew she shouldn't label her feelings because it had only been a short time since she'd spent any significant time with Silver, but there was no question in her mind that she was falling head over heels in love with Silver.

"It's not much, but it's mine. I finally feel like an adult. I bought this with my own money and feel like I'm out from under the control of someone else. I went from living under my parents' roof to living under Dara's. This is the first time I've been on my own, and I like it." Jasmine paused and hastened to add, "I don't mean to suggest I want to stay living alone forever. I just find the freedom refreshing for the moment."

When they stepped into the entryway, Silver dropped her bag and turned Jasmine around, pulling her close and kissing her on the lips. It was far too short a kiss for Jasmine, but she would take it. She only barely managed to control her breathing and the compulsion to pull Silver back into a passionate lip lock, but she was determined to let Silver set the pace. A kiss was better than nothing.

After breaking apart, Silver answered, "I understand completely. There are plusses and minuses to living alone. Sorry, I had to do that…um….the kiss…I hope it wasn't presumptuous of me."

"Presume away. In fact, you can take that presumption further. I'm not sure what the next step beyond presumption might be, but I'm up for it. Bold action? Venture into the beyond? Boldly go where no one has gone before?" Jasmine chuckled. "Sorry, I'm a *Star Trek* fan, and that was a completely ridiculous and nerdy thing to say, but you might as well know what you're getting yourself into."

"Nothing wrong with *Star Trek Voyager*. It was much better than the original series. Do you think it was a clever manipulation to name the Borg beauty Seven of Nine? Close, so close. I think I heard my lesbian friends rename her Six of Nine. An interesting play on words, don't you think?" Silver asked.

Jasmine laughed. "Oh I think they knew exactly what they were doing. It was a surefire way to attract a lesbian audience. The creators probably knew we would rename the character." She shuffled her feet and looked down. She didn't quite know how to broach the topic of where Silver felt comfortable sleeping. "Um, Silver, where would you like me to take your bag?"

Silver put her fingers under Jasmine's chin and gently lifted her face.

Jasmine looked into Silver's compassionate, ever-changing eyes. Today they were the color of a Caribbean ocean. She marveled at how they seemed to change color slightly depending on the clothes Silver wore.

"If you wouldn't feel uncomfortable, I can join you in your bedroom." Silver hastened to add, "I don't expect anything. I believe I've progressed past the point of a raging hormonal teenager. I slept better than I have for quite some time when you held me in your arms. I wouldn't mind having another night's rest like that. Oh God, I really am boldly going where I hope no one has gone before," Silver professed.

"If you're hinting at a question about who I've had in my bed, let me assure you there's been no one since I left Dara. I moved to this condo and haven't even let her visit," Jasmine assured.

"I'm sorry. I'm usually more transparent. I didn't intend to pry into your personal life. I did mention that I don't share very well, and I was hoping we could, oh I don't know how to discuss this without it sounding like a business deal. I don't know the rules for dating since I've never had to navigate those very scary waters." Silver was rubbing her left hand over her right in a nervous gesture.

Jasmine placed her hands over Silver's. "Don't apologize. I don't think I can adequately communicate how glad I am that you don't share well. That is a trait I can most definitely live with and embrace. Unfortunately, I've inadvertently shared before, and I can tell you it isn't a whole lot of fun. I don't want to have to share affections with someone else, but I'm happy to share my bed, delectable food items, and all kinds of other things." Jasmine winked.

Silver chuckled. "I do need to explore those things that are worth sharing. Lead the way to your bedroom." She picked up her bag.

Inside, Jasmine was doing the happy dance. She'd hoped Silver would want to stay with her in the master suite rather than sleep in the guest bedroom. She was prepared to accept whatever was more comfortable for Silver but saw this as a positive sign that Silver really was ready to move forward.

"You must be tired, and I'll admit that after the long week, I could probably fall asleep quickly. Do you mind if we turn in soon? I want us both to be well rested for our next adventure." Jasmine grinned.

"I don't mind at all. I'll admit I haven't gotten a lot of sleep this week due to the anticipation I've felt about this trip to Kansas. I'm dying to know what our next adventure is."

"I don't want to ruin the surprise, so I'll just tell you it involves wearing a bathing suit and reverting back to your childhood."

"Sounds delightful, except for the bathing suit part."

†

The woman wanted to smash the glass on the window when she pushed her nose up against it and saw the intimate gesture between Silver and Jasmine. When Silver guided Jasmine to look her in the eyes, the woman clenched her jaw and made a fist so tight her nails drew blood.

She couldn't spy on them anymore after they walked down the hall and entered what she suspected was one of the bedrooms. She remained plastered against the window, hoping to see Jasmine exit the room and settle into a different location.

"What is taking her so goddamned long?" she

whispered to no one.

In the quiet of the night, the woman jumped when she heard the engine of a car as it eased into the parking lot.

"Shit," she murmured as the car pulled into a space close to Jasmine's condominium.

She crouched and hoped the passengers of the vehicle wouldn't notice a strange woman hanging out in the bushes next to a large maple tree and under their neighbor's window. Fortunately, they were laughing and seemed oblivious to anyone else. The young man had his arm draped over the woman's shoulder and they were walking unsteadily to the other side of the building. She breathed a sigh of relief that the entrance to their unit was on the opposite side.

With her attention sidetracked by the couple, she wasn't able to determine if Jasmine had exited the bedroom. She didn't see any movement in the condominium and she needed to slip away before anyone noticed her.

Swiftly she walked back to her vehicle and drove away. Debating on whether to stake out her object of desire in the daylight hours, she wondered when they would leave for whatever activity Jasmine had planned for them on Saturday. Tomorrow was another day. She'd resume her observation when more information was forthcoming.

Chapter Eighteen

Silver stretched her lean body and yawned as she opened her eyes to find the opposite side of the bed empty. She'd slept like a rock last night and hadn't awakened when Jasmine slipped out of bed. She couldn't help being slightly disappointed to find herself alone with the bedcovers carefully tucked backed into a semblance of order on Jasmine's side of the bed.

When she heard noises in what she suspected was the small kitchen and her nose alerted her to freshly brewed coffee, she smiled despite the empty feeling in the room. She strolled to the bathroom where she quickly brushed her teeth and ran her fingers through her hair.

She thanked whatever higher power was in charge that it wasn't sticking up in all directions, giving her that Bride of Frankenstein look. It was always a crapshoot the next morning, because when she was restless, her hair tended to do funky things. Silver knew sleeping beside Jasmine and feeling Jasmine's protective arms wrapped around her body had settled her, but Silver must have stayed glued to one spot all night for her hair to remain relatively unaffected.

After emptying her bladder and taking one more look in the mirror to make sure she was presentable, she made her way into the kitchen.

"I swear I'll worship you every single day for the rest of our lives if I can have a cup of that glorious-smelling coffee," Silver promised.

Jasmine leaned against one of the kitchen cabinets and her lips formed a slow, sexy smile.

"I think I like the sound of that. Can I define how I want you to worship me?" Jasmine poured coffee into a mug on the counter and pointed to the french vanilla creamer and sugar.

Silver blushed. They hadn't done anything last night except sleep. After a brief kiss good night, Jasmine had rolled her over and placed her arms snugly around Silver's midsection. She could feel Jasmine nuzzle her neck and had almost turned around, giving in to the temptation to make love, but it was still too soon for her. She imagined Jasmine already knew that. It was as if she'd found the key to Silver's moods and desires without Silver feeling the need to fill her in. Silver marveled at Jasmine's innate sensitivity and believed someone had specifically engineered Jasmine just for her. She had a rare second chance at love, and she didn't intend to squander her good fortune.

Silver put a liberal amount of sugar into the cup and topped it off with enough cream to turn the coffee almost white. Naomi used to tease her about liking a little bit of coffee with her cream. She chuckled to herself as she noted that maybe she and Jasmine were a match made in heaven because they shared the same taste in coffee. She'd noted that Jasmine put almost as much creamer in her coffee as she did.

She decided to find out what Jasmine had in store for the day, rather than respond to the playful question. Her interest had been piqued ever since Jasmine had mentioned an adventure with a bathing suit. "That depends on what you have planned for me today. I haven't worn a bathing suit in years, and I'm not entirely convinced it's in anyone's best interest for me to show more skin than necessary. I have an embarrassing version of a farmer's tan, or more specifically a biker's tan. I'm going to look a bit out of place if I can't wear my shorts to cover up the fish-belly-white at the top of my legs."

"I'm prepared to lather you with sunblock." Jasmine's eyes roved up and down Silver's body. "I'm going to confess to arranging for an activity that requires a bathing suit because I was jonesing to see you in one. I can't help it if the more lecherous side of me took over. I did get a little help from Preston, who suggested this activity. Have you ever been to a water park?"

Silver took a sip of her coffee. "Ahh, hits the spot. In answer to your question, once, quite a few years back we were visiting some friends of Naomi who moved to Moses Lake. They have a small water park, but mostly we watched their kids splash around while we visited with the couple. It did look like fun, but I didn't want to be the only adult to suggest that we join in."

"Well, you are in for a real treat because the Oceans of Fun water park is nearly as famous as Disney World around these parts. There is a range of options from the mild Castaway Cove adult pool to the Constrictor, where we'll spiral down a winding double tube with three hundred and sixty degree turns. That's one of my favorite slides. Of course if you're too chicken to try the more adventurous slide, I'll understand," Jasmine teased with a gleam in her eye.

"Ha. Challenge accepted. Just try to keep up with me," Silver teased.

"It's going to be a perfect day for the park. The weatherman said it would reach the nineties today, and with eighty percent humidity, you'll welcome the cool water."

"Oh dear, I'm not used to the staggering heat. Even on the other side of the mountains where it's a bit hotter than Seattle, we have dry heat."

"And that's why God invented air conditioning."

Jasmine turned around and sprinkled cinnamon into the bowl on the counter beside the oven.

Silver noticed the frying pan on the stove and the sliced french bread on the counter. She grinned when she realized they were having french toast for breakfast. It was her favorite. She wondered if Jasmine remembered that from one of the early author spotlights she'd participated in. A reader had asked what her favorite breakfast was, and she fired back an answer on the computer without hesitation.

"Mmmm, I see you're making my favorite breakfast."

Jasmine glanced over her shoulder before placing the recently dipped bread into the frying pan. "Mmm-hmm, I know. I remember reading it when you answered that question."

"Wow, you have a great memory. I probably shouldn't stuff myself this morning if I want to have any hope of looking decent in my bathing suit, but I doubt I'll be able to stop. I don't suppose limiting myself to one piece will make a big difference this late in the game. It's not like I can drop ten pounds in less than a day before the big reveal at the water park."

"I don't think you have a thing to worry about." Jasmine rotated her body to face Silver while the toast sizzled in the pan.

Silver was worried because she was forty-five and her bikini-clad days had long since passed. Of course, she hadn't brought a skimpy bikini, but that was beside the point. Any bathing suit on a middle-aged woman was risky business if you wanted to impress someone.

"Look, Silver, I see that worried look on your face, and trust me when I say I'm one hundred percent certain you will rock your suit. You can't possibly feel any more concerned about what you will look like than I do. I'm coming up on the big four-oh, and it's hitting harder than I thought. I stood in front of the mirror the other day and looked at myself in my Speedo. I wanted to cry. I wondered when I started to sag. It just sorta sneaked up on me. One day they were perky, and bam, the next day…." Jasmine waved her hand in front of her body "This."

"I'm not seeing it, Jasmine. You are beauty personified, and everything about you is a ten plus. I'll make a deal with you. I won't worry about the thousands of calories I plan to consume this morning if you don't."

"Deal. There are a few activities at the park that will allow us to get some exercise, so we can plan to weave those into the day, and then we can forge ahead guilt-free."

†

Dara jiggled her leg as she sipped her coffee. When she'd asked Jasmine about going to dinner tonight, she'd received a cryptic response from her about already having plans. She'd wondered who Jasmine had plans with since she knew she kept mainly to herself since the breakup. Sure, she was friendly with her coworkers, but only in a polite, standoffish way. On the weekends, they all went their separate ways. She'd learned of the author's visit by happenstance.

Dara set her mug down as a horrible thought hit her. Pauline. Maybe she'd finally made her move. Now that Jasmine had transferred to that division, Pauline had every opportunity to sidle up close to Jasmine and worm her way in. Was today about Silver or Pauline? She wasn't sure; it was all so convoluted now.

Dara had very little respect for the volunteer director because she was a closeted lesbian who seemed to dance around the fringes of her sexuality. Everyone knew she was gay, but Pauline had never admitted it openly. Instead, she skulked around at the gay bars. She was worse than Dara when it came to quick trysts. Normally Dara wouldn't frequent those establishments, but on occasion she'd relented when she and Jasmine were in their off-again phase. On one of those occasions she'd seen Pauline stalking a young lesbian and following her to the bathroom. It was such a crude way to conduct oneself. Pauline had definitely changed over the years.

When she'd hired Pauline three years ago, Dara saw the telltale signs of interest as she strolled into the administrative suite and gave Jasmine the once-over. Since that first day, Pauline found the most absurd reasons to visit administration, and now that Jasmine was in human resources, she didn't have to invent reasons to interact with her. *No good deed goes unpunished*, Dara thought.

Grudgingly, Dara admitted Jasmine was a difficult woman to ignore. If the shoe had been on the other foot, she would have taken her best shot. Jealousy raged in her, as she now had to worry about yet another woman stealing Jasmine's affections from her.

She began to imagine multiple women vying for Jasmine's heart. Everything was so confusing lately, and she wasn't sure who her competition was anymore. She was imagining suitors around every corner.

Her friends never hid their admiration for Jasmine's beauty, but she didn't think that was anything to worry about because Jasmine was correct; they were a shallow group of women who were only interested in Jasmine as a plaything.

When Korrine had offhandedly mentioned on Friday that the author was visiting Kansas this weekend, Dara went into a fit of rage that she took out on her coffee cup behind closed doors in her office. She decided to call Korrine and arrange to meet for lunch. Korrine was a good friend who would help her with this problem.

She picked up her phone, jabbed at the screen to access Korrine's contact information, and made the call. Her irritation was evident in everything she did this morning, starting with how she aggressively brushed her teeth, forgoing the electric toothbrush for her manual one.

†

Jasmine was humming along with the radio as they drove to the water park. She was happy she'd kept the waterproof cell phone holder given out at the HR conference Carla had encouraged her to attend a few months ago. When the hospital's marketing department saw the clever trinket with the retirement company's logo, they'd decided to purchase some of their own and plaster their own logo across the heavy plastic. She'd snatched the marketing item and tossed it in her junk drawer with the other one. She'd never imagined she would have an opportunity to make good use of both of them.

On a whim, she'd purchased a small watertight day bag a few years ago that she could wear like a backpack. She loved to get out on the lake and kayak, but Dara never wanted to go. She'd preferred indoor activities. On occasion, Jasmine would plead her way to a picnic or day at the lake.

She rooted around in her closet until she found the unused bag and plucked it from the corner while removing the purchase tags. This would be perfect for putting their tshirts and shorts into while barreling down the roller-coaster-like ride. She was looking forward to the more adventurous attractions and hoped Silver was up to it.

Jasmine glanced over and spied Silver bobbing her head to "Happy" by Pharrell Williams. "I see you like this song as much as I do. It's awfully hard not to sing along, huh?"

Silver chuckled. "I'm going to stick to bobbing my head and not force you to suffer through my singing, but you go right ahead. Sing at the top of your lungs."

Jasmine knew she was singing off key, but she didn't care as she belted out the words and laughed with abandon.

"Oh, what the hell…." Silver began singing.

The two women filled the tight space of the car with their comingled, out-of-tune voices, interspersed with out-of-control laughter. When the song finished, they looked at each other and burst into another round of uninhibited giggles.

"I feel like a drunken college student heading to Mexico for spring break," Silver interjected between bouts of hilarity.

The unrestrained merriment was music to Jasmine's ears. "We always drove to Florida. I suppose East and West Coast have different spring break destinations."

"Mmm-hmm, but at least the jails in Florida don't require a load of cash to bribe your way out," Silver deadpanned.

"Seriously, I just can't imagine you causing enough trouble to be thrown into jail."

"Tequila is a bad, bad thing, and the worm is even worse. I was young, stupid, and wild. Oh, and the beautiful, young woman in the cantina egging me on didn't help. I've never let tequila pass by my lips since."

"I never did like tequila." Jasmine shivered. "Don't even get me started on the worm thingy. That's just wrong on so many levels."

"By the time you make it to the bottom of the bottle, you no longer care that you're about to swallow a slimy, squiggly thing that on your best day you wouldn't touch with bare hands." Silver giggled. "You know, I wouldn't trade any of my life's experiences, good or bad. One day I can write a story about the dangers of combining tequila, beautiful Mexican women, and the corrupt Mexican justice system. Life presents multiple opportunities for authors. Live like it's your last day; sing and dance like no one is looking or listening."

Jasmine nodded enthusiastically. "I'll drink to that. Not tequila though."

Silver was like a Christmas present in beautiful wrapping—every moment she spent with her, Jasmine learned something surprising as she untied another bow. This was the Silver she'd first met five years ago—the one who embraced life and viewed every twist and turn as a great escapade to hold on to.

†

Korrine sat rigid and erect in the booth at the bistro where Dara suggested they meet. Dara narrowed her eyes and wondered why she felt some kind of kinship with the oddly dichotomous woman.

The nurses at the hospital absolutely worshipped her, but everyone else in the organization cringed anytime she came near them, unless she decided to blanket them with the charm she usually reserved for the nursing staff. She had the ability to turn on a dime and show genuine gratitude for the work they did, regardless of their position in the hospital. On the other hand, when she was displeased with someone, watch out.

Dara remembered from her psychology classes the power of variable interval reinforcement. Korrine was a master at this. Instead of consistently rewarding staff with her praise, she did it intermittently, and they nearly tripped over themselves to please her. She remembered that behaviorists had discovered this trick. Constantly checking Facebook for that elusive positive post was a great example of this principle.

She wondered if she should have done that more effectively with Jasmine. Would displaying stinginess with her compliments have been more productive? Were people really like animals and this type of behavioral training actually worked? She supposed this was the kind of intellectual discussion Korrine might appreciate.

Korrine looked up and barely acknowledged Dara—again. Her normally flat affect was sometimes disconcerting. However, today Korrine looked preoccupied, and Dara wondered what had caused her pensive mood. “Thanks for meeting me for lunch.”

“Silver is staying with Jasmine,” Korrine stated. Her voice held no emotion.

“Yes, I know.”

“I didn’t expect that. I was planning to visit my sister this summer, but I don’t know if I can get away. I really expected to visit with Silver, but who knows if she’ll be there when I arrive. She seems to be rather unpredictable now. I think you might have some serious competition, Dara.”

Dara wanted to have words with the famous author. Jasmine was too starstruck to recognize the reality of her circumstances. She had zero chance of a future with Silver Lining. Dara was even willing to go through some kind of farce of a marriage if that meant Jasmine would return to her. She had to admit that making that offer hadn’t been her finest moment.

Perhaps if she made some big, romantic gesture, that would secure her future with Jasmine.

"I haven't done a good job of showing Jasmine how I feel about her. I plan to amend that as soon as I figure out what will work," Dara declared.

Korrine nodded. "Yes, I believe your contributions to the situation are necessary. I really wish you'd take care of things so I can catch her in town when I visit. I've always wanted to have an in-depth discussion with her about lesbian fiction. You do your part and I'll do mine."

The barely disguised order unsettled Dara. She didn't do well with them. She was the one who ordered, not the other way around. Dara decided to let it go. It wasn't as important as making sure Jasmine warmed her bed again, no matter what it took.

Dara was surprised to see Pauline stroll into the bistro and narrow her eyes in her direction. She felt compelled to wave her to their table. "Hmmm, all three lesbian leaders gathering at the same watering hole. What a coincidence," she mumbled.

"What?" Korrine asked.

"Oh nothing, Pauline just walked in. Small world, huh?" Dara quipped.

Korrine craned her neck to verify that their colleague had entered the restaurant. "Oh, I invited her to join us. She's the one who told me Silver was planning to come to Kansas this weekend. I figured she learned that from Jasmine and she might have more information to share. They work in the same office."

"I know that," Dara barked.

Korrine raised her eyebrow. "Oh, I get it now. You think Pauline is interested in Jasmine. Geez, she's like the lesbian Pied Piper," she grumbled.

Pauline marched up to the table. "Thanks for the

invite," she said brightly.

Dara's mood darkened. Korrine was a safe person to speak with because she had no interest in Jasmine, which she'd found a little odd. Jasmine was a striking woman, and she couldn't imagine any hot-blooded lesbian not finding her irresistible. Dara bolstered her manners and smiled politely at the interloper. She was determined to cut the lunch short and return to her plans to put her relationship back on track.

†

Silver looked up suspiciously at the Constrictor, the water slide rated "aggressive" in the brochures she'd glanced at. The brightly colored monstrosity had more twists and turns than the misshapen metal of the Experience Music Project in Seattle and no one ever intended anyone to slide down that famous contorted architecture.

After finding most everyone else running around the park in their bathing suits, Silver had reluctantly agreed to store her shorts and T-shirt in a locker and walk around in her one-piece suit and a pair of water shoes.

The only positive to that decision was seeing Jasmine in her tight-fitting Speedo that revealed her flat stomach and well-toned body. She certainly didn't look like a woman about to turn forty. Silver was glad to see that Jasmine tugged on her suit just as frequently as she did. Bathing suits tended to bunch up, and she was constantly pulling on the elastic to ensure her suit didn't inadvertently turn into a modified thong.

"The travel channel rated this as one of the five most exciting water rides in the U.S. Come on." Jasmine grabbed Silver's hand.

"Maybe I'll just sit this one out and watch you."

Jasmine chuckled. "Where's that brave woman who

took Mexico by storm?"

"That was a long time ago. When you're young you feel invincible, and then life teaches you otherwise." Silver shook her head. "I just realized what a huge stick-in-the-mud I'm being. What the hell, bring it on. If you can do it, so can I."

She wanted to start living life again, and what better way to do it than to enjoy a day in the sunshine, shooting down an extreme water tube with a beautiful woman?

"That's the ticket. I promise it'll be a blast," Jasmine enthused.

Silver thought her exuberance was infectious as they walked hand in hand to the start of the slide. "You know, I think you're right. I believe I'm about to embark on the ride of my life, and I just need to let the water flow around me."

Silver could hear the tinkle of laughter and Jasmine's scream as she barreled down the hairpin turns and followed her, feeling the rush of water flow over her as she let her inhibitions go.

Jasmine was waiting for her with her hand stretched out as Silver landed at the bottom of the ride. She noted the broad smile on Jasmine's face and thought it probably matched her own genuine joy.

"Shall we go again?" Jasmine asked.

"At least ten more times, I think, and then I'd like to hit Shark's Revenge. That looks equally promising."

"Oh yes, I've had my eye on that one as well, and then we can head over to Hurricane Falls."

"I think this is a day I'm going to remember for years to come."

"I sure hope so, I really do," Jasmine whispered.

Chapter Nineteen

Jasmine and Silver tumbled into the condominium giggling like schoolgirls. Both had pulled their hair back into ponytails, and without a smidge of makeup on either of them, the sun had made its mark, leaving a rosy glow on their cheeks. Their journey back to childhood today had done wonders for them both. It seemed as though the day in the sun had pushed twenty years of life from their faces, leaving the impression that they were women in their twenties falling in love for the first time.

"Oh God, thank you so much for this day. It's been so long since I've had such shameless fun. I feel like I'm twenty again," Silver declared.

"You know, with your hair tied back and the sunburn on your nose, you don't look a day over twenty-one."

"You are a delicious little liar," Silver teased.

"I never lie, unlike others in my life," Jasmine replied. Her tone was serious, and Silver instantly recognized the pain. She took two steps and gathered Jasmine in her arms. She rubbed her back and hesitated before letting go. "I know, and neither do I. You may not always like what I have to say, but I'll never lie to you, Jasmine. All I can say is I'm glad you haven't given Dara another chance, and I can only hope and pray that you never will."

Jasmine took Silver's hand and led her to the couch. They sat down, and Jasmine touched Silver's nose. "I think I should have offered to smear sunblock on your nose. Does it hurt? I think I have some aloe. It always tones down the heat for me when I forget to cover up."

Silver kissed Jasmine's nose. "Don't worry about me. You may want to grab the aloe for yourself though. You know, you really rock that Rudolph look."

Jasmine's expression changed and anticipation fluttered in Silver's stomach regarding where the conversation would go. She sensed Jasmine was ready to make some major declaration and wasn't sure what direction that would take their budding relationship.

Jasmine took a big breath and began, "I want so much to believe this is heading where I want it to, but there are so many obstacles. You've said you don't like sharing, and that's really the only indication that you want a monogamous relationship. I guess I'm having a hard time envisioning how that's going to work given that we live thousands of miles from one another. Have you thought about this at all?"

Silver smiled. "I have, but before either of us makes any drastic changes in our lives, I thought we should at least make it through this weekend as an official couple. Jasmine, the distance is the least problematic part of the equation. I can work anywhere, but I don't want to propagate the lesbian cliché, which is why I left my U-Haul at home. We have time, so let's enjoy these moments together. The beginning of new love contains some of the best moments in a relationship, and I don't want either of us to miss the wonder of it all with worries of the future."

"Silver, I'm not tied to Kansas, and my job is just that,

a job, not a career. All you'd ever have to do is ask and I would move for you," Jasmine stated.

"You know, I'm writing this book about a kind, sensual, genuine, intelligent woman who lives in Kansas and helps a lonely singer in the midst of despair find love again. I can write off every trip I make to Kansas as research. God, I love being a writer," Silver joked.

"I'm serious, you know. I don't want the distance to get in the way. You're far too important to me for that," Jasmine confessed.

Jasmine had profoundly touched Silver with the naked honesty of that statement. Overcome with emotion, she traced her fingers over Jasmine's lips and leaned in to capture them in a searing kiss. She wanted to impart all of the feelings she had for Jasmine as they bubbled over, spilling love deep inside her.

Silver felt Jasmine accept her love and return it with exuberance. The kiss deepened, and Silver had a hard time catching her breath. This wasn't a chaste kiss or even one that hinted at the passion ready to boil over. This kiss was the precursor to the kind of intimacy that would define the future of their relationship. For Silver, if they ended up making love, there was no going back—full steam ahead. Silver didn't offer that gift to just anyone. She'd only ever made love with one other woman, and she'd married her.

Everything felt so right in that moment, but she hesitated. She needed to be sure, so with great restraint, she pulled away.

"Wow, I felt that all the way to my toes. I would like nothing more than to drag you into my bedroom and make love with you, but I want us both ready and you're not there yet."

Silver pressed her forehead against Jasmine's. "Thank you," she whispered.

Jasmine pulled Silver to a standing position. "Come on, I don't know about you, but I'd like to wash all this chlorine off my body, and then I'm taking you for the best barbecue you've ever had in your young life."

"Sounds wonderful. Are you inviting me to shower with you?" Silver asked.

"Uh, no. I have two showers. My self-control is not that well developed." Jasmine laughed.

"Neither is mine. Whew, I was wondering how I would politely decline. By the way, I'd never uproot you without considering all the options. We'll know what to do when the time is right. I believe in the universal power of kismet."

"As long as we keep heading in the same direction, I'm okay with taking our time to get there," Jasmine assured.

"Oh we are definitely heading in the same direction. Every day I spend with you, my feelings grow exponentially. If it didn't feel so damned good, I'd be petrified."

Silver knew without a doubt that she was falling in love, and she wanted to relish every precious moment. She wasn't in any hurry; she would let her feelings marinate.

†

The woman hid in the corner of the parking lot again. It was riskier to immerse herself in a daytime stakeout, but she felt compelled to watch the continued interaction between the two women. She would recognize if things had progressed to the point of no return. If that happened, her options were limited to removing one of the obstacles to winning the object of her affection. The thought of taking things that far left a sour taste in her mouth.

With her dark glasses affixed to her face, she slumped lower into her vehicle as the older-model Honda careened into the parking lot and the two giggling women emerged. She had to admit they looked good together.

They were both casually dressed with their hair pulled back into twin ponytails. They didn't look like two middle-aged women out for a lackluster afternoon in the unexciting Midwest. Granted, Jasmine wasn't yet forty, so she wasn't sure that constituted middle age. Wasn't forty the new thirty? "Young at heart," that's what her therapist always drilled into her. She'd been convinced she was born into adulthood, having to take care of her irresponsible mother. She supposed it wasn't really her mother's fault. Bipolar was a disorder that many people did not understand.

She tried not to let her childhood and upbringing have an impact on her adult life and was smug about the fact she'd come so far. She was a successful leader in an equally flourishing organization. That made her a good catch and thus things would all work out as she intended. She might decide to return to her first occupational love with the support of a good woman.

She wasn't sure what brought her back to the complex so early in the evening. She didn't have the cover of darkness, but this one glimpse of the couple provided her additional information she hadn't possessed before spying on the unsuspecting duo. For that reason she was glad she'd taken the chance. Now that she'd seen them enter the condominium, she could leave and return later. Perhaps she could collect more data that would be useful in the future. She couldn't afford to ignore even the smallest detail.

Rubbing her head, she tried to remove the impending headache. They were becoming more frequent. It was just as well that she needed to head home because she was due for another dose of medication. She couldn't afford to be fuzzy when she returned this evening.

†

Silver whistled while she lathered soap over her body. She didn't even mind that the strong spray of the water stung her sunburned shoulders. She was in far too good a mood. Today she'd laughed and played in the water with Jasmine and couldn't remember another time she'd let herself relax, throw caution to the wind, and simply live in the moment.

Jasmine was the perfect date. She was attentive, playful, interesting, and kind, and she had such a natural and genuine charm. Silver felt she was the most important person in the world as she circled around Jasmine's orbit because she gave Silver her complete attention. Naomi used to do that. It made Silver feel special.

After her shower, she pulled a soft cotton T-shirt over her head. She hoped Jasmine wouldn't think it was rude that she'd forgone the bra, but there was no way she would subject her burned shoulders to the rub of a bra strap.

At least when she'd liberally slathered her legs in sunblock, she'd adequately protected the parts she normally covered with bike shorts. She wanted complete comfort though, so she pulled on some quick-dry camping shorts without bothering to don any underwear. She felt a little naughty doing this, but decided undergarments weren't necessary for a relaxing evening with Jasmine.

Jasmine had insisted Silver use the master bathroom while she took her shower in the guest bath. When her phone buzzed in the waterproof bag she'd set on the bathroom counter, she flipped the bag over to see who was calling. Another disturbing text glared at her with an unmistakable warning.

Are you trying to hurt me? Why are you with her? You need to stay away.

Silver began pacing the bedroom. "Shit, I can't keep

ignoring these. I could really have an unbalanced fan that might harm Jasmine."

Knock, knock, knock.

Silver jumped at the noise. This stalker business caused a hypersensitivity that she didn't enjoy.

"Hey, are you decent yet? I forgot to grab my toothbrush," Jasmine called from the other side of the door.

"Yeah, come on in. I need to talk with you about something."

"Okaaay."

Silver heard the hesitation in Jasmine's voice and knew she needed to allay her fears. Their budding relationship was still so new that insecurity danced at the edges whenever the suggestion that they needed to talk came up.

The door creaked open and Jasmine carefully entered, looking at Silver as if her whole world was about to crash down on her.

Silver rushed over and pulled Jasmine into her arms, stroking her back reassuringly with her free hand. The other hand still held the phone with the offending message. "Oh sweetheart, it's not what you think."

Jasmine moved out of the embrace and captured Silver's eyes. "Your voice sounded so serious. You scared the bejeebers out of me for a minute there."

"I got another odd text, and I think I may have failed to tell you about the other two I received on Sunday and Monday," Silver sheepishly admitted. "I should have done something about it, but someone keeps distracting me and all I see is bright skies. You've sent me into a tailspin, and I'm having a hard time controlling my emotions."

"Can you show me all of the messages?" Jasmine asked.

"God, I'm such an idiot. I should have reported this to

the police last weekend. If it was just me involved it would be one thing, but Jasmine, whoever is sending the messages has specifically called you out. Do you think this is something Dara might do? If I were in her position, I don't think I'd give you up either. Certainly, I might take a different tack, but I do understand that sometimes desperation makes us do foolish things." Silver scrolled through her messages until she landed on the first one and tilted her phone in Jasmine's direction. "See, this one wasn't exactly personally threatening, but it wasn't normal either."

Jasmine took the phone from Silver, held it out at arm's length, and squinted. "Crud, I swear one day I could read these tiny little screens clear as day, and the next day I need old-lady glasses."

Silver repositioned herself so she could hold on to Jasmine's hand while accessing the other two messages. "What do you think? Can you read them?"

"Hmmm, I got a similar cryptic message. Only the person didn't specifically tell me to stay away from you. Your person is more specific. I don't really know what to think. I don't think this is Dara's style, but she did ask me to lunch on Tuesday and made a plea for getting back together. A year ago it might have worked. She even made a half-assed attempt at a marriage proposal."

Silver's voice hitched. "Do you still love her?"

"I'm not even sure I still like her anymore. Don't mistake my complacency for real love. I should have left years ago, and now I have a good reason to stay away. I'm probably being foolish and impulsive, but a chance for something with you wins hands down over a future with Dara. I can't even explain it. I know I shouldn't get my hopes up too much because you and I are so new. We don't even have a definition for what we are. Dating? Exploring possibilities? Is it too early for the *R* word? It's definitely too early for the *L* word."

"Really? I kinda like that series. I could tuck in and watch several episodes tonight with you curled against me. I've never heard of the *R* word. Risk-takers? Readers? Roadies?" Silver grinned. "Sorry, I couldn't resist adding a little levity, but I really don't know what the *R* word is."

"Relationship," Jasmine said.

"It's all just semantics. I'm not sure if a definition is necessary. Here's what I know. When I'm around you, I forget things, my heartbeat quickens, my palms sweat, and you take my breath away. When I'm not around you, I'm thinking about you and cogitating over ways to talk to or see you again. See, you've done it to me again, because we started talking about the odd text messages and already I'm down a different path imagining snuggling up with you on the couch watching some unrealistic show about a bunch of California lesbians."

"Right. Back to the stalker," Jasmine redirected.

"Do you really think we have a stalker?"

"Yes I do, and I think it's time we took this seriously. I think we should file a report here in Kansas, and you need to file one when you return home. I don't even know how to do that. Do you think it would be overkill to dial 9-1-1 and let them direct us?" Jasmine asked.

Silver shrugged. "I'm sure they get far more mundane calls that aren't emergencies than the one I'm about to make."

Jasmine handed Silver her phone. "Here. Maybe if we're lucky some nice lesbian will take the report and because you're famous and all, she'll take it seriously."

"What are the odds of that happening?"

"Probably better than you think. I've seen quite a few suspiciously butch police officers in Kansas. There is a larger contingent of lesbians in the Midwest than most people think."

"I'm so sorry to ruin your evening with this drama," Silver said.

Jasmine waved her hand in the air. "You go ahead and make the call, and I'll rustle up some dinner. I think that barbeque takeout will hit the spot. We can eat while we wait for Kansas City's finest."

Jasmine ducked into the bathroom and came out holding up her toothbrush, smiling as she left the bedroom.

Silver pressed the screen to connect to the emergency 9-1-1 call center. "Um, I wasn't sure exactly how to report this and I apologize if this isn't the correct thing to do, but I need to report a possible stalker. I've been getting unsettling messages, and now they involve someone else…. No, I don't think I'm in imminent danger…. No, they haven't exactly been explicit threats…. Okay. I suppose I can do that…. Yes, I think it can wait until I get back home on Monday…. All right, I'm sorry to bother you. You have a good evening."

Silver sighed. She didn't blame the 9-1-1 dispatcher and had guessed what their response might be. She stared at her phone a second and then smacked her hand to her head. She selected the calendar app and programmed in an appointment to visit the police department on Monday. She also added a new notification using her alarm app, just to be on the safe side. With two reminders, even her whirlwind feelings for a Kansas beauty would not distract her from making a report.

Silver thought back to their earlier conversation about where they wanted the relationship to go. Jasmine was right, it was too soon for the *L* word, even though that was exactly where she believed this was going. She was surprised how open and vulnerable they'd been with one another, making it clear they were both seeking something more serious than casual dating. If she were inclined to define where this road led, it would definitely constitute a relationship that had the possibility of permanency—maybe even a forever commitment. Silver wanted to wait until they had more than a few days together to explore this further with Jasmine though. She wanted a partnership, not a one-sided affair.

†

Silver's contemplative look as she walked out of the bedroom and joined Jasmine in her combination kitchen-living room area didn't concern Jasmine, but did cause her to wonder how the 9-1-1 call went.

"You look like you're trying to solve the mystery of the lost city of Atlantis," Jasmine observed.

Silver shook her head and blessed Jasmine with one of her brilliant smiles. "No, not trying to solve anything as complicated as that. Although…on second thought, I suppose our situation and defining it in a way that isn't alarming to either one of us might be considered a convoluted puzzle. I think we should leave the unraveling for when you visit in July. Would that be okay? I hope I've given you enough reassurance to tide you over until then."

"You have. How did your phone call with the police go?"

"I guess I expected them to say what they did, but the report will have to wait until I get back to Seattle on Monday. I should have enough time to make it to the police department during their normal daytime hours. None of the messages were very specific with any kind of physical threat to you or me, so without either one of us being in imminent danger, they weren't inclined to send anyone out."

Jasmine was concerned for Silver's safety. She knew unbalanced fans could be dangerous. "I don't think I'm very comfortable with that response."

"I'm sorry. Should I call them back? I know it's not just me anymore that might be affected by this. I should have taken your safety into consideration when I accepted their recommendation on how to proceed."

"I'm not worried for me, I'm concerned about you."

Silver chuckled. "God, we're a pair. I guess I honestly think it will be fine if I wait until Monday. It's only a few days away."

"Okay. I trust your judgement, but—" The front doorbell interrupted Jasmine before she could complete her thought. "That was fast. I just called the barbecue place not more than ten minutes ago."

Jasmine ran her hands through her hair and turned around to answer the door. She was displeased when the young man presented her with an outrageously large bouquet of red roses. The enormous vase held at least three dozen of the flowers.

"Are you Jasmine?" the young man asked.

Jasmine nodded.

"I was specifically told to make sure these were delivered before seven. I'm glad you were home."

Jasmine accepted the flowers he handed to her and closed the door. She knew they were Dara's attempt to somehow interject herself into the day after hearing she had plans. She'd carefully left out the details, but that didn't mean Dara hadn't learned about them through one of her sources.

"Somebody has an admirer. Is there something you haven't told me?" Silver asked.

Jasmine couldn't discern whether Silver was angry, disappointed, or sad. She set the flowers down on the table after briefly considering tossing them in the trash.

"I don't even need to read the card. I know Dara, and this is her feeble attempt to woo me back into her bed. I swear there is nothing going on. We went to lunch, and I told her it wasn't ever going to happen. I thought she accepted that."

Silver narrowed her eyes. "That doesn't look all that feeble to me. Good God, there must be three dozen roses there. I think you should read the card. I'd like to know what competition I'm up against. Just so you know, I'm not going to just hand her the keys to the car. You're worth fighting for."

Jasmine plucked the card from the plastic holder and opened the small envelope. Silver sidled up next to her and read over her shoulder.

I just wanted you to remember that I love you and always will. I won't give up that easily. You need time and I'm prepared to give you that. I just want to keep reminding you of our love for each other. Love, Dara.

"Typical Dara. A big, flashy gesture with flowers I don't like. She can't even be bothered to remember what my favorite flower is," Jasmine relayed with disgust.

"What is your favorite flower?" Silver softly asked.

"Asian Stargazer Lilly. They have the most delicious smell, and it lasts for days."

"I'll remember," Silver stated.

"I know you will. You won't think less of me if I toss these in the garbage, will you?"

"Absolutely not. Toss away. I'll even help you stomp on them before they end up in the trash. You know, to get them to fit." Silver laughed.

"Oooh. I like it. You have a little wicked side to you. I was beginning to think you were entirely too perfect for me."

"Oh no, I temper my jealously, but it wants to come out and play every once in a while. I give in and let it—in completely constructive ways, of course. Stomping on flowers from another suitor is perfect." Silver grinned.

"Sounds like fun," Jasmine agreed.

Jasmine carefully pulled all the roses out of the vase and tossed them on the tile in the kitchen. She started laughing as she jumped up and landed squarely into the center of the red-and-green mess. She grabbed Silver's hand, and they both began stomping all over the flowers, giggling like schoolgirls.

The petals and leaves lay scattered on the floor, creating a collage of various shapes and sizes with the stems haphazardly strewn about. Jasmine felt a cathartic release as she symbolically stomped all over her former relationship—sending a clear message that she was finished.

Chapter Twenty

Silver felt a sense of déjà vu as she waited in baggage claim at SeaTac for Jasmine to arrive. During the last couple of weeks, they'd kept in touch every evening. Silver preferred Skype to their other means of communication, but she knew Jasmine couldn't sneak on Skype during the day just so she could talk with Silver. She was grateful for the text messages Jasmine sent throughout the day, letting Silver know she was thinking about her.

Silver thought about Jasmine all the time and had to keep herself from buying another airline ticket and showing up at her doorstep to spend whatever free time Jasmine might have with her. She was starting to appreciate how easy her relationship with Naomi was in the beginning because they lived in the same town. Silver wrestled with herself regarding how to bring up the topic of one of them moving. It was too soon, but the distance was starting to grate on her. Jasmine told her she would move if Silver wanted her to, but would that be a fair request?

She had followed through on visiting the police when she returned, but without a specific threat, they'd informed her there wasn't really anything they could do. When she hadn't received any additional messages, she let her would-be stalker fade into the background and kept her focus on Jasmine and her latest story. The writing seemed to flow like a raging river, and she was almost finished with the first draft. It was a record for her because she'd never completed a book in less than a month. She was anxious for Jasmine's feedback.

Silver kept her focus on the conveyor belt around which passengers from flight 457 had started to swarm. When Jasmine entered Silver's field of vision, the joy on her face clearly matched Silver's, and she began to run toward Silver.

She threw herself into Silver's awaiting arms and whispered, "God, I've missed you."

Silver was glad Jasmine blurted out exactly what she was thinking. Jasmine never had a filter or brick wall around her feelings, and her vulnerability was irresistible. She made it easy for Silver to let loose, and as a result, Silver didn't guard her own emotions.

"I am so glad you're finally here. This distance is very challenging for me," Silver replied.

Jasmine took a step back and repositioned her enormous backpack, which was three times the size of the one she'd brought with her three weeks ago. "Two whole weeks. I can hardly contain my excitement. I don't care what we do. I'd be perfectly content to share the same air in a room with you. We could lock ourselves in your home for the entire fourteen days and I wouldn't complain one bit."

Silver arched her eyebrow. "Hmmm, I suppose there are some pleasurable activities that would engage us without having to step foot out of the house, but I think I might be too old for that type of marathon."

Jasmine blushed. "That's not what I was suggesting,

but with the right person you're never too old."

"Hmmm, well I suppose we'll need to test that theory someday."

†

The woman breathed a sigh of relief. When she'd realized she was on the same flight as Jasmine, she'd waited until the very last minute to board and kept her bag in front of her face as she traversed the narrow aisle. She hadn't wanted to ruin the surprise just yet. She would have plenty of time to spend with her love as soon as she eliminated the competition.

The drugs she'd packed for her documented medical condition provided the perfect tools to subdue her rival. Working in a hospital afforded ample opportunity to secure the required supplies and forge the documentation needed to carry the syringes. The employee health nurse often left her door open and the box of syringes out in the open for anyone to take. Although she was prepared to make the ultimate sacrifice, she hoped it wouldn't come to that.

She realized this was the only option now after hiding in the shadows and witnessing the tender reunion between the two. She needed all of her self-control not to rip them apart and stake her claim right there in the middle of the busy baggage area.

The swarm of people gathered around the carousel waiting for their baggage reminded her of wasps circling a nest. She moved among the other wasps, keeping her distance and hiding in plain sight. She didn't mind thinking of herself as a wasp. Wasps stung repeatedly, revealing their strength and irritation over the audacity of another creature horning in on their territory. The interloper would feel her sting, that was a given.

Silver and Jasmine would arrive at Silver's house before she had a chance to secure her rental car and find the home, but she wasn't concerned about the delay. Having Silver and Jasmine settle in worked to her advantage. They wouldn't expect her arrival. She'd been extremely patient so far and had sent multiple warnings. She had hoped it wouldn't come to this, but her warnings had gone unanswered.

She muscled her way to the bags circling on the conveyor belt, plucked her nondescript black suitcase from the rotating carousel, and walked briskly to the rental desk. She masked her irritation over how long the incompetent clerk took to prepare her paperwork. The delay darkened her mood. Every moment she permitted Silver and Jasmine to spend together created additional consternation. She didn't believe they'd crossed the line to become intimate yet, and she simply could not allow that.

Imagining that her one and only might feel the caress of another disgusted her. The other women hadn't meant anything to her at all—they were just pleasant distractions. She needed to be the only one to touch her creamy skin and cause the ecstasy that came from finding that special spot. Being a skilled lover of women was a special talent, and she was convinced she would send her love to new heights of passion.

She imagined how she would squirm under her control as she kept bringing her close and holding back until she begged for release. Yes, their first time together would be perfect.

†

Jasmine marveled at how much sunshine remained late in the day in Washington. Kansas had long summer days, but not nearly as long as where Silver lived. It was close to eight and there would be at least another hour of daylight. The summer nights always energized Jasmine, and she usually needed a lot less sleep because she wanted to take advantage of every minute in the day.

Jasmine wondered about the sleeping arrangements. They'd already opened the barn door when Silver stayed with her in Kansas and the second night she'd spent at Silver's home, but would Silver invite her into the bed she had shared with Naomi, or would that be too distressing? She didn't want to cause Silver any pain by opening heartbreaking memories.

With her backpack securely fastened, she followed Silver into her home, still wondering where she would be sleeping. The answer came quickly.

"I never want to assume anything, so I need to know if you're okay staying in the master suite with me. I don't want you to feel uncomfortable, because you know—"

Jasmine grabbed Silver's hand. "Honestly, I'm not the one who needs to feel comfortable about the sleeping arrangements." She felt an overwhelming sense of sadness. She wondered if she could ever match up to Silver's first love, but the sorrow she felt over Silver's tragic loss was even more profound.

Silver turned her around and gently kissed her. "Oh God, I'm so sorry to leave you with the wrong impression. I've made peace with my past, and you, my love, are my future. Please don't be sad. The master suite it is. It's a lot more comfortable than the guest bedroom."

Jasmine wondered how long it would take to avoid feeling as if they were walking on eggshells around the subject of Naomi. Jasmine didn't want Silver to avoid the subject, but she also didn't want it to remain a focal point of discussion. This was a quagmire she didn't know how to extricate them from, but at some point, they both needed to face the issue head-on.

†

Dara felt a sense of urgency as she waited for her rental car. She hoped it wasn't too late. As soon as she'd learned what was happening, she'd changed her travel plans. She'd already intended to make the trek to Washington, but she hadn't planned to leave work early.

Dara should have seen the signs—they were all there. It had been a fluke when she'd overheard the conversation in the professional services building where the human resources division had their offices. She'd needed to meet with Carla and had inadvertently learned about her plans.

Dara hadn't wanted to blow everything out of proportion because she believed she could talk some sense into her. She couldn't do that by phone, because Dara wasn't sure she would answer the call. Dara felt a certain amount of responsibility for this whole mess and was determined to correct it all before anyone got hurt. There was no sense it bringing anyone else into the mix. No good would come of that.

†

Silver glanced at the dresser where the picture of Naomi and herself had previously held a prominent place. The dresser looked naked without the comforting photo.

She'd spent the last week packing up Naomi's clothes and safely tucking away the mementos, including the picture. She'd cried and called her sister for support as she symbolically packaged her old life into boxes to start a new life.

Silver noted Jasmine watching her carefully and marveled at how sensitive Jasmine was to her thoughts and moods. She was sure Jasmine had noticed the melancholy glance, but wasn't sure what to say or do. She'd felt her squeeze her hand, and that was enough.

Not wanting to put a damper on the evening, Silver shook away thoughts of her old life with Naomi and sent Jasmine a genuine smile. She felt such joy as she anticipated their upcoming time together.

"Do you need to freshen up before we head out to the back porch? I thought we could have a glass of wine and watch the sun set."

"Why? Do I smell or something?" Jasmine teased.

"As a matter of fact, yes you do." The shocked look on Jasmine's face was priceless. "Heavenly. You smell delicious like orange spice. I noticed it the very first time I hugged you," Silver quickly added.

"It's the handmade lotion I buy from this woman at the farmers' market. I'll be sure to tell her what a hit it is. Lead the way. I don't need to freshen up, and I can unpack later." Jasmine slipped the bag off her shoulders and set it in the corner.

Silver was glad Jasmine didn't want to take the time to unpack, because she was anxious to address the elephant in the room. She'd sensed they needed to talk about how they were both treading lightly on the topic of Naomi, and she didn't want that to get in the way of their budding relationship.

When they reached the kitchen, Silver pulled a bottle of wine out of the refrigerator. "Go on to the backyard and I'll bring the wine. We should have another hour or so before the sun sets. I absolutely love summer in the Pacific Northwest."

"All right, I'll be communing with nature until you

bring the libations."

†

Jasmine sat in one of the lawn chairs facing the mountains that created the perfect scenic backdrop. The multitude of lush greens instilled a sense of peace in her, and she came to a sudden realization. When she'd made the declaration about moving to Washington, she thought Silver hadn't taken her seriously, but not only was she willing to move, she wanted to live in this miracle of nature. The mountains and the trees suited her far better than the boring Kansas landscape.

"You look like you're pondering the secrets of the universe," Silver stated.

Jasmine turned her head as Silver approached. Silver handed her a glass of wine and pulled up another lawn chair.

"It's peaceful here. I feel settled. I meant what I said before. All you'd have to do is ask and I'd move in a heartbeat," Jasmine reiterated.

"Excellent. I have a tiny recorder in my pocket and I've captured every word, so you can't take that back because I have proof now," Silver joked.

"I know it's too soon to make definitive plans, but I can't help how I feel. My compulsive need to share every little thought and feeling with you is definitely out of control. I don't know how you've managed to tap into that part of my psyche so easily, and I hope you aren't scared away by it."

"On the contrary, I find it refreshing, and you have the same effect on me, which brings me to something I want to talk with you about," Silver said.

"Sounds serious. Should I be concerned?" Jasmine asked.

"No, you shouldn't be concerned, but I do want to get

this out in the open."

"Open communication is best," Jasmine agreed.

"I don't quite know how to resolve this, but we both have been tiptoeing around the topic of Naomi. You've never made me feel like I can't talk about her, but I think you wonder if it causes me pain. I hope you don't think you'll never be as important to me as Naomi was, because that couldn't be further from the truth. Sure, I sometimes get nostalgic, and I can't guarantee it will never cause me some amount of pain to remember her, but I don't want that getting in the way of us. If you have any suggestions, I'm all ears."

"I think what we're doing now is the answer. Talking about it openly and honestly is the key. I suppose life is filled with both pain and joy. As much as I don't want to see you in distress, I'm glad I can be by your side to support you. I know it's good for you to talk about Naomi, and I don't feel like I'm the sloppy seconds. I do admit my discomfort is more about sensing your sadness and wanting to fix it, but that's my issue to deal with, not yours. I'll work on reframing my perspective. Oh God, I sound like some self-help book—reframing my perspective. You know what I mean, right?" Jasmine chuckled.

"I do know what you mean. I used to be what Naomi called a 'fixer.' She told me once that she didn't need fixing—she just needed someone to listen. You listen and you're much better at letting me talk without trying to fix me than I ever was with Naomi. I must have done something right in this life for the universe to send you to me. Who knows, maybe Naomi was the one to orchestrate this from the great beyond. She would have loved you and I'm sure would have approved."

Chapter Twenty-one

When the woman had arrived thirty minutes ago, she hadn't counted on a locked gate. Silver's choice to live in a gated community didn't fit with what she knew about her. That seemed too pretentious for the famous author, but maybe she had crazy stalker fans to deal with.

She decided to turn around and wait a safe distance away for another resident of the community to open the gate. Finally, a car activated the right blinker and she realized this was her chance to follow them into the secure neighborhood.

She didn't see any cars in the driveway, but that didn't necessarily mean anything because the house had a garage. A part of her recognized how odd showing up unannounced may seem, and she hesitated for a moment before parking her car in the cul-de-sac in front of the house.

The woman looked at the large house surrounded by trees and flowering plants. It was lush and alive, just like its owner. Those qualities were what made Silver so attractive to others, and recently she'd let that part of her shine through again. She'd worked out what she would say to them when she arrived. It had all made sense, but now that she was here, she began to question her plan.

She grumbled that the cause of her confusion was the damn dull ache that was her constant companion these days. She refused to acknowledge that the lesions were back.

Pressing the doorbell, she waited patiently for Silver to answer. Rubbing her temples, she shifted the weight to her other foot and her irritation increased at having to wait so long. It didn't make sense that Silver wouldn't answer the door, unless the unthinkable was already occurring. She imagined them tearing each other's clothes off and acting like animals in heat. The panic manifested itself in her quickened heartbeat and the increased pounding in her head.

Musical laughter finally made its way into her consciousness and drove away the nightmare playing in her head. She realized the two women were in the backyard, and this added another layer of complication. She almost decided to turn back around and wait for another day, but she was already here and there was no time like the present.

Walking toward the laughter, she rehearsed what she was going to say.

†

Silver was facing the driveway when a strange woman crossed the grassy area adjacent to her back patio. The woman was smiling, and Silver wasn't sure why she felt a shiver travel up her spine, but there was something off about this person.

"Um, can I help you? Are you lost or something?" Silver asked.

Jasmine turned in the direction of the stranger. "Pauline?"

"Hello, Jasmine. I'm sure you don't remember me, Silver, but I met you about five years ago at the Lesbian

Literary Society conference. I'm a big fan. I saw Jasmine there too, but I didn't know her at the time because I didn't start working with her until recently." Pauline smiled.

"What are you doing here?" Jasmine asked.

The woman's presence was causing Silver increasing alarm at what she considered a violation of her private refuge. She didn't appreciate surprise visitors, especially those who traveled from thousands of miles away. It wasn't normal, and her thoughts traveled to the strange texts.

"I blame myself for all of this. I don't want Dara to feel cornered. She needs our help and compassion. You may not know this because you met Dara after her health challenges, but Dara and I went to nursing school together. She began getting headaches, and they found lesions on her brain. I noticed the personality change and encouraged her to seek medical care. I thought the neurosurgeon got them all, but apparently, they've come back. I think Dara is your stalker. She's on her way here, and I want to help. Please don't call the police. I think I can honestly convince her to get help again. It's not her fault—she doesn't know what she's doing. The lesions are causing the obsession. If you care about her, you won't have her arrested and you'll let me handle this," Pauline explained.

"Are you two involved?" Jasmine asked.

"Yes. I'm sorry, Jasmine. I know I should have told you, but I didn't want to hurt you. We reconnected as lovers after you broke up this last time. I honestly thought that since you were exploring things with Silver, you wouldn't mind," Pauline admitted.

"I don't. I never knew you were a nurse. I thought you always worked with volunteers," Jasmine said.

"I got tired of the bullshit and politics in nursing management. Dara was always much better at that than I was," Pauline responded.

Silver narrowed her eyes at Pauline. Something wasn't ringing true about her story. Her eyes were cold and the smile seemed forced.

"Why don't we go inside and we can talk more about what we should do. Jasmine, do you think Dara is dangerous?" Silver asked.

Jasmine shook her head. "I just can't see Dara getting violent. She can be verbally forceful and doesn't give up easily when she wants something, but I've never seen her become physical."

Silver wasn't sure she shouldn't call the police, but her manners kicked in and she gestured for Pauline to enter her home. "Pauline, that's your name, right? I'm sorry, I am horrible at remembering names. Would you like to come inside? Can I offer you something to drink?"

"Thank you. I appreciate your hospitality. Can I please use your restroom? I drove straight from the airport. I wasn't sure when Dara was due to arrive." Pauline pushed the strap of her bag back up on her shoulder and followed Silver into the house.

"Of course." Silver gestured to her right. "There's a washroom through that door leading to the mudroom, and then on your right is the bathroom."

After Pauline left the combined kitchen and living room area, Silver whispered, "Don't you think this is strange? I think we should call the police. Something seems off to me. How well do you know Pauline?"

"Well apparently not that well, considering I didn't know she was a nurse or that she was sleeping with Dara. She's always been very nice to me—almost protective. At one point, I thought she was coming on to me, but I just ignored her flirtations. After I moved to human resources, I suppose they got more blatant, but I always found a way to politely decline her invitations. I would use the excuse that I was still trying to recover from a failed relationship. Even though everyone knew about Dara and me, I never actually used her name."

Silver heard the door to the bathroom open and ceased her conversation.

Pauline emerged from the mudroom clutching her bag as she held it securely against her hip.

"Why don't we sit down in the living room and figure out where to go from here. I'd offer you some wine, but I think it best if we all remain clear-headed. How about some coffee or tea?" Silver offered.

"I'd love some tea," Pauline answered. "If you don't mind, can I have a few moments to talk with Jasmine alone? There are a few very sensitive things I'd like to talk with her about, especially since I've already violated some of Dara's privacy. I'd like to protect some of the rest of the story."

"Um, I don't know. I think that if this concerns the both of us, I'm entitled to all of the information you plan to share," Silver responded.

"Some of it is very private and not at all related to you. Please, there are some things I need to say to Jasmine," Pauline insisted.

"It's okay, Silver, I want to hear what Pauline has to say," Jasmine interjected. "Remember, we can both take care of ourselves because neither one of us need fixing." She winked.

"Okay. I'll just be in my study," Silver agreed.

Everything in her whole being was screaming at her to not turn her back on this woman or leave her alone with Jasmine, but she didn't want to come across as controlling or overprotective and push Jasmine away, so she reluctantly retired to her study.

Closing the door behind her, she felt ridiculous pressing her ear against the hard wood. The study was around the corner. All she could hear were murmurs, and then it was quiet—too quiet. She strained her ears and thought she picked up a rustling outside of the office. *Screw it.* If Jasmine labeled her overprotective or controlling, so be it; her instincts screamed at her to act. She'd written this scene in her books on multiple occasions with different variations, but truth was stranger than fiction.

She flung open the office door and stood face-to-face with Pauline, who held a syringe in her right hand in the same manner that Norman Bates clutched his knife in *Psycho*. Before she had time to react, the sting of the needle pricked her neck. Wide-eyed, she swung at her attacker, striking her in the face but causing no visible damage.

"Where's Jasmine?" Silver slurred.

She felt her muscles relax, and an uncomfortable fog enveloped her before complete darkness hit.

†

Jasmine felt a soft tickle on her cheek. "Silver?"

"No, baby, it's me. Silver is tied up right now."

Jasmine forced her eyes open and stared into Pauline's stormy-gray eyes. She tried to force the cobwebs out of her head. Something was wrong—terribly wrong. Pauline just called her baby. *What the hell?* As her brain started firing again, her first thought was Silver. Was Silver all right?

"Silver," Jasmine croaked. "Please don't hurt Silver."

"She's not the one for you, sweet baby; I am. I've loved you since that day I saw you at the convention. I'll admit Silver is a looker and a damn good writer. I wasn't lying when I said I was a fan. I know she'll understand about soulmates. I'll explain it to her, and then no one will get hurt. You'll see that we're meant for each other. I've been waiting patiently for five years to make my move. Dara and I go way back. It was only a matter of time before she screwed up again and you left her for good. Silver shouldn't have been able to sweep right in and take you away from me. I was willing to let her be your rebound, but then I just couldn't let her touch you like that. It wasn't right. Don't you see?"

Jasmine glanced around and noticed she was in Silver's guest bedroom. She had to find out what Pauline had done to Silver. "Pauline, Silver does understand romance. She is a lesbian romance writer, after all. I know you don't want to hurt her."

"Of course not. See, I knew you would understand. I did have to take a few precautions though. I tied her up, just in case she didn't understand our love for each other. She hasn't woken up yet; I gave her a bigger dose. When she wakes up, we'll both explain it to her. You can let her down gently, and then we can go anywhere you want to for vacation. Okay?" Pauline smiled brightly.

Jasmine gingerly pushed herself to a sitting position.

Ding-dong sounded through the house.

When the doorbell rang, she wasn't sure if that was a good or bad thing.

Pauline frowned. "It's late, why would anyone be visiting this late?"

Jasmine didn't want anyone else drawn into the danger and quickly answered, "It's probably Sally, Silver's petsitter. She wanted to come by and meet me tonight."

"Why not wait until tomorrow? It's late," Pauline stated.

Jasmine had no idea where the lies that flowed from her mouth came from. "Um, I think she was planning to go camping for the long weekend and wasn't going to be available."

Pauline nodded. "You need to shake off the effects of the drug and get rid of her." Her eyes narrowed and the friendly coworker no longer existed. A very dangerous woman had just taken her place.

Ding-dong ding-dong.

"Hurry up. I'll be listening at the top of the stairs. Don't let that doorbell ring again. It hurts my head." Pauline pinched the bridge of her nose.

Jasmine scrambled down the stairs, and when she opened the door, she thought that maybe she'd fallen into the *Twilight Zone*.

"Dara?" She slapped her hand over her mouth, realizing Pauline could hear her.

"I swear I'm not trying to stalk you or cause you any grief. I'll admit I entertained the idea of having a talk with Silver because I wanted you back so badly, but it's Pauline—"

Jasmine shook her head vigorously and placed her finger over her lips.

"Well looky here. I guess the gang's all here now. Dara, you should have kept out of this. I told you there wasn't a snowball's chance in hell that Jasmine would take you back. I just didn't tell you why. We're together now."

Dara cautiously took a step inside. "I can see that now. Where's Silver, Pauline?"

"She's a little tied up right now." Pauline grinned.

"Pauline, remember back in college when you got those really bad headaches? It wasn't your fault then, and it's not your fault now. Let me help you. Are you in pain right now?"

"I'll manage. I don't want them cutting me open again, Dara. They shaved my head. I had to wear a wig for months."

"I'll be there for you again, Pauline. I promise. Why didn't you tell me why you lost your last job? Let me help you. We can fix this and you can go back to nursing. You were always an amazing nursing leader. The nurses adored you. I'll find you a position as soon as you're back on your feet again. Please, Pauline."

"I don't need your help, Dara. You left me when you met Jasmine. I can see why now and I forgive you, but Jasmine doesn't care if I'm a big-shot CNO or just the volunteer director, do you, Jasmine? She's not shallow like you are."

"Oh Pauline, I'll always care about you. You were my first love. I'm so sorry I hurt you. Please, Pauline, I know you must realize those damn lesions are doing it again. I know there's some amount of lucidity left," Dara pleaded.

"Stop it. Please stop it." Pauline held her head. "You're just trying to confuse me."

Jasmine watched the scene unfold in horror as Dara tried to wrap Pauline in her arms.

Pauline lifted the syringe in her hand and viciously plunged it into Dara's neck.

Jasmine screamed as Dara stumbled and then sat heavily on the stairs trying to maintain her consciousness. The war was lost as she slumped against them.

"I can get rid of her and she'll never bother you again," Pauline offered mechanically.

"No," Jasmine shouted.

"Okay. Whatever you want, my sweet. Don't worry. She shouldn't stay asleep too long. I didn't even give her as much as Silver. I didn't have a lot left over. Knowing where the major veins are is a plus. You know it takes several minutes when you inject into a muscle versus the vein." Pauline cocked her head. "How long will it take you to get ready?"

"I'd like to take a shower, please. I still feel a little off kilter and I think it might help."

Jasmine was hoping this would give her some much-needed time to think of something, and maybe by then Dara and Silver would wake up, and three against one was much better odds. She didn't want to harm Pauline, but they needed to subdue her and get her medical assistance.

†

It was pitch black in the room when Silver pried her eyes open and felt the ropes digging into her wrists. Everything clicked into place. It was never about Silver—it was always about Jasmine. The stalker was after Jasmine, and Silver's arrogance had put her in danger. *Jasmine*. She needed to get out of these restraints and help her. It was all crystal clear to her now. She loved Jasmine and wanted to share her life with this remarkable woman.

Silver concentrated on the sounds in her home. She could hear voices down the hall in her guest bath. That gave her hope. She didn't think Pauline would harm Jasmine, but she couldn't be sure. The woman clearly danced on the edges of sanity.

Tugging on the ropes, she tried to ascertain how tightly Pauline had tied her to the bedposts.

Socrates jumped on the bed and started biting on the rope and playing with the fringes.

"Good boy, Socrates. Help Mommy get free and there is a big treat for you," Silver whispered.

Socrates kept gnawing at the rope and Silver glanced over to see it had weakened. She tugged hard and the rough material tore into her skin, but she didn't care because she could almost feel how close she was to freeing her left hand. Another quick pull and the rope snapped, startling Socrates, who jumped in the air and scrambled away from the bed.

Leaning over and working her fingers through the thick twine was awkward. Finally, she'd freed both hands and worked feverishly to untie her legs. Her head was pounding, making it difficult for her to think clearly. Her mouth felt like she'd swallowed a box of cotton balls.

Silver tiptoed out of the guest bedroom and carefully made her way to the master suite. When she looked down the stairs, she noticed a body slumped at the bottom. She crept down and nearly gasped when she realized Dara was lying there unconscious, and her panic rose quickly.

She pressed her fingers against Dara's neck and breathed a sigh of relief that the woman was still alive. Even though she'd only met Dara once, she remembered her. Jasmine was unforgettable when they'd first met at the conference, and Silver had noted the woman who seemed glued to Jasmine's side for the entire event.

Silver would deal with Dara later. She looked around for something, anything she could use to subdue Pauline without hurting her too much. She suspected the story Pauline had provided about Dara having lesions was very familiar to Pauline because she'd been down that road with her own health and she knew all the signs and symptoms. People were predictable and incorporated knowledge of events they were familiar with, rather than inventing something completely out of the realm of their personal experience. *Where's the convenient baseball bat when you need one?* That scenario only worked in the movies though. Real life had real problems. She couldn't find anything handy to use. She could creep into her kitchen and grab a knife, but she was afraid of doing irreparable damage with a weapon that could kill.

Silver remembered the heavy Tiffany lamp with the metal base in the guest room. That would have to do. She carefully made her way back up the stairs and quickly unplugged the lamp, removed the dragonfly stained-glass shade, and lifted the heavy brass lamp, wielding it as a club.

Carefully she soundlessly eased into the hallway and walked softly to the guest suite. She listened at the door as Jasmine pleaded with Pauline.

"I'll go with you, but only if you promise to let me call the police and an ambulance to make sure Dara and Silver are okay."

"Why would you care so much about those two? Hasn't Dara hurt you enough? Silver will eventually hurt you as much as Dara. She'll never get over her dead wife. You'll always play second fiddle to her."

Silver experienced such an acute rage that this woman would create doubts about her feelings for Jasmine that she rushed into the bedroom and swung without thinking. Silver made a solid connection with Pauline's shoulder, causing her to stumble and reach for Jasmine, pulling her down as she crashed to the floor.

Jasmine flailed about on the ground and began to kick as she pushed Pauline away. One of her fists connected with Pauline's head.

Pauline grabbed her head and screamed, "Make it stop, make it stop." She curled into a ball.

Silver felt a wave of pity for the woman in the fetal position who was obviously in pain, and her anger quickly dissipated.

"We're going to get you help, Pauline. Just hang on." Silver held the lamp tightly, just in case Pauline was putting on an act so they'd let their guard down.

Jasmine scrambled away from Pauline. "I'll make the call," she said.

†

One paramedic shined a light into Jasmine's eyes while the other started his assessment of Dara, who was still unconscious at the bottom of the stairs.

Jasmine insisted she was fine and didn't need medical attention. She wanted them to concentrate on Silver and Dara. "I've been awake longer than Silver." She pointed at Silver, who was hanging on to the bannister, looking unsteady on her feet. "Can you please check her out? I wasn't given as strong a dose as she was, and can't you see how unstable she is?"

Dara was slow to revive, but finally blinked and opened her eyes. The medic wrapped a blood pressure cuff around Dara's arm, pressed the pump, and then released the valve slowly. "One hundred over sixty. Is your blood pressure usually this low, ma'am?" the medic asked. He began shining the light in her eyes while simultaneously checking her pulse.

Dara nodded. "I think I'll be fine. Nothing a good night's rest won't cure," she croaked.

"Do you think we can go into the living room and have these nice young men check us out there? I wouldn't mind sitting down," Silver suggested.

Silver, Dara, and Jasmine gathered in the living room with the assistance of the two paramedics who had remained to assess their medical conditions. An earlier pair of paramedics had sedated Pauline before transporting her to the hospital. When Jasmine had first dialed 9-1-1, one ambulance pulled in quickly with another aide car following shortly thereafter. Jasmine was thankful that two separate emergency vehicles had arrived after she'd told the dispatcher there were multiple victims.

The paramedic continued his assessment of Dara while his partner began working on Silver.

"Your vitals seem stable, ma'am," the medic reported to Silver.

"I'm sorry. I'm so sorry. I didn't want any of this to

happen," Dara insisted.

"This isn't your fault, Dara, but you should have called the police if you suspected Pauline was about ready to break. Do you think another surgery will help her?" Jasmine asked.

"I hope so, Jasmine. She was a different person when we first met, and then our relationship became a challenge. Her mood swings were hard to deal with…so I left. I didn't know about her condition until later, and by then I'd met you. She had her surgery and I was there for her during her recovery. Remember when I was gone for a month and we had that big fight because I wouldn't tell you where I had been? I didn't think you'd appreciate me spending time with my old girlfriend, but I owed her that much."

"Where will they take Pauline?" Dara asked.

"The main hospital is about half an hour away," Silver said.

"Well, if none of the rest of you plan on going to the hospital to get checked out, we'll get out of your hair," one of the medics said.

Both medics collected their bags and let themselves out.

Jasmine was thankful they had gone. She could sense their discomfort as they began to discuss what had happened.

"Will you stay with her and help her through another surgery if that's what she needs?" Jasmine asked.

"I will. She's a good person, and she used to be an excellent nurse. I just learned they let her go from her last job for diverting medication. I didn't know. I honestly thought she was burned out and wanted to try something new. That's why I hired her for the volunteer role. I came as soon as I put all the pieces together. Can you recommend a good hotel?" Dara asked.

Silver glanced over at her before answering. "Umm,

there's no need for you to get a hotel. I have a perfectly good guest room. Look, Dara, I know this is all very awkward for everyone, but I wouldn't feel right about sending you off to a hotel. However, that doesn't mean I don't have some rules...."

"I can guess. You and I are competing for the same woman—"

"No, we aren't competing here, because Jasmine isn't some trophy we can win in a game of love. I'm not playing for Jasmine's affections. I'm offering my love freely without strings or expectations. Jasmine is the only one who gets to decide what's right for her.

"My rules are simple, really. Jasmine doesn't need me to protect her, yet I won't be party to anything I believe is disrespectful, controlling, manipulative, or hurtful. If Jasmine wants to talk with you privately or has any other wishes regarding how this all will unfold, that is completely up to her, but if she says no, then you have to respect that. I abhor bullying and have no tolerance for it. I can handle awkward, if it won't ruin Jasmine's vacation."

"Thanks, that's very generous of you. Jasmine?"

"I don't know. Silver, can we talk about this privately? I don't want to be unkind, but honestly it could get extremely uncomfortable and I'm not sure I'm okay with that." Jasmine cringed. "God, I can't believe I'm telling you who you can and can't invite into your home. I take it all back. I can make things work."

"I'll get a hotel. I suppose this will go down in history as the very first selfless decision I'll ever make. Maybe there's hope for me yet. I'm going to back off, but if you two don't work out, I'm going to make another play...um...I mean I'll still be around in case you want to give us another shot." Dara shrugged. "You can't expect a leopard to change all her spots immediately." She stood up and wobbled a bit.

"Look, we're all adults here. I really think you should rest a bit in the guest bedroom before you get in a car and drive to the hospital. I don't want an accident on my conscience. They probably have to do a mental health evaluation on Pauline, so I suspect it will take a bit of time. Come on, I'll show you to your room, but don't make me regret my generosity," Silver warned.

"Do you need any help? You were a bit shaky earlier. Maybe I should show her to the guest bedroom," Jasmine offered.

"That's okay, I feel fine. You stay here and I'll be right back, or if you'd rather head to the bedroom right now, I'll meet you there. I think we could all benefit from a good night's sleep. Things will be clearer in the morning," Silver stated.

"I'll follow you both upstairs. I think turning in for the night is a grand idea," Jasmine agreed.

†

Silver wanted to despise Dara, but she was having a hard time matching her obvious compassion toward Pauline with the cheating, shallow woman who'd treated Jasmine so poorly.

Yes, she still didn't deserve Jasmine, but there was a good person deep inside the image she presented to most everyone. Silver worried that Jasmine recognized that side of Dara and might think repairing their broken relationship was worth a try. She hadn't given any indication of that, but they were still so new and Silver suddenly felt extremely vulnerable. The one bright spot was Jasmine's discomfort over Dara staying at the house.

After she'd settled Dara into the guest bedroom, providing her a towel and a new toothbrush, she took a deep breath and walked into the bedroom. She needed to determine if anything had changed between Jasmine and her in light of the events and revelations of the evening.

Silver heard the water running in the master bath and noticed Jasmine's bag was open. She decided to join Jasmine, who was probably brushing her teeth. Her mouth felt dry and she wanted to root out the stale, metallic aftertaste that remained from the drug Pauline had used.

As she entered the bath, she marveled at how normal and domestic it felt to watch Jasmine spit out her toothpaste as she leaned over the sink. She shuffled over to the other sink and silently opened the drawer to retrieve her tube of toothpaste.

Jasmine shot her a weak smile, and Silver proceeded to squeeze a ribbon of paste onto her electric toothbrush.

Jasmine ran her fingers through her own hair and squeezed Silver's arm as she brushed past her on her way back into the bedroom.

The master bath wasn't particularly small, but she suspected Jasmine might feel uncomfortable hanging out in the bathroom waiting for Silver to complete her nightly ritual. Silver didn't mind; it was oddly reminiscent of when Naomi and she would get ready for bed and often brush together, but maybe this was foreign to Jasmine.

After Silver finished brushing her teeth, she quickly washed her face, removing her makeup and rubbing in some nighttime Oil of Olay. When she entered the bedroom, Jasmine was already nestled under the sheets but propped up against the headboard. Sinbad, Plato, and Freud, her three older cats, had curled themselves at the foot of the bed. Silver suspected she wanted to talk, and for a minute panic set in as she wondered where the discussion might lead.

"Stop looking like you're ready to enter the gallows. You're scaring me," Jasmine declared. "What is it you think

I'm about to tell you?"

"I can see why you were with Dara. She's not what I expected. Are you sure it's over between the two of you?"

"Oh I see. That's why you look like you just lost your best friend." Jasmine patted the bed. "Come here. Apparently I haven't done a good enough job of letting you know how I feel."

Silver crossed the room, pulled back the covers, and crawled into bed. "I'm feeling a little vulnerable right about now," she admitted.

"Oh, hell, I might as well just come right out and tell you that I'm sure I'm falling in love with you. I've probably been slowly heading in that direction for the last five years. Of course, I never would have admitted that or acted on my feelings if Naomi was still alive or you weren't ready. I need to know you are ready, really ready to move on, because at this point nothing is holding me back from loving you," Jasmine confessed.

"God, we are a pair. I'm ready, really ready. I'm falling for you too. I'm sorry I can't say that I've been falling for the last five years, but I think I can honestly say I've been falling for the last six months. I've been allowing myself to feel again and didn't realize that until the first weekend you visited. Maybe at the time I put that contest out on my Facebook page it was a stupid idea, but now I can honestly admit your review was easily the best review I've ever received. It brought you to me."

Socrates and Artemis were doing their nightly racetrack impersonation by chasing one another around the bedroom and across the bed.

Jasmine started giggling. "Do your kittens do this often?"

"Every single night, and I hope you're prepared for their activity in about…." Silver reached over and pressed the button on her tablet to note the time. "Oh, I'd say four hours. Four thirty is their favorite time to rouse their mama. I think I've spoiled them because I'll wake up, play with them, and then start writing. They think that's a normal time to wake up. Socrates likes to inch his way up the bed in the middle of the night until his paw is touching my face or neck. He has a loud purr, and he'll butt his little head against me until I wake up and pet him. He's a spoiled little bugger, but so loveable that he's hard to resist. Are you sure you still want to explore a future with me and my five cats?"

"Are you kidding? I'll believe I've reached the Promised Land when they start cuddling with me in the middle of the night. I'd love Socrates to wake me up. I promise I'll pet him every time if he starts snuggling against me," Jasmine enthused.

"Should I be getting jealous, or will I get the same treatment? Can I wake you up in the middle of the night and you'll pet me?" Silver teased.

"Um, I think we need to make it past first base before we talk about waking each other up in the middle of the night for creative calisthenics."

"I'm using that terminology in my next book. *Creative calisthenics* is another word for sex, right?" Silver asked.

Jasmine blushed. "Yes, it is. My grandma had a strange way of describing just about everything related to sex or women's body parts. She used to tease that my breasts were future milk dispensers. I tried to tell her that since I wasn't planning to pop out any kids, they were likely intended for someone else, but she wasn't listening."

"As much as I would really like to explore that other use, I think the effects of the drugs and the fact your ex is across the hall are having an impact on any grand plans that are suddenly making an appearance in my head. All this talk about breasts and petting is giving me ideas, but I want our first time to be perfect. I just feel like tonight is not that night. Do you mind if we just get a good night's rest so we're prepared to unravel our suddenly complicated relationship tomorrow?"

"Not at all." Jasmine scooted down in the bed and turned toward Silver.

Silver stretched her left arm to click off the light and rolled over to face Jasmine. She reached over and pulled Jasmine into an embrace as she kissed her tenderly. Silver resisted the urge to deepen the kiss, and Jasmine seemed to accept the tempered gesture of affection.

"Good night, Jasmine."

Jasmine laid her head on Silver's chest and settled into a comfortable position with Silver lying on her back and her arm draped protectively across Jasmine. "Good night, Silver."

Silver lay awake for several minutes as she listened for the even cadence of Jasmine's breathing. Socrates jumped up on the bed and was inching his way to a spot right between the two women. He settled on Silver's chest with his head tucked underneath Jasmine's chin. The last thing Silver heard was a contented sigh from Jasmine before her eyes closed and she entered her own dreamland.

Chapter Twenty-two

Jasmine opened her eyes and felt the warmth of Silver's arms as they wrapped around her center. She fit perfectly spooned against Silver as her body molded tightly to her lover. She rolled the word *lover* around in her mouth as if it were a delectable piece of chocolate. They hadn't actually made love yet, but their connection was as intimate, maybe more so than her relationship with Dara. Everything felt right. It was only a matter of time before they'd take the next step and share their physical love for one another.

Jasmine didn't want to disturb this perfect moment, but she was anxious to start the day and make some decisions about what to do regarding Pauline and Dara. She hoped Silver would agree with her and not press charges against Pauline. If what Dara had said last night was accurate, Pauline needed support and love, not the harshness of the criminal justice system. Her medical condition was certainly grave, and Jasmine hoped another surgery would give her a fighting chance at turning things around in her life.

Silver's hand stroked her stomach and she turned to face her. "Good morning. Are you ready for the craziness of the day to descend upon us?" Jasmine asked.

Silver chuckled. "I sure know how to show a girl a good time, huh? How do you feel this morning? Do you have any lasting aftereffects from the drugs?"

Jasmine stretched and blinked twice. "Actually, I feel pretty darn good for an almost-kidnap victim. You must have a magical antidote in your fingertips."

"You haven't seen anything yet—wait until I show you all my moves."

"Is that a promise?"

"Sure is, one you can take to the bank," Silver vowed.

"How are you feeling this morning? You got a much stronger dose than I did."

"I feel fine. I think the ten hours plus of sleep did both of us a world of good," Silver responded.

"As much as I would like to remain in bed and collect on that promise, I'll bet Dara is anxious to go to the hospital and see how Pauline is doing. If I know Dara, she's already done research on the top hospitals to have neurosurgery."

Silver pressed her lips to Jasmine's. "All right, but after we get everything settled, I'd like to take you to dinner and try to turn this vacation into something you'll remember for the right reasons."

"That sounds wonderful, but just being here with you is enough for me. We could hang out in rocking chairs and watch the sunrise and sunset, not leaving the house for the next two weeks, and I'd be overjoyed."

"Come on, lazybones. Last one to the bathroom is a rotten turnip," Silver joked.

"I think the saying is 'rotten egg.'"

Silver jumped from the bed. "I'm a writer, we always take poetic license. 'Turnip' sounds more original, don't you think?"

Jasmine scrambled out of bed and gently pushed

Silver aside on her way to the bathroom, giggling along the way.

"Cheater," Silver called out.

†

"Oomf," Dara cried out as a small, gray kitten pounced on her stomach and quickly scrambled off the bed. Shortly after, two rambunctious kittens ran across the foot of the bed several times. She'd opened her eyes and found a large, orange tabby curled up next to her purring. She'd leaned over and petted his head. She assumed it was a male tomcat because of his size. He was the biggest cat she'd ever seen.

"Well hello, big boy, aren't you a handsome fellow."

Dara yawned and glanced over at her watch sitting on the dresser. It was already nine, so she decided to take a quick shower while she waited for Jasmine and Silver to awaken.

She made her way down the stairs clutching her smartphone in one hand. She'd do some research into places for Pauline to get the best care for what she knew would be another surgery.

As she sat on the couch, she began to ponder her current situation. She had to admit it was obvious there was a connection between the two. She didn't want to give up on Jasmine, but the reality she might never get that second chance was hitting her full in the face. It felt like a shock of cold water. She didn't understand how quickly it happened, but she was sure they were in love with one another. Jasmine looked at Silver in a way she'd never looked at Dara. It severely bruised her ego, but Dara needed to analyze how she was really feeling. Was it simply a blow to her confidence, or did she truly love Jasmine enough to fight for her?

Dara sighed. She supposed if she really loved Jasmine, she would wish her happiness and not try to cajole her back into an unhealthy relationship. That was a sobering thought for Dara. She realized she'd not been the best partner, and the most loving thing she could do at this point was let Jasmine go. Jasmine was without a doubt the most beautiful woman she'd ever laid eyes on, and that had been the primary reason she hadn't let go. If she were honest with herself, they weren't as compatible as what she'd had with Pauline before she got sick. Dara suddenly felt uncomfortable taking a deep dive into her motives. What she'd become wasn't pretty. Perhaps this messy situation would lead her on her own path of growth.

Dara accessed the Internet and began researching neurosurgeons. She was happy to learn the University of Kansas was in the top twenty. Barnes-Jewish Hospital in St. Louis ranked higher and that wasn't very far away, so that was also a possibility.

She heard footsteps on the stairwell and looked up to see a smiling Jasmine and Silver. The fact that their hands were linked didn't bypass Dara's inspection. When they rounded the corner and Dara caught Jasmine's eye, they quickly broke apart.

"Good morning, Dara. I didn't realize you were up already," Silver noted.

"I woke up about an hour ago. I didn't want to disturb the two of you. I've been doing some research on neurosurgeons, and I think we should arrange to have her transferred back to Kansas or Missouri. No offense, but I didn't find any Washington hospitals in the top twenty and I'd be able to care for her better closer to home anyway. The sooner we are out of your hair, the better."

"How will you arrange for a transport?" Jasmine

asked.

"Probably the best thing to do is to coordinate with AeroCare. The closest airport they serve is Arizona and it could get expensive, but I think that would be the best option. I don't think I should try to take her back myself. She's too unpredictable at this point. I have some connections at both hospitals and the transport service. I'll make the calls after I try to talk with Pauline. I'll see if I can take advantage of any window of opportunity when she's lucid enough to make a decision. Her parents aren't alive anymore, but she has a sister I can call," Dara explained.

"We can get some breakfast on the way, then we'll drive to the hospital and you can follow us," Silver offered.

"Thanks. Under the circumstances, I'm not sure I'd be as gracious as you've been," Dara admitted.

"We're all human works in progress. I think you might be on the right path now," Silver said.

Dara smiled. She felt good about her progress. She'd taken the first honest step in looking closely at herself and her motives. Maybe it wasn't too late to evolve into a real human being who didn't first think about *what's in it for me?*

†

Pauline woke up in a panic as she looked around at her unfamiliar surroundings. Her terror increased when she realized she was in some kind of restraint. She tried to recall the events of the night before, but everything was foggy. The monitor to her right started beeping, and thirty seconds later, a young woman entered the room.

"It's okay. You're at Kittitas Valley Healthcare. The restraints are for your own protection. I can give you another dose of medication to calm you," the young woman soothed. "My name is Shelby and I'll be your nurse for today."

"No, I don't want to be sedated, please," she croaked.

Pauline desperately wanted to grab her head. The pain began to envelope her again and she wasn't able to find relief by massaging her temples.

"All right, Ms. Thompson. Is there anything I can get you while we wait for the doctor to make his rounds?"

Pauline groaned. "My head is killing me."

"I'll be right back. I need to check with the doctor to see if I can give you any pain medication for some relief."

As the young nurse walked out of the room and pushed the curtain aside, Dara strode through the door, followed by Silver and Jasmine.

"Dara? What's going on? I can't think clearly. I think someone drugged me," Pauline declared.

Dara approached the bed and took Pauline's hand in hers. "Pauline, we need to get you some help. I believe your lesions are back. Please let me arrange for your transfer to Barnes-Jewish Hospital. I've talked with your sister, and she's agreed that is the best option. I'll be there with you for every step of your recovery. I promise I'm not going anywhere this time. Let me help you."

"I don't believe you. Why am I here and restrained?" she asked, the panic rising again.

"It's not your fault, Pauline, but the lesions have affected your reasoning and you acted on some delusions. You drugged all of us. Please let me help you," Dara pleaded.

Pauline looked into the eyes of her friend, and the events of the previous night flooded back in bits and pieces. "What does Emily say about all of this?"

"Your sister has already talked with the doctor and given her consent to transfer and treatment in the event that you weren't able to make that decision on your own. Silver and Jasmine have agreed not to press charges, but only if you permit us to make the arrangements for surgery."

Pauline sighed. "You'll stay with me?"

"I've already contacted Carla to start the paperwork to take a personal leave of absence." Dara pushed the hair from Pauline's forehead and stroked her cheek.

Pauline grimaced as pain shot through her head. A tear leaked out. "It hurts."

Dara turned and acknowledged the young woman who bustled into the room.

"I hope you have something for the pain," Dara barked.

"The doctor ordered a cocktail of Dilaudid and morphine. I've got it right here. We don't usually give this for migraines, but the lesions are very large and the doctor suspects her pain is much greater than a patient with a typical migraine."

The nurse pushed the medication into the IV line. "That should help in a few minutes. The doctor should be along shortly to talk with you about her treatment. Her sister has already been in contact with us, and she mentioned that a Dara would arrange for transport to Barnes-Jewish Hospital in St. Louis."

"That's the plan, and I'm Dara."

The nurse nodded and walked out of the room.

Chapter Twenty-three

Silver looked across the table as the soft candlelight framed Jasmine's face, showing off her extraordinary beauty. The craziness of the last twelve hours hadn't affected how much she longed to take Jasmine in her arms and explore every inch of her body.

Jasmine smiled at her as she brought the wine to her lips and took a sip,

"I'm glad Dara decided to stay at a hotel while waiting for the transport tomorrow. I'm looking forward to spending the evening with you, without the drama," Jasmine revealed.

"So…now that I have you all to myself, I hope a quiet evening back at home will be enough to keep you entertained."

"Honestly, all I really need is to spend time with you. We could order out every night and snuggle on the couch for the rest of the time and I'd be perfectly content. I would like to read what you've written so far on your next novel. I kinda like being a beta reader."

"The first draft is almost done. I'm a little nervous about it," Silver hedged.

The waitress approached the table. “Would either of you care for dessert?”

Jasmine leaned back in her chair and patted her stomach. “Oh God, not for me, I’m totally stuffed. It was wonderful. Don’t let me stop you from enjoying a tasty treat,” she said. “I’ll bet they have some decadent chocolate delight for you.”

“We do. We have a triple chocolate torte that is to die for. Shall I bring that to the table? I’ll bring two forks, just in case.”

“Sold. I’ll never pass up the chance to stuff myself with chocolate. It’s the reason I didn’t finish my meal. It was spectacular, but I didn’t want to waste my valuable stomach space on the mashed potatoes when dessert was just around the corner,” Silver answered.

The waitress picked up their plates and hurried off to serve another couple.

“That reminds me. Preston and Bruce want to get together while I’m in town. He swears he’s a culinary specialist. I’m embarrassed to admit that he may be my only true friend and I’ve talked to him over the last couple of weeks almost as much as my calls with you. I suppose if I move here, that would be an added bonus—a built-in friend I can share all my deep, dark secrets with, besides you of course.”

“Okaaay, but can we have a few days to ourselves, before we entertain the tornado of energy?”

Jasmine laughed. “He is rather effervescent, but I think he has a really good heart and I like him.”

“I’m sure if you like him, I will as well. I get the feeling I might connect with his boyfriend—Bruce, right?—a bit better. He seems like the strong, silent type.”

“Yes, it’s Bruce, and you’re right, he does seem to ground Preston. I usually only hear him chastising Preston in the background when we talk."

The waitress smiled when she brought Silver a gooey, rectangular slice of decadent chocolate cake. The dessert oozed creamy goodness, and Silver couldn't wait to dig in. She plunged her fork into the treat and held out a large bite in front of Jasmine. "Come on, I know you want a taste."

Jasmine chuckled and lunged at the forkful, wrapping her mouth around the rich chocolate. "Mmmm, that is definitely calorie-worthy. Honestly, that's all I want, the rest is all yours. I can taste the echo when I kiss you senseless after we head to your place."

Silver stuck the fork in her cake and broke off a new bite for herself. "Deal." She savored the bite and let out her own moan of delight. "Almost better than sex," she joked.

"Damn, now I have to compete with a piece of chocolate cake. I'm afraid the bar will be too high to reach."

"I don't believe it'll be out of your reach at all. No pressure, Jasmine, but I'm ready to take the next step."

"If it will get us back quicker, let me help you finish." Jasmine grabbed the other fork and separated a large piece.

"Oh now you want some of my cake."

"Indeed I do." Jasmine raised her hand and caught the waitress's attention. "Check, please."

"Hey, that's my line."

"Just finish your cake." Jasmine grinned.

†

Jasmine was anxious to get back to Silver's home because the sultry looks Silver kept giving her were driving her crazy. The drive back was only ten minutes, but every few seconds Silver would glance over at Jasmine and smile.

The minute Silver had put the car into gear, she'd grabbed ahold of Jasmine's hand, turned it over, and continued to stroke her palm the whole way home. Her own palm was one of her most favorite places, and Jasmine assumed it was a special erogenous zone for Silver as well.

Without saying a word, Silver led Jasmine into the house, up the stairs, and directly into her bedroom. It was too early to go to sleep, so Jasmine knew there was only one reason Silver had brought her to this room at just after seven thirty.

The kittens, Socrates and Artemis, started to follow the amorous couple into the bedroom until Silver warned, "No, babies, we need a little alone time. Mama will let you in a little later."

Silver closed the bedroom door quickly with her foot, and stereo meows penetrated the solid wood barrier for several minutes. Jasmine assumed they'd given up when silence prevailed.

Jasmine guessed the other three cats had curled up in the guest bedroom, and now they were all alone—just the two of them. Jasmine's palms began to sweat, and she was sure Silver could feel the moisture, but she hadn't mentioned anything yet. It was too late to declare her insecurities now, and she didn't want to slow things down anyway. She craved Silver's touch and wanted to feel Silver move beneath her. This was the point of no return.

For a brief moment, they stood awkwardly in the middle of the room until Silver seized Jasmine's lips and began to nibble on the fleshy lower part. Her tongue wandered out and found its way inside, taking a leisurely journey within Jasmine's receptive mouth.

Jasmine enveloped Silver in a warm embrace and their bodies moved as one, closer to the bed.

Silver's hand traveled to the interior of Jasmine's shirt and covered her breast in a light, teasing touch. Jasmine could feel the caress through the silky fabric of her bra, and it drove her crazy. She was anxious to feel skin on skin, but Silver didn't seem to be in any hurry.

Jasmine reached for the buttons on Silver's shirt and began undoing them as her hands roamed all over Silver's velvety skin. She could hardly contain her excitement as she uncovered Silver's beautiful body.

"God, you are beyond stunning," Silver whispered.

"I can't believe I'm about to make love with you, Silver. This is more than a fantasy come true for me. You're no longer some untouchable object of desire. The person behind the curtain is so much more. I was in lust with you from afar, but now that I've come to know the person under the beauty and beneath the beautiful words you write, I can't imagine my life without you in it." Jasmine allowed Silver to take her hand and lead her to the bed.

Silver pulled back the comforter and the cool cotton sheets, enticing Jasmine to crawl inside the bed and continue their tender ministrations.

Jasmine wasn't able to control her beating heart as it pounded quickly in her chest. Silver's hands traveled over her body, and she felt as though Silver was worshipping every inch. When the tips of her fingers brushed against the neatly trimmed hair of her pubis, Jasmine's breath hitched.

Jasmine parted her legs to let Silver penetrate that last barrier to intimacy, and she eagerly returned the favor. Both women found their way to each other's pleasure center, and their excitement soared.

"God, you're so wet and ready. I hope you're as close as I am because I'm not sure how much longer I can hold out," Jasmine expressed.

"I'm close, so close. Please don't stop," Silver uttered.

Jasmine continued to rub in small circles using the moisture from Silver's excitement as Silver continued to caress her sensitive bundle of nerves in return.

They moved together sensually as a wave of desire overtook their bodies and the simultaneous orgasms crested, creating a multitude of ripples. They shuddered in each other's embrace and let the pleasure flow over them.

Silver tenderly kissed Jasmine. "Thank you. I didn't think anyone would ever make me feel this good again. It's not just about the physical release, it's so much more. I've fallen in love with you, Jasmine. Despite my hesitation to ever fall in love again, you've managed to turn my whole world upside down."

"I don't have pretty words for you because I'm not a writer, so will *I love you* do?"

Silver chuckled. "It will."

"It's still early, I hope you weren't expecting to fall asleep just yet," Jasmine asserted.

"Of course not. I may be more mature, but I think I've still got a few tricks up my sleeve, and I'm not the least bit tired. On the contrary, I'm quite energized. Besides, I haven't tasted you yet, and I've been so looking forward to a second dessert."

"Can I just say *ditto*?"

"Absolutely. We'll both be keeping each other healthy," Silver added.

Jasmine quirked her eyebrow. "Care to expound on that?"

Silver chuckled. "I was reading this Facebook post the other day, and apparently someone conducted research and found that, um…I don't quite know how else to put this, so I'll just quote the article. Apparently, the most important meal to eat is a vagina, according to research done at the State University of New York. They went so far as to say it can save you from fatal conditions such as cancer or heart disease."

"Get out, you are pulling my leg," Jasmine stated

skeptically.

"Honest, I'm not making this up. There are hormones such as DHEA and Oxytocin that the body produces whenever cunnilingus occurs." Silver laughed.

"You need to weave that into your next book because, oh my God, that is hysterical."

"Done. The minute I read that, I knew I had to use it. I'm serious about protecting my girlfriend from cancer and heart disease. Now where were we?"

"About to engage in some healthy eating," Jasmine remarked.

Chapter Twenty-four

Silver tugged at her fitted shirt and wondered if she should change into something more comfortable. She didn't believe she needed to impress Preston or his boyfriend, Bruce, but she did want to look good for Jasmine. She wanted Jasmine to feel proud that she was her date for the evening.

They'd spent five glorious days mostly in the bedroom, and Preston kept leaving pointed messages until they finally relented and agreed to travel to his house in Bellevue. Silver didn't care for the city of Bellevue because there was a Microsoft executive around every corner and they tended to be a pretentious bunch. The area overflowed with money, but people there had little respect for employees in the service industry and that was a pet peeve of Silver's.

Silver felt Jasmine's arms wrap around her stomach as her lips descended on her neck. Silver adored it when Jasmine kissed the back of her neck. It always sent delicious shivers up and down her body.

"If you don't stop that teasing right now, we're not going to make it to Preston's, and then he'll start his nonstop barrage of text messages. I fully expect you to run interference for me. His exuberance is exhausting." Silver turned around and gave Jasmine a peck on the lips.

"I promise to keep Pretty Preston occupied while you spend time with Bruce. He's a good guy and so is Preston. He just has ten times more energy than Bruce does, but he means well. He's so excited for us, especially since he's been there from the very beginning of our blossoming love." Jasmine grinned.

"All right, let's go before I change my mind and come to my senses." Silver stroked Jasmine's face and kissed her again. Kissing Jasmine was something she thought she'd never tire of doing.

†

Jasmine supposed that either Preston was a remarkable speaker or Bruce had a lot of money. Preston told her Bruce was some kind of computer genius, but she hadn't put two and two together until Silver mentioned that Bellevue was the central location for Microsoft.

Silver's home was beautiful, but Preston's house was magnificent. Nearly every vantage point in the expansive home had unobstructed views of Lake Washington and the Seattle skyline. Their home was located on Meydenbauer Bay, and Preston and Bruce had their own private dock with the requisite powerboat resting peacefully in its stall. Jasmine could tell Silver was impressed.

Jasmine was looking out one of the windows at the imposing view with Silver holding her hand as Preston pranced up to them. "Isn't the view to die for? I do all right in my job, but Brucey here is my little sugar papa. I tell him all the time that I'm just a shallow gold-digger, but he doesn't mind."

Bruce walked up to the trio and handed Silver and Jasmine each a glass of wine. He pecked Preston on the cheek. "None for you, because you've already started your fibbing."

Preston laughed and pulled Bruce close and kissed him full on the mouth. "I'm just having a little fun, my adorable little dough boy."

"Don't believe a word he says. He makes every bit as much money as I do, and on occasion substantially more. I'm the one who snagged him for his money and silver tongue. He makes his living using his considerable charm, and I was a goner the minute I heard him speak."

"Oh yes, lover, I do have a silver tongue and I definitely know how to use it, don't I, big boy?"

Bruce shook his head. "You promised you were going to behave tonight."

Jasmine giggled.

Preston waved his hand in the air and turned toward the kitchen. "Fine, I need to get back to my masterpiece anyway." He grabbed an apron with the saying *Eat My Meat* in big block letters and grinned as he pointed to the words. "How do you like my apron, Jasmine? I have another one that says *Kiss the Chef* with an arrow pointing to my gloriously large—"

Bruce ran over, slapped his hand against Preston's mouth, and dragged him into another room.

Jasmine heard loud whispers, but couldn't make out what they were saying to each other. "I think my good friend Preston is getting his butt chewed out. Were you offended? I bet if I ask him to tone it down, he will."

"No, it's fine. He's slightly humorous, but don't ever tell him I said that," Silver admitted.

Bruce and Preston came back into the combination kitchen and living room and Preston had a serious look on his face. "I'm sorry. Bruce helped me understand that my raucous humor does not go over as well with lesbians as it does with our gay friends. You're the first lesbian couple I've entertained. I promise to be a little more cognizant of what I say to you in the future. You know I was only joking, right?"

"It's okay, it isn't like we've lived in an Amish community all our lives," Jasmine answered.

Preston smacked Bruce in the chest. "See, I was right. They aren't offended."

"Maybe not, but I'd really like to get to know these lovely women and not be sidetracked by your gay humor," Bruce insisted.

"Oh all right. Spoilsport. Well, if we can't take it down the dirty-innuendo road tonight, I want to know every little detail of the past three weeks. Don't leave a single thing out. I love hearing falling-in-love stories. You two look so adorable together I just want to pinch your cheeks and eat you right up. But if I did that, I wouldn't have room for the scrumptious meal we're about to have."

"That's the first honest thing he's said all night." Bruce laughed.

†

"So how awful was tonight?" Jasmine asked.

"Honestly, I like them both for different reasons, so it was fun. Preston does seem to have taken a shine to you almost as much as I have. I think he's just a little in love with you. If he was straight, I might be jealous."

"He is definitely not my type, and there is nothing about any of his equipment that interests me. Now if you ever want to borrow his apron, I would be more than happy to kiss the chef in the exact location the apron suggests."

"I like the sound of that. I'll have to ask him where I

can get one." Silver grabbed Jasmine's hand. "Come on, I think there is a king bed calling our name—time to kick the furbabies out again."

"They're going to hate me for taking their mommy away so much," Jasmine lamented.

"No they aren't. They're just happy there is another person to shower them with all the attention one mere mortal cannot possibly manage by herself."

"I like the sound of that."

Chapter Twenty-five

Silver stood in the middle of a crowd of rushing travelers and brushed the tears from Jasmine's eyes. The airport was now her least favorite place in the world. She didn't want to say good-bye again. They'd danced around the topic of how they planned to make their long-distance relationship work.

Silver wanted to beg Jasmine to quit her job and move in with her, but when Jasmine had found her staring in front of the glass door at her back patio and asked what she was thinking about, she'd answered honestly. No matter how hard she tried, she still thought about Naomi from time to time.

Silver could see the pain she'd caused with her honest admission. Damn, she'd wanted to quickly follow up with something, anything, to reassure Jasmine, but no words came to mind.

Later she'd wrapped Jasmine in her arms and insisted she loved her but was still wrestling with her feelings. She was sure about one thing and that was she wanted Jasmine in her life. She'd asked Jasmine to be patient with her and promised she'd work through everything in time.

Silver shook her head. Jasmine had said something and she missed it, thinking about the pain she'd caused a few days earlier. "I'm sorry, honey, what did you say?"

"I've got to go. They'll be starting to board the plane in a few minutes. I'll call you when I arrive in Kansas. I love you." Jasmine brushed her hand down Silver's face and offered a chaste one-second kiss. Her fingers continued to travel down Silver's arm until she squeezed her hand one last time before they separated for good.

"I love you too. Please don't forget that, or me, when you land in Kansas," Silver whispered.

Silver felt like a vise was squeezing her heart as Jasmine walked away. She knew a piece of herself was leaving with Jasmine, and she almost called her back to grovel before the women she loved. She wanted to tell her that she needed Jasmine by her side to help her work through her remaining issues with letting Naomi's ghost go, but instead she let her walk away.

†

Jasmine was sitting at her desk with her head propped up by her right hand as she stared into space. Although the other team members had resolved many of the day-to-day issues in her absence, they'd left her desk piled high with papers that required filing, positions that needed posting, and evaluations Carla had asked her to record in the database. Her Monday had started slow, and there was an eerie silence in the office. Pauline's office door remained closed, and no one had mentioned anything to Jasmine about how Pauline was doing. She'd called Dara, who informed her Pauline was recovering nicely, but probably wouldn't return for quite some time.

Everyone was walking on eggshells around Jasmine

and it was taking a toll on her. The staff had been polite saying hello and asking if she'd had a nice vacation, but the topic of Pauline was strictly off-limits.

It was already ten and the pile of papers was nearly as high as when she'd arrived at the office at seven thirty. She needed to stop thinking about Silver, because it certainly wasn't helping her productivity.

She thought about how she'd left Silver in the airport and wondered if the future she imagined was in the cards for her. She'd wanted to yell at Silver to ask her to move in, but she knew it was too soon and Silver was still thinking about Naomi. Even though she'd assured Silver that she understood, it hurt. It had caused her far more pain than she was willing to admit, and she suspected Silver had seen through her bravado.

The phone call on Sunday night felt stilted, and after a few minutes, she gave up and rushed the call, telling Silver she was exhausted and needed to head off to bed so she wouldn't fall asleep at her desk on Monday.

As if her day wasn't bad enough, Korrine barged into the office.

"I see you're back from vacation. There are a few postings on your desk that I hope you'll be able to get to today. I'm leaving to visit my sister in Washington tomorrow, so I'd like to review any applicants that come forward as soon as I return. Can you hold on to them for me?" Korrine asked.

Jasmine listened to Korrine's clipped tone and was thankful the powerful woman wasn't yelling at her like she had before. She wished she could return to Washington, and once again, thinking of Silver hijacked her attention.

"Well? Did you hear my request or not?" Korrine asked.

"Oh, I'm sorry. Yes, of course I'll collect all the

résumés for you and place them in a folder for you to look at when you return."

"Thank you." Korrine pivoted on her heel and brusquely left the office.

Carla pushed open the door and leaned against the counter, frowning at Jasmine. "Are you okay, Jasmine? Did Korrine treat you poorly again? If she did, I'll have another talk with her."

"No, she was fine. She just wanted me to collect the résumés for her." Jasmine sighed.

"You seem a little down today. I thought the vacation would reenergize you. I heard a little about what happened. You're okay, right?"

Jasmine nodded. "It's okay, you don't need to tread lightly. I called Dara, and Pauline is doing fine. I want her to recover and honestly don't have any ill will toward her at all. I'm just in a quandary about what to do with a new long-distance relationship. Oh dang, I didn't mean to talk about my personal life at work."

Carla chuckled. "Why on earth would you think you can't talk about your personal life? Everyone else does."

"Well not with their boss, do they?"

"Yes, as a matter of fact, they do. I know all about everyone's kids, spouses, significant others, pets, you name it. You're the only one who doesn't share anything. I had to learn about this Silver person from Pauline. I had no idea she was so fixated on you. She seemed more interested in that author friend of yours. She wanted to know what I knew. I'd honestly told her I didn't know anything. Am I going to lose you to this person?" Carla asked.

"If she asks me to move, I would in a heartbeat, but I'm not about to worm my way into her life. I think she's still struggling with the loss of her wife and her feelings are conflicted."

"Love is a powerful thing, Jasmine. If the two of you are meant to be, those conflicting feelings will unravel and leave a clear path for you to come together, and when that happens, I'll wish you the best of luck." Carla smiled, waved, and returned to her office.

Jasmine decided she needed to call Preston and ask his advice. She wasn't sure how she'd be able to cross the sudden continental divide in her budding relationship with Silver. Normally she ate at her desk while she worked, but today she'd take that half hour and interrupt Preston. He wouldn't mind; he'd told her to call him after she'd cried over the phone last night. The minute she'd ended the call with Silver, she'd phoned Preston. He'd been reassuring and gentle with her. She needed to hear his assurances again. She'd avoided asking him what she should do next by telling him she didn't want his advice—she just wanted him to listen. Now she was ready for his sage counsel after letting her feelings marinate.

†

Silver was pacing in front of her sliding glass doors. Normally when she looked outside, she let the beauty of her property envelop her. She thought of Naomi, and how much she loved living in their rural corner of the state, surrounded by majestic mountains and lush greenery.

Today was very different; she couldn't expel the look on Jasmine's face as she turned to leave.

She'd only experienced this kind of angst once in her life—when Naomi had died. She wasn't able to change that outcome, but she sure as heck could affect what was happening right now.

"Naomi, I need you to give me a sign, something to tell me you're really okay with me moving on." Silver glanced up at the sky.

The day had been dreary with misty rain blanketing Naomi's favorite mountains. She almost missed the triple rainbow when she turned her back to the glass, but then Sinbad jumped on the door chasing a raindrop. She saw the beautiful sign and smiled.

"Thank you, Naomi. I will always love you, but I'll take this gift you've just given me," she whispered.

Her smartphone buzzed in her pocket. She almost let it go to voice mail when she didn't recognize the number, but the person on the other end—undoubtedly a telemarketer—was about to receive a huge piece of her mind because it was the perfect outlet.

"Hello," Silver barked.

"What the hell do you think you're doing?"

"Preston?" Silver asked.

"Who else, unless you think I'm Jasmine's fairy godmother. Hmmm, I guess I could fall into that category. Oh never mind, I'm doing what any good friend would do and telling you some things I was hoping your sister would take care of, but obviously hasn't."

"Don't be too sure of that. Meredith gave me an earful this morning."

"Good. Look, I've seen a lot of lezzie couples, but never have I seen two people absolutely made for one another. Why isn't Jasmine packing up her office right now and making plans to move to Washington? More specifically, why didn't you ask—no, beg—her to move?" Preston bellowed.

"We've only just started dating. I can't ask her to uproot her life after two weeks of bliss. Besides, I hurt her."

"No shit, Sherlock. You hurt her by not taking a chance. She understands she'll never replace Naomi, but that doesn't mean you don't have room in your heart for a new love. I don't believe for one minute that there is only one soulmate for us—that's a bunch of hooey the Hallmark people and you crazy romance writers push. She's your next great love, and you're about to lose her. Do you honestly think Dara is going to stand aside while you get your shit together? Jasmine's special and Dara knows that. Hell, even crazy Pauline knew that," Preston lectured.

"Has Dara made another play for Jasmine?" Silver started to panic.

"Not that I know of, but she won't let the grass grow under her feet once she learns what an idiot you are. She'll pounce for sure and take advantage of the situation. Get off your ass and do something, because Dara is not the right person for my bestie, you are."

"She's all I've thought about since she left. What can I do to convince her?" Silver asked.

"Something big. Oooh, I know. Go to Kansas and make a surprise visit. Before you make an appearance at her office, get some Christopher Elbow chocolate and then beg her to come with you. Pick her up like Richard Gere in *An Officer and a Gentleman* if you have to. God, now that was romantic. Of course, it would have been better if he'd scooped up Brad Pitt over his shoulder. Yummy."

"Um, Preston, come back to earth, please, and stop fantasizing about Richard Gere and Brad Pitt," Silver interrupted. "I don't think chocolate has the same impact on Jasmine as it does on me."

"Have you finished your latest book yet?" Preston asked.

"I'm supposed to get the printed copy any day now. Why?"

"It's about you and Jasmine, right?" Preston asked.

"Yes, it has a lot of parallels, and I didn't even have to think about it, the dedication to Jasmine flowed from my fingers," Silver admitted.

"I have just the right personal note for you to inscribe in the book."

"What about Dara?"

Preston giggled. "Oh, she's still taking care of Pauline. I tossed that in to get your jealous juices flowing."

"Why you little...."

"A fairy godmother's got to use every available tool at her disposal. It worked, didn't it?"

"Yeah, it worked. I'm hanging up now. I need to make some arrangements, and thanks, Preston."

"Just make sure I get an invitation to the wedding—correction, I want to be Jasmine's best mate at the wedding. I look positively dashing in a tuxedo."

"Bye, Preston." Silver pushed the button to end the call. Her excitement bubbled over. It wasn't too late. She envisioned a future with Jasmine, and nothing would get between them, not even Naomi's ghost.

Chapter Twenty-six

Jasmine tossed her bag on the kitchen counter. She was finally home after a long, very unproductive day. She just couldn't seem to focus. She'd barely managed to catch up and had stayed a few minutes later without recording her time because she'd felt bad for staring off into space and not concentrating on her work.

She needed to talk to Silver and try to close the emotional distance. She couldn't do anything right now about the physical distance, but she could try to mend the discomfort. Even though she knew Silver didn't have regular sleep patterns, she wanted to call before it was too late in the evening.

When Silver answered her phone on the third ring, Jasmine breathed a sigh of relief.

"Hi. I'm so glad you called. Listen, I don't have a lot of time to talk tonight, but I wanted to tell you there's a surprise coming, and if you can just be patient for a little while longer…," Silver started.

"Oh, okay, I'll let you go, then. It sounds like you're busy." Jasmine was disappointed. She wanted to have a more meaningful conversation and get back to their ease with one another.

"I love you, baby, and I'll talk to you soon." Silver's hurried tone came across the wires loud and clear.

"I love you too."

Jasmine ended the call and wondered what had just happened. She supposed she should feel good about Silver telling her she loved her, but the conversation was just plain odd. It left an unsettled reverberation in her heart.

†

Silver knew she'd sounded strange on the phone last night, but she still had so much to do before leaving at o-dark-hundred the next morning. She'd managed to get the first flight the next day, but had spent most of the rest of the afternoon, after talking with Preston, trying to get an advance copy of her new book. Finally, a nice young man had delivered it to her house at seven and she had to thank a friend of a friend of a friend, who had made the arrangements.

She had run around her house pulling together her clothes and called Sally to have her take care of her brood of furbabies. The phone rang in the middle of her pulling out various outfits and placing them on the bed for consideration. She noted it was Jasmine and didn't want her to get the wrong impression by letting it go to voice mail, but she'd chastised herself later when she had time to reflect on how she may have come across. She was sure she had appeared abrupt and uncaring when she'd answered the call.

Silver had almost called Jasmine back after she'd finished packing and was winding down for bed, knowing morning was just a few short hours away, but she didn't quite know what to say and worried she might let slip her surprise visit.

She'd tried to fall asleep on the long flight to Kansas, but the speech she intended to make to Jasmine kept rolling around in her head. She was tempted to write it all down again, but discarded that idea. She hoped when the time came, she'd be able to recite everything and speak from her heart. That was for the best anyway. Jasmine didn't need a stiff, well-rehearsed speech; she needed to hear Silver's raw emotions and the depth of her feelings.

She'd googled where to pick up Jasmine's favorite flower and hoped that GPS provided accurate directions to the flower shop. So far, everything had fallen into place, and this was the last piece.

Silver was still in a mental daze as she deplaned and walked through the airport. As she continued to play the words in her head, accepting some and discarding others, an unfamiliar woman interrupted her mental gymnastics.

"Silver?"

Silver looked at the middle-aged woman with light brown hair hanging limply to her shoulders and matching faded, coffee-colored eyes. Silver tried to search her memory for where she might know this woman from, but came up empty. Not wanting to appear rude, Silver answered, "Yes."

"What are you doing in Kansas?" the woman asked.

Silver thought that was an odd question and hesitated before engaging in conversation with a person she didn't recognize. "I'm sorry, have we met before?"

The woman stuck out her hand. "I'm Korrine Carson, but you probably know me as Nurse Executive. I was on my way to Washington to visit my sister, and I was hoping we might get a chance to visit with one another, but now you're here in Kansas. I met you at the conference five years ago before your wife died. You know I've been a big fan ever since. I was hoping I would be the one to win that contest."

Korrine shrugged. "I was upset for a while when Jasmine beat me to the punch, but I guess she won fair and square. Although I wouldn't mind getting advance copies and doing beta reading for you in the future, and then maybe I'd have a fighting chance next time."

Silver thought the woman was brash, but she didn't get the danger vibe from her—not like when she'd first met Pauline. "What a small world. You're the Korrine that works with Dara and Jasmine. I don't think I'll offer another contest like that in the future. That was a one-time thing. I'm glad Jasmine won though, because I never would have found love again if she hadn't. Who knew how much the power of one review can change a person's life."

"I suppose Jasmine is hard to resist. I've probably treated her unfairly over the last couple of years. She seems to have women falling all over her, and I just assumed she was an emptyheaded tart. I'd be thankful for one woman gushing over me. I decided the only reason Dara hired her was because she was sleeping with her and that irritated me. Her new boss set me straight." Korrine chuckled. "Well, not literally, only figuratively. Now that I've learned all about Pauline's break with reality, I'll bet my private message to you several weeks ago letting you know I'd be in your neck of the woods sent you into a panic."

"It did cause a bit of consternation. I'm glad we ran into each other or I might have unfriended you, assuming you were another crazy person—not that Pauline's crazy. That was probably not the right word," Silver admitted.

Korrine waved her hand in the air. "Oh, I completely understand, and I'm glad we crossed paths as well." Korrine set her bag down and began rummaging around inside. She pulled out one of Silver's earlier novels. "Would you mind signing this for me? I was hoping to track you down and do that while I was in Washington. I would have been very disappointed to miss you. I'd also hoped we would get a chance to talk about the future of lesbian fiction, maybe some other time."

"Um, sure," Silver agreed.

Korrine handed her the book, and Silver pulled a pen from the bag draped around her shoulder. She quickly scribbled, *Thanks for the support, Peace, Silver*, then passed the novel back to Korrine.

"I've got to rush, but I really would like to have coffee with you sometime when I visit Washington again, or rather coffee with you and Jasmine." Korrine winked. "Go on and get the girl. I presume that is why you are here. I was rooting for Dara, but somehow I don't think she has the same twinkle in her eye that you did when you mentioned finding love again. I might be a bitch, but deep inside I'm a romantic and I really do wish you the best."

Korrine pivoted and gave Silver a small wave before rushing down the corridor toward the security checkpoint.

Silver shook her head and thought how interesting and coincidental everything was. They'd both assumed Nurse Executive was Silver's stalker and it ended up being Pauline who was fixated on Jasmine and not Silver. Now Silver was about to become the stalker, but hopefully in a good way. She was determined to convince Jasmine to come live with her and wasn't about to accept any answer but yes.

Chapter Twenty-seven

Jasmine looked down at her keyboard as she furiously typed up the minutes she'd taken for the division's monthly meeting. She prided herself on getting them out the same day while everything was fresh in her memory. Carla had often praised her for her accuracy and promptness, and she didn't want to let her boss down.

"Hello, Jasmine."

Jasmine thought she was having auditory hallucinations due to her incessant thoughts of Silver—morning, noon, and night, and the person who had approached her desk sounded exactly like Silver. She added olfactory delusions, as she smelled the distinct sweet odor from her favorite flower. Jasmine lifted her head and could not believe her eyes. Silver stood in front of the desk with a beautiful bouquet of Asian Stargazer Lilies, her favorite flower. Silver had remembered.

"Silver? What are you doing here?"

"Aren't you happy to see me?"

"'Happy' would be an understatement. I'm overjoyed, but I don't understand."

"I'd been rehearsing a speech the entire flight here, and now for the life of me, I can't remember a word." Silver shoved the book at Jasmine and offered the bouquet. "Please read the dedication. I've always been better with the written word."

Jasmine set the flowers on her desk, accepted Silver's new book titled *Second Time Around*, and opened to the first page. In beautiful cursive script, Silver had written, *I can't imagine my life without you. Please consider moving to Washington and building a future with me, by my side, for the rest of this precious time we have on the planet.*

Jasmine flipped to the next page and read the dedication.

To Jasmine, who is the love of my life.

Jasmine looked up with tears in her eyes. "You had me at hello."

Silver chuckled. "That was the third option Preston gave you when you first came for a visit, right?"

Jasmine nodded. "Yes, my answer is yes, to this, to everything, and if down the road you ask me another question, that answer will also be yes."

"Good to know. I suppose you'll just have to wait until I write another book. I'm a writer, after all, so all the really important questions are asked in dedications."

"I can't wait to review this book if it will get you working on the next."

"Reviews are good, really, really, good. Maybe the next book I write will be titled *The Review*." Silver laughed.

"Now that's a book I look forward to reading."

About the Author

Annette Mori

Annette is an award winning author and healthcare executive living in the beautiful Pacific Northwest with her wife and their five furry kids. Well, actually, it might be more than five, but they do not count the ones they only feed. Annette believes it is not too late to try something new. As an avid reader, she is pleased there are thousands of good books to choose from, and hopes that one day hers will be one of the many for readers to consider. She reads at least three to four books a week, so please, keep them coming. She has a habit to feed, after all.

No matter if you loved it or hated it, Annette would love your comments. Feel free to email her at annettemori0859@gmail.com.

She believes she will always be a WIP (work in progress—she just learned that), so feedback is a gift. Follow Annette's blog at: https://annettemori0859.wordpress.com/

Other Books from Affinity eBook Press

South of Heaven by Ali Spooner
Kendra Drake thinks her life is complete. She has taken over as Captain of her father's shrimp boat. As a favor to her father, Kendra has agreed to give fellow shrimper Lindsey Bowen a chance to work on the boat. Kendra is fighting against mother nature, the open waters, and herself. Still, Lindsey finds a way into Kendra's heart. Will it only last for the summer?

Catch to Release by Lacey Schmidt
On the verge of finally releasing her own record label, lesbian folk-rock star, Shay Greenaura, finds herself caught up in more than just her music. Addison Weller, a former Diplomatic Security Services agent is called in to assess the threats against Shay. Follow this fast-paced adventure to its surprising romantic conclusion.

Ready for Love by Erin O'Reilly
Kylie Wilcox's life dramatically changed with the death of her husband. Dr. LJ Evans, a renowned archaeologist, needed and wanted nothing but her work for her happiness. Their worlds are about to collide and lives will be altered forever.

Neptune's Ring by Ali Spooner
In the sequel to *Venus Rising*, Nat and Liz, owners of Venus Rising, invite Levi and Vanessa to join them in a venture for a new club on another island. They find the perfect place in

an unfinished resort, Neptune's Ring. While on the island, Levi is drawn into a mystery involving secret compartments and a murder. Join the characters in this page-turning adventure, filled with steamy romance, intrigue, and an unsolved murder.

The Ultimate Betrayal by Annette Mori
Lara is a successful, beautiful, charming financier. She is also a total control freak, so whatever Lara wants, Lara makes sure she gets. Rachel is Lara's fun-loving, charming, irresistible wife. Sophia's surprise visit to see Lara sets in motion a number of life-changing events for them all. Hell has no fury like a woman scorned.

Keeping Faith by TJ Vertigo
Join the antics of Reece, Faith, Cori, Vi, and even The Animal, one last time in *Keeping Faith*. Faith has finally made the big screen, but how will Reece handle her success? Will the love that they share be enough to save their relationship and soothe The Animal?

Bound by Ali Spooner
A rogue master vampire threatens the existence of the New Orleans vampire clan. Lord Jordan enlists Devin Benoit, sister of the Baton Rouge Alpha, and her witch lover, Tia, to assist with cleansing the city from potential disaster.

The Circle Dance by Jen Silver
Jamie Steele has moved to another town, trying to forget the heartbreak of losing her lover of six years. Sasha Fairfield finds her thoughts taken up with her ex-lover and thinks she wants Jamie back. Follow this captivating romance as love dances through the lives of these women to its surprising conclusion.

Search for the White Moon by Natalie London
Kathryn Austin, a government agent, is given opera singer, Adriana Desi, as her new assignment. Their lives and futures are in danger as the White Moon terrorists hunt them. Immerse yourself in this fast-paced romantic thriller by debut author Natalie London.

Take Me as I Am by JM Dragon & Erin O'Reilly
When Jo Lackerly and Thea Danvers meet, an unexpected friendship develops, proving a catalyst for both women to change their lives irrevocably. Follow them on a journey of discovery that will have your heart smiling, blood boiling, and senses entangled in a wonderful romance.

Carved in Stone by Jen Silver
Join the characters from *Starting Over* and *Arc Over Time* in this final book from the Starling Hill trilogy. Ellie Winters thinks she might be going mad when the ancient queen wants a proper burial for herself and her consort. *Carved in Stone* has romance, adventure, a treasure hunt, and happy endings for all, living and dead.

Anywhere, Everywhere by Renee MacKenzie
Gwen Martin's life in the Ten Thousand Islands area changes irrevocably when Piper Jackson comes into her life. Without trust, can the budding relationship between Gwen and Piper survive? Or will the answers to the questions continue to haunt them?

Venus Rising by Ali Spooner
Levi Johnson arrives at Venus Rising, an exclusive lesbian-only tropical resort in the Virgin Islands and finds more than she expected—a sizzling-hot love triangle. Torn between her

attraction to two women, she struggles to choose the right woman to share her life.

The Devil's Tree by Ali Spooner
Torn between her love for the pack and her need to find what's missing in her life, Devin Benoit travels to New Orleans. Will the previous happenings at the Devil's Tree help or hinder Devin in the fight of her life, and the life of Tia, the woman who now owns her heart?

The Beggars' Coppice by Erica Lawson
Edda Case is a woman in crisis who discovers that things are not as they seem. Is it truly a message for her from beyond the grave or is something more sinister taking place? Can Edda solve the mystery of *The Beggars' Coppice*?

Locked Inside by Annette Mori
How much does the power of love matter to someone who must overcome obstacles far greater than most people face in a lifetime?

Line of Sight by Ali Spooner
Sasha and her lover Kara are back. Continue the thrilling adventures of this couple from the Sasha Thibodaux series.

Requiem for Vukovar by Angela Koenig
Requiem for Vukovar continues the Refraction series and the exploits of Jeri O'Donnell and her partner, Kelly Corcoran. In an epic siege largely ignored by the wider world, Kelly, who was prepared to give up comforts and certainties when she became part of Jeri's nomadic life, encounters more than physical danger. Her ability to maintain her core integrity is assaulted by the inevitable ugliness of war. For Jeri, the true battle is confronting her attraction to violence as she

struggles against losing herself in the exhilaration of combat.

Against All Odds by JM Dragon
From award-winning and bestselling author JM Dragon, with significant updates by Erin O'Reilly, comes an original tale of romance where everything seems to be stacked against two women whose destinies bring them together. Life however takes a twisted path, setting both Steph and Louise in directions they never thought possible. Will love win out against all odds, or will love be forever lost?

The Settlement by Ali Spooner
The outpouring of love and friendship toward Cadin helps her on her path to healing and learning to trust her heart to love once again. Join bestselling author Ali Spooner on this sensational journey that ends with a heartwarming romance.

Once Upon a Time by Alane Hotchkin
Raven only wanted to escape the blows that life had dealt her. She longed to be on the open sea and free. When she came upon a beautiful young girl sitting alone in the middle of a meadow, little did she know that her destiny would be changed forever. Will they become the pawns of the ancient vision, or will both paths lead to the same port of destiny? Find out in this exciting high-seas adventure that will capture your imagination.

E-Books, Print, Free e-books

Visit our website for more publications available online.

www.affinityebooks.com

Published by Affinity E-Book Press NZ LTD
Canterbury, New Zealand

Registered Company 2517228

www.ingramcontent.com/pod-product-compliance
Lightning Source LLC
Chambersburg PA
CBHW052022020726
47501CB00004B/1194

* 9 7 8 0 9 0 8 3 5 1 9 5 4 *